THE OVERLANDERS

Inspired by true events

MARY SEATON

SWEETSPIRE LITERATURE
MANAGEMENT

CHAPTER 1

1946

Tom stepped up into the saddle and swung his horse around to face the north. As he spurred his horse into a canter a smile broke out over his face, he felt free.

Tom was going droving. He would travel from Mable Downs over five hundred miles northwest of Mataranka, the three hundred miles to the rail head in Katherine with a herd of seven hundred head. The cattle would do the rest of the journey to Darwin by rail.

Tom had been droving since he was twelve and knew no other life. Before he was twelve, he'd accompanied his father on the trail and earned a little cash helping the cooks. He was unable to stand his father's drunken rages and lit out on his own. Tom understood exactly why his mother had run off first chance she got. He heard last year that his father languished in prison where he was doing time for belting his new wife. As far as Tom was concerned, he could rot there.

After fourteen years on the trail, he had made a name for himself and was an eagerly sought-after trail boss. He was well known for getting cattle to their destination with minimum wear and tear and with most of them making the journey. In fact, he averaged one or two losses over a few hundred miles. Tom was also well known for the professional way he handled himself and the team he picked.

He loved the life and could never imagine himself doing anything else. On this particular trip though Tom would be nursing a broken heart. His fiancée Emily had explained her being in bed with one of his mates by telling him she could never be a drover's wife. She said she was sorry and should have told him sooner. 'Anyway' she'd finished, 'I can't have a decent conversation with you. All you talk about is bloody cattle.'

'But Rodney's a bloody drover' he'd cried at her, 'when he can manage to get his lazy arse out of bed'. He took a deep, shaky breath and ploughed right on. 'Tell me Emily, what does he talk about in the sack? You're just a slut you know that?'

'Well, he might talk about cattle but at least he's good in the sack. Anyway, Janet told me you were going down there to see her. So that makes you a slut to Tom hay. And you started it!'

'Don't be fuckin daft Emily, I wouldn't touch her, and you know it. I only ever loved you. Why'd you have to be such a bitch? Well to hell with the lot of you, I won't ever be back.'

'Well, I can't wait Tom. If I'm a bitch it's because I got tired of waiting around for you. You were always away for months at a time and never once wrote me a letter. And as soon as you get back to town you get drunk. You're just like your father you are, just like him. Go on Tom, bugger off then.'

Tom smiled at this point; he didn't know why. He took a deep breath and said quietly, 'I'm nothing like my father Emily and you know it. I always gave you all the money I could. What did you do with it Emily? What did you do with my money?'

'Why, do you want it back big shot?'

'No, I just reckon you probably spent it on yourself, and you were supposed to be saving for a home for us. Bitch!'

Tom turned around to walk out the gate and found his legs were like jelly. He heard her yell 'good riddance' from the doorway, and he turned to look at her. He studied her for a few moments and shook his head. 'Dunno what I ever seen in you.' He said softly and smiled.

Emily's breath caught in her throat; he had a sexy smile she had to admit. Too late she realised she did love him, loved his smile, loved his manner, and loved his loving. She also knew she didn't love Rodney.

Oh, she wished she'd never met Rodney, this was all his fault. He'd talked her into this, and she'd been gullible.

She turned to walk inside and found she didn't want to. Tom noticed for the first time how much weight she was carrying and how badly she dressed. Her hair was always a mess, and she gave the appearance of being unkempt, even dirty. Probably lying-in bed all day he thought bitterly, most likely with his mates.

'No bugger it' he said and climbed up on his horse. He rode off to join the herd two miles away and never looked back.

Ernie the old camp cook hailed him as he rode up and drew his horse to a halt. Tom hadn't seen the old man for a long time and shook hands with him. Smiling he said kindly, 'g'day Ernie. Glad you're cooking for us this trip mate could do with some good tucker.' He patted his stomach and laughed heartily with the old man.

"How's things young fulla, heard you was taking this camp on. How are you son?'

'I'm fine thanks Ernie.'

'How's that young woman of yours, are you two married yet?'

'No Ernie we're not. She left me for that bloody Rodney Gaskill, remember him?'

'Shit she'll be sorry she did that Tom. He's nothing but a no hoper. I heard he got two young girls pregnant and ran out on them both.'

Tom smiled, yep, he'd dodged a bullet there he thought and went off to check over the stores. The old cook followed along behind him, troubled by what he had heard. He knew how keen Tom had been on that young woman, he scratched his head.

Satisfied with the stores, Tom told Ernie he had done well and getting on his horse, rode over to meet the blokes and look over the herd. To his surprise there was a young woman in their midst. Just the sight of her set his nerves to jangling, bloody women he said to himself, bloody everywhere. Couldn't they stay out of anything?

Tom rode up to her and said with a polite smile, 'and who might you be young lady? I don't think we've met.'

The woman looked him up and down and waited until he'd dismounted. He turned and held his hand out to her which she ignored as she scrutinised him. He was tall and slim with light brown hair. The smile died and he let his hand drop to his side.

'You're a bit young to be the boss here, aren't you?' She demanded as she looked him up and down again. 'I'm Sue Ellis and I own most of these cattle. I'll be accompanying you on this drive. I trust that will be in order Mr...' She shrugged one shoulder indicating she cared not a jot if it was, or it wasn't, nor did she care what his name was.

Tom looked down at his boots. Oh, shit he thought. He hated when these bloody owners decided to come on trail drives, they always interfered. Couldn't help themselves. And they knew nothing about cattle or how to look after them. But they knew plenty about throwing orders around from the shade of a tree though. Well, he wasn't going to put up with it, he'd see her father if he had to.

'Why' he asked simply?

He watched her and noted that she was shocked by the question, hadn't expected it. He was pleased by that and watched as she regained her composure. When she did, he saw she wasn't very pleased with the question at all. She stared at him for a moment not knowing what to make of him except that he was insolent, and she didn't like him. She decided that she'd need to put him in his place.

'I don't think I need to explain anything to you... I don't see what it has to do with you.'

'Well, I have been entrusted with getting all these cattle to Katherine, so it has everything to do with me. You see I think your being here promises trouble. I'd just like to make it clear I don't want you on this drive.' He went to turn away, but she wasn't finished.

'Too bad Mr. whatever your name is...'

'Tom Cooper, people...'

'Yes, whatever you say. I am going to see my cattle to the rail head, and you can...'

'Well, I've already told you I don't like it.' Tom turned to the men who wore amused looks on their faces and scowled at them. 'I'm going to see Mr. Ellis. You men wait here. I'll be back tonight ready to break camp in the morning.'

'Oh, you needn't bother daddy has already agreed to it.'

Tom smiled thinly and through his teeth he said, 'yes I'm sure he has Miss, but I have not.'

Tom turned on his heel grabbing up the reigns he swung up into the saddle with the ease that comes from doing it nearly every day for most of your life. He was offended and he was bloody sure he wasn't taking any damn woman on any bloody shopping trip. He galloped off to the sound of that woman yelling something after him. He'd had a gut full of women for one day, shit were they all the bloody same.

When Tom stood in front of Mr. Ellis the short, heavy set, balding man grinned up at him. 'What can I do for you Tom? This got something to do with my daughter. Has she rubbed you the wrong way already?' He shrugged his heavy shoulders and hurried on, 'I'm sorry but she has a mind of her own, I hope you're not here to refuse the job. I need...'

Tom was frayed, 'I don't care what you need.' He knew his voice was too loud, but he was highly offended. 'See Mr. Ellis, there are a number of jobs I could take up right now. I did not sign on to escort a flipping woman on a shopping expedition.'

'I know son' Mr. Ellis was using his most practised placating tone. 'I would be eternally grateful if you would. She's driving me crazy here son. Listen I'll make sure you get a decent sized bonus... on top of your other bonuses, if you could keep a bit of an eye...'

'She has informed me that a number of the cattle are hers.' Ellis smiled and shook his head. Tom rushed on, 'I don't know what you find so damned funny. For two pins she could take her own cattle to Katherine and you to. It's over a month and she's not exactly... umm...'

'She's downright bloody rude and obnoxious' Ellis leaned close dropping his voice. 'Her fuckin mother's the same. Don't s'pose I could trouble you to take her to...'his voice trailed away.

There was a brief silence. Ellis' voice took on a pleading tone now, 'now son, only a few of the cattle are hers, they are mostly mine, and she knows very bloody little about them. Dunno why she got a bee in her bonnet to see them to Katherine. If she gets in your way you have my permission to get her out of it, yeah. The bonus would be sizeable'.

'How bloody sizeable?'

'Well… see now… lets…'

'I said how bloody sizeable?'

'Well, what about fifty quid.'

'And I have your permission to tell her to butt out?'

Ellis nodded. 'You have that son; you have that, and I'd like to be there to see it.'

'Make it seventy and I'll think about it'.

'Daylight robbery son but I'd do anything for a bit of peace. Okay done. So will you do it son?'

Tom nodded and swung back up into the saddle. He was still fuming but he'd need the money now that his bitch of a fiancée had taken him to the cleaners. He was done with women that was for sure. He headed off to the pub to get a beer. He wasn't looking forward to facing that bloody woman again especially seeing as she'd gotten her own way. Tom suspected she got her own way quite a bit.

❧

As Tom suspected she was gloating, and the men were smirking when he informed her, she would in fact be on the drive. 'You will stay out of my way Miss, or I will run you off.'

'What?'

Tom ignored the question and stormed off.

'So how much did the old buzzard pay you to take her?'

Tom turned, the question was from Ernie and was deliberately spoken loud enough for the young madam to hear. Tom shook his head, 'not nearly enough cook, not nearly enough.'

The company pulled out by Eight o'clock the next morning. To Tom's chagrin they'd had to wait for Madam to be ready.

As they rode out Tom sidled up next to her and leaned across and spoke loudly. 'Next time you are not ready Madam we will leave you behind. I like to pull out by no later than seven, six whenever we can. We will not wait for you again. There are those things we would wait for, but you are not one of them. Be on time or find yourself on your own.' He kicked his horse into a gallop and left her in his dust.

Sue sat her horse, her hand poised on the reigns and her mouth hanging open. Who the hell did he think he was she thought indignantly as she watched him gallop away?

He sat a good saddle, tall and broad shouldered, long slim body, and legs. One of the men had told her that his fiancée had dumped him. Well, she said to herself, who could blame her? She'd put him in his place right away.

'You'll do no such thing' she caught up to him. 'I must stay with my…'

'Your father's cows? Apart from your rudeness and your insufferable air of privilege and entitlement and your annoying chatter Miss, you are a liar. Go behind and bring up the rear.' Without looking at her he gave his head a flick in that direction.

'I'm not going back there in all that dust… I'm…'

Tom stopped and grabbed her by the arm almost pulling her clear out of the saddle. 'You'll do as you're told Miss if you want to stay with this drive. So, help me if you give me any more trouble, I will run you off. Nothing would give me more pleasure Miss so go on. Git behind, in the dust where I can neither see you nor hear you.' He almost unseated her again when he threw her arm down and sat glaring at her.

Sue was shocked to the core; she turned her horse about and rode off to take up the rear. She'd have her day with him she vowed, but for now she'd wait. She had to get to town without Daddy. Herbert would be waiting there for her. Oh Herbert, dear, sweet, civilized Herbert. Yes, she had to make it to Darwin but first she had to make it to Katherine.

They stopped for a quick lunch at midday and Sue rode up with the men laughing at something Jimmy a young stockman had said. The sound of it grated on Tom's nerves, he rode up to her. 'In this outfit', he said 'we take it in turns to watch the herd. You will stay with Jimmy and take your turn now Miss while the rest of us go to lunch. Maybe Jimmy can keep you amused until we return. And maybe somebody will bring you back some lunch.' He shrugged his broad shoulders.

'Won't I have time to have my…'

'Your lunch Miss? No… no you won't. We have to make up some time since we got off to a late start.'

'I can't eat my lunch back there in all that dust!'

'Why the hell not? Jimmy does.'

The sun was getting low on the horizon when Fred, a big ringer from Queensland rode up beside him. Fred was a huge rough looking character with lines crisscrossing lines on his leathery face which was permanently covered in dusty stubble. When Fred opened his mouth to speak though everybody listened. His voice was so at odds with the rest of him. It was soft and smooth, and he spoke the Queens English perfectly and in very polished tones.

He eyed Tom for a moment and said 'Tom, are you being a little hard on the young lady?'

'No.'

'Alright Tom just as you say. Listen Tom is it right what I am hearing? That you have broken up…'

'Yeah.'

'How are you feeling Tom, are you okay?"

'Never better Fred. I went to see her and found her in bed with Rodney.'

'Rodney Gaskill? Good God man.' Fred studied his saddle horn very carefully.

'That's him but I don't want to put it around. She's going to need to find someone else sooner or later. When a couple of other women catch up with him. No, I'm better off out of it Fred. I never felt less like babysitting a spoilt brat though.'

The small note of desolation in Tom's voice was not lost on Fred and he made up his mind to keep an eye on the youngster. He liked Tom; he was a good man. He could see this woman they had with them was a handful he didn't need. Fred had to admit he didn't like her nor trust her, and he'd be glad to see the back of her. He thought they all would be.

'Alright Tom, let me know if there's anything I can do'. Fred smiled and rode back to flank the cattle. Tom watched him go, he'd ridden many times with the man and had absolute trust in him. He might have to hand ball this particular problem off to his old friend.

❧

The cattle were bedded down in a grassy field and Fred and Jack took first turn to sleep out there with them. The rest Sat around the campfire each man alone in his thoughts. Tom was pleased with the distance they had made today. They'd made up for the late start this morning, but they'd had to push the cattle hard and he didn't like that.

Suddenly he was aware that Sue had sat down beside him. 'What?' He didn't bother to look at her but kept his eyes on the fire, the calming effects of the flames relaxing his taught body.

She looked at him for a moment and when she spoke her voice held a certain forced politeness which tickled Tom for some reason. 'Tom, is there somewhere I might bathe?'

It was just what Tom needed, he started to laugh. He laughed and laughed, louder and louder. She'd been so polite and to no avail. 'No there isn't' he snapped his face setting back into a frown. Now he did look at her, 'and if I hear you've been wasting water on washing yourself, I'll run you off. Just give me half a reason girlie. Bath indeed.'

Sue looked so angry it was comical and it pleased Tom no end. He started laughing again. After a while he said. 'Why don't you give Ernie a hand with the dishes. That's woman's work and at least your hands will be clean hay.'

He laughed again and suddenly a picture of Emily and Rodney flitted, unbidden across his mind. The smile died on his lips, and he forgot about Sue. The very next memory he was treated to, was the sound of the bloody pair of them grunting like pigs as they kept screwing right in front of him not knowing he was there. His Emily, laying under that bozo squealing her bloody pleasure.

'Well, hello' he'd said and watched them grabbing at the covers to hide themselves. Well fuck the pair of them, but Jesus it hurt.

He rose abruptly and went to his bedroll. He knew Sue irked him more than she should and thought to thank Emily for that. Jesus, he hated women right now. Tom lay for hours looking at the stars wondering what he should make of his life now. At any other time, being on the trail made him happy but not this trip, he hated every minute of it. Was it the women or was he getting sick of this beloved life? The thought that it might be the latter was almost unbearable.

Tom was happier the next day because they got started before seven o'clock. The other thing was that he had sent Sue to the flank with Fred. He was relying on Fred to keep her out of his hair. Tom grudgingly admitted that she was a very good rider and knew how to hustle cows. But she was an annoying spoilt brat, and he couldn't stand her.

He also noticed as the day wore on that Fred was guiding her and she was learning fast. Oh God he hated the bitch, even the bloody dogs tripped over each other in front of her. He needed to get to Katherine, needed to get her to Katherine and get shod of her, then he needed to get a gutful of grog in Katherine. Tom realised he had a cruel thirst.

At lunch time Tom took his turn along with Fred to Stay with the herd. The two men sat in the shade and Tom dozed off. He came to with a start to the sound of Fred cursing up a storm.

'Jesus what is it, Fred?"

'Bloody wasp, bit me right on the end of it. Least ways I think it was a wasp.'

'How?'

'Well, I went behind the tree to relieve myself Tom. I'd just finished when I felt an excruciating pain. Must have peed on him or his nest or something.'

'The females have nests Fred. Only the females.'

'Is that right mate?'

'I dunno Fred. You want me to have a look at it?'

'I don't know little mate, it hurts like a bastard, but it would, wouldn't it? A bloody wasp.'

'Yeah. Go and get some cream off cooky, he'll have a look at it.'

'Hell, no I'll see how it is tonight'.

'How come you weren't looking Fred? You usually watch when you get the old fulla out don't you?' Tom looked puzzled.

'Not now Tom the others are coming back. Thank God to, I'm starving.'

❧

About mid-afternoon Tom noticed that Fred was sitting awkwardly in his saddle. He rode up and leaned towards him. 'Are you okay Fred? You're hurting, aren't you? We'll need to have a look at it, Fred. We'll catch up with cooky, he knows about these things. That's half the reason why he is always picked to go on these long drives, his knowledge of all things medicine. Together with his medicine chest of course.' Tom smiled his kindest at his old friend.

Fred sat shaking his head, but Tom wasn't to be put off, he knew these things could be serious. He went on, 'I'll tell the others we are needed up in front and you Fred will come with me. That's an order old man.'

Fred rode off at a canter towards the tucker wagon with Tom, he continued to protest. 'Tom I'm alright. I don't need to…'

Out of earshot Tom leaned towards Fred and without looking at him he asked, 'Were you… you know? Were you Fred?'

'Well, she's… she's very attractive damn it.'

Tom put his head back and howled with laughter. He couldn't stop and drew his horse up to enjoy it. The tears sprang to his eyes. He looked at Fred but the look on Fred's face only set him off again. At last, he got it under control and said, 'I knew she was trouble; I bloody knew it. By Jesus if anything…'

'Tom, if you say anything about this I'll leave.'

Tom looked at Fred's face and the look on it made him gulp. 'Jesus Fred, you aint got feelings for the bitch…? Fred, you got no chance with her. Jesus, man.' Tom put his hand on the older man's arm, but Fred pulled it away.

'Well, I don't want to marry her… I… I don't actually… even like her or anything. Now can you just shut up Tom. Can you just please bloody shut up.'

At the tucker wagon Ernie had a cream which he let Fred put on himself. 'Just in case it goes off again. Yeah, yeah… I know… you wasn't Pullin' on it was ya.' Ernie laughed and set Tom off again. 'Did the bastard of a thing at least let you get finished?'

'Oh, fuck off the pair of you. Come on Tom let's get back…'

'Oh no son' Ernie was shaking his head and trying not to giggle, 'you can't get back in the saddle. No son, no… infections you know. No… no more rubbing on this today I'm afraid.' Ernie pointed at Fred's swollen appendage, he could hardly talk for giggling now and he tried desperately to pull himself together. 'If it doesn't go down by sundown, we'll have to start thinking about getting somebody to suck the poison out. Maybe that nice … young lady.' The two men laughed until their ribs hurt.

Ernie straightened up and looked serious, 'wonder what made that wasp sting you. Must have been a male and he thought you was looking for his girlfriend.' The two men were doubled up.

Tom and Ernie came to their senses and Tom looked at Fred his face sobering completely. 'What? How long for Ernie? How long before he can ride?' He glanced at Fred who now had a half smile on his face and was lounging back on a bag of flour his hand over his appendage. 'And for Christ's sake put that frightful thing away Fred.' Tom grimaced at him.

'Couple of days lad. If it doesn't start going down soon or if he gets a fever he'll have to be taken to the hospital.'

Tom rode back to the herd minus Fred. Shit, he thought, the rest of them would have to cover for him. He'd no sooner got back than Sue rode up and asked where Fred was. He glared at her 'none of your business' he snapped. 'Get back to work.'

'You know I'm getting a little tired of your brutish attitude Tom.'

He leaned forward his face registering his contempt. 'Are you now Miss high and mighty? Are you now? Well clear off home to your Mummy then. I will give you a good horse.'

'Sorry, not going to happen.'

Sue thought the look on his face was quite murderous, so she dropped her hoity tone as she went on. 'Well, you might want to look at Jimmy he's been hurt. He rode into a tree branch, and I think he has a splinter in his face.'

Tom stared at her in disbelief. He'd left this bloody woman with Jimmy and now he was hurt. Jesus where would it end this trouble, she seemed to bring with her? And she was so bloody casual about it. And Jimmy, a married man!

'Bloody marvellous' he blurted out and as he pushed past her, he snapped, 'Would you just stay away from my men. From now on you'll bring up the rear on your own. If I see anyone near you, I will send them packing with you.' With that Tom rode off to look at Jimmy. Tom didn't like the sound of this at all, it was bad enough being one man down.

Tom always dreaded infections; he'd seen men lose limbs in the time it took to get from dawn to dusk.

As Tom rode up to Jimmy, he watched the man carefully. The look on Jimmy's face told Tom what he was going to ask. He said now, 'so how did you manage to find a tree branch Jimmy, and then get it into your face. Tell me.' Tom was trying to smile.

Jimmy started to splutter about studying a cow and not watching where he was going. 'I thought it was hurt.' He looked at the ground as Tom began to remove a rough bandage gently from his face. He smiled at Jimmy to ease at least some of his discomfort.

'I tend to agree that she's a cow young Jimmy and I don't doubt you were studying her.'

'Sorry boss.'

'It's okay Jimmy. Let's see what we got here.' He pulled the bandages away and sat up straight. 'Hells bells man, you got half the bloody branch in your face here. Splinter my arse.' There was a large stick protruding from the young stockman's face beside his nose. Tom looked at it carefully, he didn't want to touch it, he could see the young stockman was in pain. It looked clean enough, but he couldn't take any chances. And then there was the chance of considerable bleeding. Tom didn't know how far in it went.

'I'm sorry Tom. I'll be right, let's just get to work hay. Just pull it out and put the bandage back on.'

Tom put the bandage back on Jimmy's face. 'No buddy. I need to get you to a doctor. It's okay Jimmy you can go with Fred.'

'What's wrong with Fred?'

'A wasp stung him. Come on now Jimmy let's go.' Tom could see Sue sitting idle on her horse and rode up to her.

She turned smiling sweetly at Jimmy, 'how are you J…'

Tom exploded. 'Just shut up and listen woman. You get Jimmy up to the tucker wagon as fast as he can ride. Tell Ernie to get these two back to Mataranka. He'll take them there in the truck. Tell Fred he is to go to and ask him to send some help, at least one bloke, if they can't make it back.'

Sue stared at him, 'why m…'

'Git' Tom yelled. 'Now what did I tell you to do? Tell me.'

Sue repeated it word for word. 'Should I come back here as soon as I've done that?'

'Of course, there are four more men you have not yet put in hospital. I would rather you did not, but your father paid me to take you the hell off his hands for a little while.' Tom knew this last comment had been purely to hurt and he didn't understand why himself.

Sue stared at Tom with big doleful eyes full of hurt. A tear slid down her cheek and she said softly, 'of course he did Tom. Of course, he did.'

Tom didn't know what to do so he just sat there glaring at her. Finally, she turned to Jimmy, 'I'm sorry this has happened to you Jimmy. Come I will take you to Ernie. I'll come straight back Tom and do all I can to be of some help.'

Tom's face was red with temper. 'Just stay wherever the tucker wagon is, Ernie will leave behind some food for us. See if you can mind it. We'll catch up.'

'Alright Tom' Sue held her head down her eyes on her saddle horn. Jimmy sat quietly.

'Right' Tom said and wheeled his horse around and rode off. He didn't want to feel sorry for her!

Tom and the herd caught up with Sue who was waiting at the tucker wagon a couple of hours later. The sun was going down and so they needed to get the cattle settled as soon as possible. He was surprised to see the truck was still there, a frown crossed his handsome features. He decided to find out what had happened.

'Ernie' he said as he rode up leaving the men to see to the herd. He swung down out of the saddle with practiced ease and turned to the cook. 'What goes on mate?"

'Well son, Fred's swelling has gone down a fair bit and I knew he'd be okay. When I had a good look at Jimmy's face, I found it looked worse than it was because of some swelling mainly and the width of the stick. I got the stick, which wasn't all that long, out of it with the plyers and put some ointment on it and bandaged it up nice and clean. Fred can go back to work tomorrow, but Jimmy will take a couple days more. I'd like to keep him out of the dust for a bit.'

Tom clapped Ernie on the shoulder a big grin on his face. 'Now that's why your doctoring is almost as good as your cooking. Thanks a lot mate I am eternally grateful. I was a bit worried his face would bleed too much but he seems alright hay.'

'Yeah, well it did bleed a lot young Tom, your instinct was spot on. But with a bit of pressure, I got it to slow up and nature did the rest. He'd be in a fair bit of pain as well, so I'd like to keep him in the truck for a few days. What happened Tom?'

'Oh, he's got struck down by Sue itis. Too busy looking at her, Ernie and didn't see the tree galloping down the road towards him.'

'Maybe you should send her in the truck.' The two men laughed.

Tom grinned at his dear friend; he shook his head. 'Nah, I need the truck Ernie and God knows I couldn't do without you to put the walking wounded back together.' They both laughed again.

'Righto son, I must get the camp set up.' Ernie went about his tasks and Tom got back in the saddle.

That night around the campfire the conversation was kept very low and a lot of laughing went on. Mostly at poor Fred's expense who took it pretty good naturedly. Tom noticed that Sue was sitting away by herself eating her tea. She looked pale and drawn. She was one of his crew whether he bloody well liked it or not, so it was his job to ask her if she was okay. So, he asked her and was surprised when she didn't bight his head off.

'Of course, I am' was her response. 'Does my father pay you extra for this service?' Her voice held only tired resignation and she smiled thinly up at him.

'I dunno, maybe' he smiled now even though it hurt his pride. 'You did alright today. You know… getting Jimmy here and Ernie says you helped with him. Thanks.'

Tom walked away and got into his bedroll. Sue was flabbergasted as she watched him go. Oh, she could see how he could be insufferable, but who was going to tell him? She smiled and got into her bed; she was worn out. She couldn't ever remember being this tired before. She'd curl up and think about Herbert for a while. Dear, sweet Herbert, oh she couldn't wait to be in his arms.

Ernie had watched the exchange with interest and saw Tom go and get into bed. Maybe he thinks he hates her he said to himself and went to his bed scratching his head.

The camp was soon quiet, only the noise of some night creatures and the odd howl of a dingo. Just as Tom liked it yet he tossed and turned trying to figure out what worried him the most.

CHAPTER 2

After her exchange with Tom, Emily walked straight back in the bedroom and looked at Rodney. He was dressed and gathering up his wallet and comb his hanky and makings and cramming them into his pockets. She was standing in the doorway. 'So, you're going to run off after him, are you? He'll do you if you try it.'

'Well, then he won't do me at all because I aint going after him and I'm sure not going to try it. Jesus I should a never have done this to Tom, he's me mate. I must o been nice and drunk.'

'Don't think he's your mate anymore, do you? I wouldn't want to be you next time he sees you.'

'We'll see, won't we? Anyhow he's right about you though you're nothing but a slut.'

'So are you. You talked me into it, you mongrel.'`

'Well, I didn't have to do much talking did I? How many others of his mates you been with? What all of them? Get out of my way woman I'm off.'

Emily stood aside and as he walked past her, she said softly, 'Yes, I may have been with a lot of men, but you were my biggest mistake. I know now why they call you limp dick.'

Rodney pulled his fist back and punched her on the nose. Emily's head shot back and hit the door frame, and she fell unconscious to the floor. Blood spurted from her nose and head. Vaguely she was aware that she hit the side of her face on the other door frame as she went down.

Rodney stepped over her and ran. He'd have to run a bloody long way now; Tom wouldn't take too kindly to this. Anyhow he knew those other two women were gaining on him, probably wasn't responsible for any of their bastards either. Yeah, he'd head for Adelaide.

When Emily came to it was almost dark. Her head hurt and she wondered why she was laying on the floor. She needed to have a lay down on the bed but when she tried to get up, she found she was having trouble. She tried and tried but she was beginning to panic now.

Emily lived in the small cottage that her parents had left her, and the nearest neighbour was across the road. She took a deep breath and tried to quell the rising panic in the pit of her belly. Finally, she got to her hands and knees and crawled slowly and awkwardly to the door, calling for help as she went. She found that only one of her knees would do as she wanted it to do. The other one sort of dragged behind her.

Emily couldn't remember what had happened to her, in fact she didn't remember much of anything. She made it to the front door after a long struggle. It was almost dark, and nothing looked familiar. She knew she was bleeding and the darkness in her head was threatening to engulf her. She vomited and the taste of blood worried her. Where were her parents she wondered vaguely?

Collapsing on the veranda she lay for a moment and cried. The thought which was to the forefront of her mind was that she needed help and soon. She started calling to someone, anyone. 'Help… help… please help me.' She was weak and stopped to get her breath. And then she cried out, again and again.

A light came on across the road and a man came out to have a smoke in the cool breeze. 'Please Mister, can you help me? Please help me…'

She heard the footsteps running towards her and she cried with relief. The tears ran down her face. The man, whose name was Albert and she had known him all her life, was a stranger to her now. He dropped on a knee beside her bellowing for his wife to bring a torch.

He said softly to her now, 'Emily, what has happened to you?'

'I don't know' she said and sobbed loudly. 'I think I'm hurt.' A light blinded her, and she screamed with fear.

'Jesus, Mavis, run along to Ned's and tell him we need to get Emily to the hospital and can he bring his horse and gig. Now Mavis! Oh, holy mother of God, Emily girl…' Albert took a deep breath, 'Just relax Emily, we are here now love. We'll get you to the hospital and you'll be right girl. The doctor will patch you up and when you get home me and Mavis will take good care of you.' All he could do to comfort her was stroke her hair which had a calming effect.

Mavis came back and stood looking at the girl she'd known since she was little, her hand clasped over her mouth and tears in her eyes. She looked more dead than alive to Mavis and her body was twisted in a funny sort of way. 'Oh God almighty' she moaned. Coming to herself she said 'Ned is getting the horse harnessed up now. He says he'll take her along to the Thompson's and they can get her there quicker in their motor car. He said he'll put a mattress in the back. Is she… she looks…?'

'Bad', Albert nodded. 'Mavis' Albert was yelling now, 'get some towels woman. And a pillow there's a good girl.'

'Is my name Emily?'

Albert sniffed and wiped away the tears and said 'Yes Emily it is. Don't worry, that silly old name will come back to you presently. You've had a shock girlie. Jesus!'

Emily passed out in his arms. All Albert could think of was the blood. It was everywhere, coming from her nose and mouth and somewhere behind her. Her nose was bent to the side so that was broken. He wondered what the house looked like. He suspected someone had done this and vowed he'd get his hands on them someday.

'He'd finished mopping up most of the blood when Ned got there. He got down from the gig and took a look. 'Holy mother, man what the hell happened?'

Albert sniffed loudly, relieved to have someone with him. 'She doesn't remember anything Ned, not even her name.' Albert sobbed and Ned put his hand on his shoulder. He'd known these people for many years and was at a loss.

He said now, 'Jesus Bert! The poor little bugger. Here give me a hand and we'll get going hey.' They got her settled on the mattress. Both men were glad when she didn't come round when they moved her.

Mavis handed Albert a jacket and a blanket and said, 'go with her Albert hay. She is like a daughter to us, go with her love.' Albert nodded and kissing his wife he said 'course I will love, course I will. Be back soon hay.' He couldn't bring himself to say to her that everything would be alright. No, Albert had never lied to her.

On the way to the Thompson's Emily woke up a couple of times and held onto Alberts hand for dear life. Ned carried on bellowing and pleading with the horse to give him some more. A stockman riding home had volunteered to gallop on back to the Thompson's and alert them.

At the Thompson's Ted was waiting for them in the car. They put Emily in the back and Albert climbed in with her. Ned looked in the window and put his hand on Albert's shoulder, 'well good luck old man. I hope everything will be alright.'

'Oh, thanks Ned, thanks for all your help.'

'Anytime mate you know that glad to be of some help. See you when you get back mate' and the big black Humber super snipe sped out the gate and down the road.

Ned watched until the lights were out of sight and climbed back up in the gig. He wondered what had happened to the girl and like Albert he suspected someone had helped her to get in the shape she was in. Which wasn't good by any stretch of the imagination.

He also wondered if Emily would make it to the hospital, he hadn't liked the look of her. He knew something was wrong with her legs. He shook his head, only time would tell. Ned set off home, he'd call in and see Mavis.

Emily made it through the night and early the next morning the doctors operated on her. They straightened and set her nose, but it would never be perfect. They told Albert that they suspected a blunt object, most likely a punch had broken her nose due to lack of lacerations. A sharp object, probably a door frame had done the rest of the damage. The blow must have been considerable given the gash and the swelling. Other cuts to her face had needed suturing as well.

The big doctor sighed and went on, 'it is the head wound that is our main worry here, how bad it is, only time will tell. We have patched her up and stopped the bleeding, but the swelling will take time. She's lucky you got her here so quickly. She appears to me to have some paralysis down her left side. This could be due to swelling but if it is damage to the brain she may be crippled or partially crippled for the rest of her life. As I said, only time will tell. I'm sorry the news is not better, and I cannot be more specific. If it is any comfort to you sir, I believe she will survive this.' He smiled kindly at a broken Albert and waited patiently while the man tried to get his feelings under control.

Albert couldn't and sobbed right there in the corridor and the doctor took him into a small room. He sat down in front of Albert and talked. 'We will keep her here and in time we will know what we are up against. We have a physiotherapist on staff here and we'll help her all we can. Your other options are to take her to Darwin or Adelaide.'

'What do you think we should do?"

'To be honest Albert I don't think there is much anyone can do. If you like I will get in touch with a surgeon I know in Adelaide and ask his advice on that. But I will wait until we know a bit more about her condition. She can't travel as she is anyway. Then I will get in touch with Darwin Base Hospital and see what they have to offer, and you will have some information to help you to decide. Have you anywhere to stay?' Albert shook his head. 'Well, I will send you over to the nuns they have some rooms for families of patients. Is she your daughter?'

Albert shook his head, 'no she isn't but her parents were killed, and we have always watched out for her. We have no children, and she is it for us. We live across the road.' Albert pulled his hanky out and blew his nose.

'Where is home?'

'A little railway siding about forty miles from here. Damper Creek. There is a pub and a store and post office there. Plus, about twenty or so houses.'

'Albert, would you like me to get word to anyone regarding Emily's condition?'

Albert nodded and broke out sobbing afresh.

Mavis got the message from the good doctor and arrived the next day and stayed in the room the nuns had made available to Albert. They took it in turns to sleep and watch over their girl.

Emily woke up from time to time and didn't know either of them, and didn't remember how she got there. But Emily was glad to have them, and she told them so daily. She couldn't use her left arm at all well and the doctor doubted she would do any better if not worse with her left leg. He was right, Emily's leg was going to be a problem.

The following week went by reasonably incident free for Tom. Fred got back in the saddle and so did Jimmy. Jimmy's face looked a fright, and no doubt would be badly scarred. They were making good time and Tom was pleased. He avoided the woman as best he could, she grated on him. He left Fred to do the babysitting and told him to watch out for wasps.

Tom was sitting at his usual position at the fire where he could see everything. Sue sat away from the fire a bit as she was won't to do. He'd noticed she had a little brief case which she never let out of her sight. He'd noticed also that she always took it with her tied to her saddle. Never leaving it in camp.

He was staring into the fire waiting for his tea when he heard her gasp and saw that Fred had picked up the little bag. She jumped up and pulled it from his grasp screeching at him to leave things alone.

'Well, you can't just leave the bloody thing laying around for people to trip over.' He snapped back at her.

Cecil the aboriginal stockman from the Alice said quietly, 'you got the crown jewels in there, Missy?'

'You shut up and mind your own business. Who do you think you are? You still believe in kadaicha men you ignoramus.'

Cecil laughed softly as was his habit whenever confronted. Tom could see he was very nervous, and that the stockman wished he'd never opened his mouth. His eyes darted to Tom then back to the ground.

'Shut the hell up the lot of you' Tom bellowed rising to his feet, thinking that would be the end of it. He hadn't reckoned with Sue. God he was sick of the bitch.

She went on at Cecil now, 'how would you like me to point the bone at you? I know all about the little rituals you think you hide so well.'

Cecil got up and left the firelight, his face a blank.

Tom looked scathingly at Sue, 'you know', he barked 'this is the last straw. First thing in the morning you get out of my camp.' With that he went after Cecil. He couldn't find him; the man had disappeared. He hurried back to camp to saddle a horse; he had some idea where to look. There was a tribal camp not far off.

Fred looked apologetically at him, and Sue glared. 'I'm…' Fred began but Tom held up his hand. 'It's alright Fred this was not your fault.'

He saddled his horse and Fred asked, 'can I come with you…?'

Tom said 'No Fred, I'll need you here. Jack, get saddled you'll come with me.' Tom was well aware that Jack was her latest conquest and may stick up for her.

Tom held up his hand and Fred fell silent studying his boots. He understood Tom's decision.

When tom spoke it was quietly and authoritatively to Sue who had backed away. 'Give me that bloody bag' he ordered.

Sue shook her head looking almost fearfully at him. 'It's none of your business Tom.' She put it behind her back and glanced at Fred. Fred shrugged.

Tom reached out and after a struggle got the bag away from her. 'No one will look in this you have my word unless I need to.' He took a step and threw it in the truck. Turning to Fred he said now, 'I leave you in charge here Fred. If she tries to regain this bloody thing tie her up. No do it now, I mean it, get some rope, and tie her hands and feet and tie her to the truck, Jimmy, go get some rope. She will remain thus until I figure out what to do with her.' He looked at Jimmy, 'you lend him whatever support he needs.' He turned to Nevil, a quiet man who nobody knew much about. Tom found him to be very good at his job and never caused trouble, so he was alright with Tom. 'Can I count on you Nevil?'

Nevil nodded to Tom looking him straight in the eye, 'you can boss.' He wore a knowing look and worry lines had appeared on his face so Tom knew he was aware of the danger they could be in.

Tom looked at Ernie and said quietly, 'break out all the firepower we have Ernie. Make sure everyone is armed except her. That little crack about seeing their rituals will probably bring the whole fuckin tribe down on our heads. Douse this fire soon and watch. We can't afford to try and save the cattle at this stage we may very well be flat out saving ourselves if they come.' He turned to Sue now, 'I will turn you over you know. If they want you, I will turn you over to them. This is all on account of you and your big bloody mouth.'

Tom climbed up into the saddle and watched Fred tie her up. He looked at Ernie 'if I don't make it back hand her over Ernie. Save yourselves, and the cattle if you can.'

Ernie looked up at Tom, 'wouldn't we be better off sticking together lad?"

'I'll have a quick scout around Ernie and come back. I should be back way before they get here and anyway, they'll have to get passed me.' He took a few steps and turned back, 'put a gag over her mouth no telling what the idiot will do next.'

Tom and Jack disappeared into the night leaving Ernie wondering if the next time they met, would they be up yonder? 'In that great cattle drive beyond the stars' he murmured to himself.

'I hope you are satisfied girlie' he said loudly now to Sue. She went to open her mouth and Ernie pointed a rifle at her. 'Gimme a reason girlie. They're good men you've sent out there to face God knows what. Yeah, go on girlie, open your bloody mouth.'

Fred was behind her now and said quietly 'go on open it I want to put the gag in it.'

Sues eyes flicked down. Shaking her head, she said 'you're not putting that dirty...' the rest of what she said was muffled.

Ernie, Jimmy, Fred, and Nevil settled down in the dark to watch and wait, Ernie and Nevil had a rifle each and the other two had pistols. They waited for about half an hour when a footfall brought their attention to the direction Tom had gone in. It was horses but the little party did not relax a muscle.

Soon a familiar voice hailed them, it was Tom. Thank God breathed Ernie. When the two riders came into view Ernie could see in the moonlight that they carried a body with them.

Ernie was up and went quickly to Tom. 'What's happened' he asked quietly?

Tom sounded tired when he replied. 'It seems we got lucky Ernie. We found Cecil laying on the ground gibbering about bad spirits, devil devils and bad luck.'

Tom handed Cecil down to Fred who stood looking up at him. Ernie stood near and he could feel the heat emanating from Cecil. He knew the man was in a bad way and that there was probably nothing they could do for him. He would probably die, and they all knew it. All except Sue.

As the days went by Cecil worsened and they all took turns to sit with him at night. He was feverish and yelled and thrashed around until morning. He slept all day. Tom had no choice they had to move the herd along.

Everyone there knew that if Cecil had made it to the camp they might not be around. Sue was unaware and unrepentant. Tom left her tied up when there was no one to watch her and only put her gag on when she started swearing at them.

They'd been back on the drive about a week. Tom woke up, it was sometime near morning when he heard Cecil talking calmly and quietly to himself. He had eaten only when delirious and didn't know what he was doing. He drank very little.

Tom crept over to him, 'what is it Cecil' he asked gently?

'The crown jewels… no. The family jewels. The family…'

'What Cecil? Where?'

'The bag… The bag… the bag. No don't trip over the bag, it's important Tom. Fred's right.'

'Shit!' Tom had to get a look in that bag.

He got up and went to the truck. He heard voices in the dark and one of them was Sue. 'Oh, come on baby, hurry. We need to get it back; you have to help me.'

Tom crept closer and saw that Sue had Jack entwined in her legs. Jack was starting to make similar noises to that which… Tom shook his head. He bent down beside Fred and woke the big man gently.

Fred opened his eyes and saw that Tom had his finger to his lips. Fred stayed silent as he got out of his bed. Tom pointed to the two people by the truck. Fred shook his head to clear it.

'Will you help me Fred' Tom breathed?

'Course'. Fred could see that Jack was trying to get astride Sue, but the ropes were making it hard.

'Alright Jack that's bloody enough of that' Tom's voice was low but harsh. Jack sprang away from her. Tom shook his head at him, and Jack kept his mouth shut. He'd been caught and he knew it.

Fred found his voice, 'well I'll be fucked Jack. You got a wife and three kids you dirty bastard.'

Tom spoke, 'Jack, you get your horse saddled and make ready for the road. I don't want you in my outfit. Go on Jack.'

'Tom, I just wanted to get a bit. Honest Tom.'

'You can't fire him Tom see. He's working for me.'

'Put that gag back in Fred then see this bastard out of the camp. I catch you sneaking around Jack, I'll shoot you stone dead.'

Fred came back just in time to gape at the contents of the briefcase. It was full of money. Tom pulled the gag out of Sue's mouth. 'Tell me you didn't steal this from Daddy.'

'You mind your own business. It's my money.'

'He'll come after us you know.'

Emily improved slowly and eventually; the decision was made to wait it out in the St. John Of God Hospital. She started with physio after only a week. Everyone but the good doctor thought it was too soon but after seeing the improvements after a month, those people changed their minds.

But Emily still had no memory of who she was. The good doctor was starting to talk about psychiatrists.

Such talk made people very uneasy. All except Albert who embraced the idea. Out of his own pocket he paid for sessions with the man who came down from Darwin every month.

Nothing worked until about nine weeks after her accident she woke up screaming. Albert was beside her bed doing the night shift, he asked her what was wrong as he picked up her hand and rubbed it.

'He punched me in the face.' Albert's heart broke. He felt it, felt it all. He also knew who it was, he'd seen that bloody Rodney Gaskill light out that morning. He didn't think it would do to try and get in touch with Tom.

As the weeks went slowly by the story of how Emily got hurt came out. Albert told Mavis that the psychiatrist was money well spent. 'But I would sorely like to get my hands on that bastard' he told her as the tears ran down his face, 'he could've killed her. He nearly killed her.' Albert was heavy weight champion several times in his youth and would make short work of Rodney. If he could catch him.

'Albert, what about Tom, shouldn't we…'

Albert shook his head. 'We should be careful to avoid that subject, it's not like she remembers Tom. Jesus Mavis, Tom was a bit of a hot head but he'd a never have done anything like this. My heart bleeds for the both of them, I know how much he… how much she… Oh, Hell Mavis. Wait until that comes back to her.' Albert dropped his head in his hand then looked up at his wife, Despair on his face. 'It was that mongrel Rodney. I suspected all along.'

'Me to love, me to. Well, it's out now and she remembers us even if it is vaguely.'

Mavis was beaming and Albert took her in his arms and kissed the top of her head. Pulling back, he looked at his wife, 'you know, vaguely will do Mavis, we can build on that. And she is getting a little movement in her left arm, and she can move most of her fingers now. That's real progress Mavis. We just have to keep going and get her as good as we can. That is all we can do.'

'I wish we could call Tom though. We need help.'

'It'll only upset her Mavis and who knows how much it would set her back.'

After they had stashed the money under the seat of the truck Tom decided he should go and see if anybody was trailing them. He had an uneasy feeling growing in the pit of his belly. He'd go day after tomorrow.

The next day a rider was spotted coming up fast from the rear. 'Fuck' cried Fred who was looking through the binoculars, 'it's that bloody Jack. Jesus we better let Tom know about this.'

'You go mate, I'll stay with this.'

Fred left Nevil and galloped up to Tom. Tom looked surprised 'what's up' He asked?

'We have a rider about half a mile behind us, we spotted him from the top of the rise. It's Jack and he's coming up fast Tom.'

'Okay Fred, I think you and I better go back and see what he wants don't you? You still got your rifle with you?'

Fred nodded; he didn't like this. They rode back to see what he wanted. 'Keep your eyes peeled Fred'.

At last Jack drew up and said 'G'day. How goes it, Tom?'

'Yeah Jack, what's going on?'

'Tom, I ran into some pretty rough looking characters, there were six of them in all, be about twenty miles back. I stopped to chew the fat and I asked them what they were doing, and they told me it was none of my business. Not a good thing for a start. Well anyway after a bit more talk, they asked me if I'd seen any drovers about. Told me that these drovers would have a woman with them and a herd of about seven hundred. You think they're looking for you Tom?' It was more of a statement than a question. He went on now, 'they had an old bloke with them didn't open his mouth. Short dumpy man with a bald head. That sound like her father Tom?'

Tom nodded his head then put it down, he felt sick. 'What did you tell them Jack?"

'I told them that I had come from Bella Downs, fifty miles ahead. The old bloke nodded his head he knew where it was. Well anyway I said I didn't see no bloody drovers but there's plenty of darkies about and that they tried to rob me. Then I tell them that I'd heard a droving team had pulled into Water Loona, ten miles to the west of here and they were looking for drovers. Told them I'm looking for them myself to get some work. When I rode off, I headed in that direction to make it look so.'

Jack sat and waited for Tom to speak. Tom lifted his hat and wiped his brow. He looked at Fred, 'I bloody knew it.'

'You did,' said Jack. 'I'm sorry Tom, she had me turned against you. I'm here Tom and I'll throw in with you, you just say the word. You was a good boss Tom… I dunno…'

'Jesus, I wish I could Jack, God knows we could do with your help, but she'll just get at you again.'

'I give you my word Tom. I will never let you down again Gods honour. I'll stay away make camp away from you a bit. You know Tom… away from her. I know what a fool I was Tom.'

Tom looked at Fred. Fred swung round towards him and said, 'sounds like we might need him.'

Tom looked straight at Jack now, 'If I was to take you on Jack, I may find myself having to deal with you as well as them. I can't afford to have anyone in my own team, in the camp, turn on me. Do you understand Jack, I cannot give you a gun that you may decide to use on me or my…?'

'Tom, it's me. I won't turn on you, let me help you even if it's just reloading magazines. I hadn't intended to betray you Tom I just wanted a… I was missing Julie…'

'Well, you ought to be downright ashamed of yourself Jack' Fred put in. 'However, I do know how she gets to you.' He looked at Tom, Fred knew they had to take a chance on him, and so did Tom.

'I am Fred. 'Jack put his head down.

'Alright Jack' Tom sounded defeated, 'but I still can't give you a gun and if these blokes get nasty you might need one.'

Tom turned back for the herd and so did Jack and Fred. Jack sidled up to Tom. 'Are they looking for Sue?"

Tom nodded and kept his eyes to the front.

'Has it got anything to do with that bloody bag Tom?' again it was more of a statement. Tom nodded.

''How much?'

Tom stopped his horse and looked at Jack, 'you're asking a lot of questions Jack.'

'Well yeah, why don't we just give them the bag of money and they'll leave us alone.'

Tom looked thoughtful and he said to both the men, 'because I don't know enough about where that money came from. These two Ellis and Sue claim it belongs to them say. So, who's to say it doesn't belong to someone else entirely. A third party who is also interested in its whereabouts. And may be interested in who knows what...'

'Well, what do we care Tom? We hand over the bag and Sue.'

'If we do that, they may very well decide we know too much any way. It might just be that Sue is our only ace to play... who knows. I need to get back to the tucker truck and have a word. Can the two of you get back to the herd?'

'Sure Tom, be glad to' Jack grinned. He was glad to be back, and he'd never let Tom down again.

Tom climbed down off his horse at the truck as Ernie was setting up camp. Tom launched straight into the story.

'Ernie we are being followed, Jack came all the way back to warn us, I'm pretty sure it's Ellis' he noticed Sue's head snapped up. 'He has about five blokes with him, all armed, so they mean business. Jack has come back to help us but he's not to have a gun. He's also got to camp away from us, and we'll need to take turns to keep watch anyway. Ernie start wearing a side arm will you and keep madam tied to the truck, remember to keep your distance though, if she gets hold of it. I'm gunna have to send Nevil to help you babysit the bitch.'

Ernie nodded, 'it's that bloody money. As soon as I saw it, I knew it weren't hers. Why don't we turn her and the bag over Tom, what do we care?'

'We might care if it's stollen money and they know we know about it.'

'We could leave her tied to a tree...'

'Jack told them we are over at Water Loona. We'll keep sending someone to watch our back Ernie. That bloody woman aint going with us to Katherine though, we'll ditch her before then.'

'You can't do that...' Sue was indignant.

Tom didn't look at her, 'we can, and we will. We'll leave you tied to a tree at the next road we come to.' Ernie went off to find firewood and Tom walked across to her, he hunkered down beside her, keeping his voice low. 'Sixty thousand is a fortune Sue, so where'd you get it?'

'What! What? You miserable bastard…'

'Be very careful Sue. If you give me a reason, I will put you on my horse and travel back a ways and tie you to a tree for them to find. Along with the money. How about that Sue?'

'Like I said, miserable bastard.'

'Right now, let's start again, shall we?' Tom studied the fire.

'You can't keep me tied up Tom its…'

'Where did you get the money? I'm assuming from your father since he is after you.'

Sue nodded, she was beaten, and she knew it.

'Right so where did he get it?'

'A job he did involving rustled cattle.'

'Right! Are these those cattle Sue?'

'Course not he's been paid for those hasn't he, and you have the bloody money. That's a discrepancy of ten thousand Tom. He's not going to like that if he gets hold of me. What do I tell him Tom? What do I tell him?'

'I'm sure you'll think of something Sue, women like you always do. You've dragged us all into this you bitch. Men may die you know but that won't bother you right? Right?' Tom stood up 'are these cattle stollen?'

Sue shook her head. 'You can't just throw me to the wolves Tom…'

'I can though, and I will. You threw Cecil to the wolves, didn't you? You are prepared to throw every-one of us to the wolves. Tell me Sue, how had you planned to get away?'

'I'm to meet a man in Darwin. He is waiting there with a small plane.'

Tom nodded and rose to his feet; He'd have to get her to Darwin. He'd get her to the train for Darwin and put the bitch on it.

Tom walked over to Cecil, dropping to his hunkers he looked the man in the eye. 'How did you know about the money Cecil?'

'Tom is it alright if I go. I won't say anything about all this Tom, any of it. I know what goes on here. You're a good man Tom, it's thanks to you that I'm still alive. It was just a guess Tom, just a lucky guess I swear it.'

'You may go Cecil when you are a little better.' The two men eyed each other Tom couldn't turn him loose and Cecil knew he couldn't. Cecil settled back down to wait. His head snapped up 'well I might as well be some bloody use, Tom. At least put me back to work. Tom, you saved my life. Give me something mate, put me back to work. I'll finish the drive with you Tom.'

Tom stared down at the man looking eagerly back at him, he didn't doubt the man's word for a minute. He nodded 'okay, starting tomorrow you'll ride up front opposite me.' He went to turn away then looked back at the man sitting on the ground, 'at full pay' he grinned.

Tom knew he'd need all the help he could get. He had to keep these cows moving, had to reach Katherine before Ellis caught up with them.

Bradly Ellis didn't know whether he should believe the story Jack had told him or not, He knew that Tom should be following this trail but if he did have injured men, he might be over in Water Loona. He scratched his head and chewed on a stick. Getting up he announced to his men they would keep on their present course. The worst that could happen was that he'd get in front of Tom.

He did realise that by now his daughter would have done quite a job on the young drover and probably all the others as well. He had to get his hands on her before she reached Katherine.

He swung up in the saddle with a remarkable agility and ease for a man of his age and stature. All he wanted was the money, he had no animosity to Tom and his men. He could understand though that Tom might make an attempt to outrun him. Especially if he knew where the money came from. Bradley wasn't concerned with that. Who was going to take Tom's word over his? But his bloody daughter! He had to get his hands on her, he had an idea she'd be headed for Darwin.

He kicked his horse into a canter and headed along the trail. There was evidence of a large herd passing this way very recently, but he had no way of knowing if it was his. This was a well-used trail by drovers from all over, there was plenty of water. But Bradley had been following it from Damper Creek, so he was pretty sure it was them. He had to keep moving if he was going to intercept them and get his daughter and his money back.

There was a road up ahead, maybe he'd send one of his men back to check if they went that way.

❧

It was three days later that Tom's men spotted the riders behind them from a rise. They were just visible, but Tom knew they'd have him within the week. He'd have to play dirty, though he hated to.

Tom loved horses and the idea of shooting them for no good reason was repugnant to him. He knew Fred was their best shot, so he sent him and Jimmy back to take out three of their horses. That way they'd have to double up. Tom had known Bradley Ellis for years and knew he'd never leave behind men to walk out of this country.

He sat his horse now with a heavy heart as Fred rode up to him. He'd watched through the binoculars as the horses went down. Then he'd watched as Bradley inspected his horse and seen them double up on their horses. His plan had worked.

At that moment he figured he hated that bloody woman more than anything in the world. He had a sudden urge to go back to camp and shoot her.

❧

Over the next few weeks Tom never saw the riders again. When he was a few days out of Katherine he stopped on top of a hill. Looking back, he could just see the riders through the binoculars. he tethered three of his horses near some trees with water and feed. Tom judged them to be about ten miles back and knew he'd outrun them. They'd take two days to reach the horses.

He left a note in the saddle bag he'd left over one the horses' backs. The note said simply, 'I did say I didn't want to take the bitch. She's been nothing but trouble, but she has convinced me she is afraid of you. I am most sorry about the horses. Please leave these horses saddles and bits at the Katherine stable.'

Bradley scrunched the paper up in his fist. He should've bloody listened. He was bloody glad to see the horses though and knew he'd judged young Tom correctly. He knew however that he would never catch them now, but he would eventually catch up with that bloody daughter of his. The only thing she could be counted on was for running out of money. Then she'd come crawling back. He'd put the little bitch in a nunnery.

In Katherine Tom delivered the cattle to the rail head where they were booked on a train for three days' time. He then delivered Sue to the Katherine hotel. He told her he hoped he'd never have the misfortune of running into her again.

He told her, 'You have three days before daddy turns up. I don't much care what happens to you, but I would like to see you get on that bloody train and as far away from me as possible.' He turned and walked away.

He got to the end of the street and changing his mind he turned round a retraced his steps. There was a train due out in two hours. That'd do. He went back and got her.

Tom hurried along the platform now carrying Sue's bags as she hurried to keep up. 'For God's sake Tom I…'

'Just shut up and move woman' Tom snapped. 'I want you on that fuckin train and out of my hair.'

'Language…!'

Tom stopped and turned to face her, 'language! You have the bloody cheek to talk to me about language. The abuse you have levelled at me and my men over the last few weeks. How you swore and cursed at us was just fuckin shameful. Just hurry up, I want bloody rid of you. It's a wonder you didn't get us all killed.'

'I don't doubt that Tom, that I nearly got you all killed, but how was I to know? And anyway, what do you think daddy will say when he finds out…'

Tom had swung round and grabbed Sues arm 'you tell him what you want you. You went through every one of my men. Yeah, even the married ones. You're worse than a cat on heat you bitch of a thing. What'll daddy think? Probably just that you want to diminish what you did and rope others in to share the blame with you. Go right ahead but I'll be denying any fuckin knowledge of any of it.'

Tom opened the carriage door and threw her bags inside. Turning he grabbed Sue by her oxters and practically threw her in after them.

'I didn't fuck all your men.'

'No, there's me and Ernie and I don't think Cecil would have wanted to touch you with a barge pole.'

'Well fuck you Mister high and mighty, you thieving mongrel.' Sue hesitated at the look on Tom's face, the slow grin spreading across it. Something happened to his face when he smiled.

Tom banged the door shut in her face and heaved a sigh of relief. He was glad to be rid of that. Tom still had things to do before closing. He turned his back on the train and hurried off.

Sue sat back on the train and heaved a sigh of relief also. This was the last leg of her trip; in just hours she would be with Herbert. Dear sweet Herbert, she'd be safe in his loving arms. Sue closed her eyes and let the desire for him wash over her.

Then onto his plane and off to more civilised shores to a more civilised life. To hell with Tom, to hell with all the Tom's and that included her father. Sue was through with this bloody country. Through with the heat and the dust and flies, through with the loud, rough, course men and their arrogance and their hardness. She closed her eyes and sighed.

As Sue entered the Astra Hotel the next morning Herbert was in the foyer. She was stung at the sight of Herbert, dear sweet Herbert with his arm wrapped around a woman old enough to be his mother.

She hesitated just inside the door, almost completely hidden by a plant and watched as he talked to her. His face was flushed and serious as he talked to her in earnest. In horror she watched as Herbert tried to snatch a kiss and copped the woman's handbag in his face.

Herbert staggered backwards trying desperately to keep to his feet. He was within a few feet of Sue when, stepping from behind the plant, she lashed out and hit him in the back of the legs with her suitcase. Herbert crashed to the floor at her feet.

She watched horror stricken as his face registered that he recognised her. Just as horrified she felt a revulsion fill her at the smarmy smile which spread across it. He tried to scramble to his feet.

Sue felt every one of her hopes and dreams evaporate as she stood there. Herbert had made it to his knees and bent forward to gain his feet. On an impulse she drew her foot back and kicked him as hard as she could in his backside. The older woman cackled like a witch.

As Sue watched the love of her life take the plant with him and land in soil and manure at the feet of the woman, she let out a cry. The woman he'd been trying to kiss laid into him with her handbag. 'You no good thieving bloody scoundrel. You need to leave town you are finished here. When I make it known around town what you are, no decent woman will look the road you're on. You asked me to marry you and I find out you are already so. How dare you? I should get the police onto you; you are a cheap con man. I have it on good authority you can't even pay for your hotel room.' The older woman turned on her heel and marched out of the foyer. 'Have nothing to do with that one' she said to Sue as she marched passed her.

Sue stood staring open mouthed at the man she'd risked all for. For the first time she noticed he was pasty faced, overweight and bleary eyed. He looked unkempt and shabby. Sue's heart broke in two, how had she been such a fool? Her breath caught in her throat as suddenly she realised, she was comparing him to Tom. Sue forced this thought from her mind as she watched her beloved prince charming turn into a toad right before her baby blues. She hoped he wouldn't speak, prayed he wouldn't open his smarmy mouth and speak.

But this was Herbert and he'd watched a few of his own hopes and dreams turn to steam. He turned to Sue and smiled as sweetly as he could. 'Please don't listen to her darling, she is a lying old biddy. I never asked her to marry m…'

He was walking towards her and tried to take her hands in his. Sue swung her bag and caught Herbert on the chin. She was repulsed and picked her suitcase up and turned away from this man she had fallen for. Had thought herself in love with, tears making it difficult to see where she was going.

With as much dignity as she could muster Sue walked to the desk and checked into a single room. She turned at the bottom of the stairs and looked askance at her boyfriend brushing furiously at his pants. Sue fought the urge to rush back down and give him a good thrashing.

She walked up to her room and fumbled with the key. She could feel hot tears spilling from her eyes. She tried to hold them back. But the memory of Herbert trying to kiss the woman in the foyer was threatening to choke her. Oh, she'd like to choke him.

Suddenly she saw herself as others saw her. A fool! She shook her head at this thought, anything but that. She let herself in the room and caught a glimpse of herself in the mirror. How she despised herself at this moment. That bloody Herbert had hoodwinked her for the money. And now she couldn't even go back to daddy. Sue found as she got angry her pain lessened and so did her despair. Well, she told herself she had a fortune in her bag. She'd start taking care of herself. And she'd find a way to regain her self-respect. She just needed to pick a city.

Sue threw herself on her bed and cried. When she was through, she sat up and wiped her eyes, she was sick of crying. No more of it! What now she wondered?

❧

After he put Sue on the train, Tom picked up his cheque from the bank and paid the men. He shook hands with Fred and Ernie. 'What now Tom' asked Fred?

'Well, I'm dry so it's the pub for me. Anybody want to join me?'

The three men walked into the bar where they met up with Jack and Nevil. Tom settled himself on a barstool in the corner and his first drink hardly touched the sides he said as he ordered another. How he wanted to forget all about the fairer sex.

Three days after Tom had reached Katherine Ellis and his men arrived. Bradley Ellis found Tom horribly drunk in the Drovers Rest. He got two of his men to carry young Tom to a hotel room which he paid for and put him to bed. He'd seen men in a worse state after spending much less time with his daughter. As soon as Tom came to, he'd find out where she'd got to. As if he didn't know.

Bradly settled himself down on a barstool downstairs and sank a few beers. He wondered about his daughter and the money. On a train to Darwin, he guessed. He'd be quite happy to go home without her, but it was a lot of money she'd taken from him. He'd like to get it back and maybe find out who else knew about it.

He started with a couple of whiskey chasers and asked himself how he had brought all this upon himself? Why did his children not respect him? Must have something to do with the fact that his bitch wife disrespected him and abused him from the time he got in the door to the time he made it back out the door.

Bradley Ellis had no idea why his bitch of a wife hated him; he had loved her at first. Well, it was sort of love. They had been thrown together by their parents he knew but she had seemed keen. But hate him she did and now he hated her back, with every fibre of his being he hated that bloody shrew.

Ellis wanted to talk to Tom and see if he could find out what, if anything, the young drover knew. Tom was just the sort of young man he'd like to see his daughter with. A cut above those bloody lounge lizard gigolos she usually brought home. Sleazy bastards who were more interested in poking around the place ascertaining how much the woman was worth or would be worth when daddy died.

But his wife seemed taken with the trash and not only allowed them to stay but encouraged it. Finding good qualities about these good for nothing lay abouts where there were none as they sat about eating the food on his table that he'd put there. All the while washing it down with his finest bottles of wine.

Yes, Bradly could see her with worse than Tom Cooper. Salt of the earth was Tom. By the time Bradly staggered upstairs to sleep it off he'd forgiven Tom, no matter what his involvement in all this. Hell, he'd made up his mind if he ever got his hands on that money, he'd give it all to Tom to take his bitch daughter off his hands.

And he told himself as he lay his head on the pillow, if his bitch wife had anything to say he'd sell her to the first dero he came across. Or maybe he'd have to give the dero a bottle of wine to take her. Bradly chuckled as his head hit the pillow and the blessed blackness that only drink could bring, engulfed him.

CHAPTER 3

Just over two months after Emily was brought into the hospital, she got out of bed and walked out. She shuffled when she walked but she was improving all the time and the doctor said he wanted her to keep going to physio. Her arm was inclined to swing about, so she mostly kept it tucked into her waist. She could use it to help her other hand a bit, but it would never be the same. Emily had lost a lot of weight which helped her with her walking.

She had regained a lot of her memory though many details surrounding the incident which left her permanently disabled did not return to her. She asked Mavis one day if she'd had a boyfriend.

'Yes dear' said Mavis 'you did but you don't see him anymore.'

Both women left it at that but Emily, although she didn't know why, knew she should be sad.

When Emily walked into the house, she looked about her feeling less familiar than she thought she would. She didn't know it, but Ned and his wife had cleaned the house from top to bottom as well as tended her garden. They'd been saddened by the state of the place, particularly all the blood. They both liked Emily but they knew how fond Albert and Mavis were of her. It was a most upsetting business all round and they prayed everything would work out for the young woman.

Now Emily stood in her kitchen, thanking everyone for their help. She wished they'd go home and leave her to her thoughts. Albert sensed this and announced that maybe Emily should lay down and get some rest. 'Of course,' said Ned. 'It's been a big day for you. My wife left a stew in the fridge for you love, you just need to heat it up.' He smiled kindly at Emily, and she miled back, she was pretty sure she liked Ned.

'Thankyou' said Emily as she said goodbye to Albert and Mavis at the front door. Alone at last, Emily walked through the house some of her memories of it returning. She sat at her kitchen table and looked about her. She did realise that she had never seen it so clean. She liked it and made herself a promise that she would keep it clean. It was a nice big kitchen with plenty of workspace and cupboards.

The pantry which was just off the kitchen had always been well stocked with bins of flour and salt and sugar etc. Emily loved to bake and saved a lot of money baking for herself. She often baked bread and people bought it from her along with vegetables from the garden and fruit when it was in season. Emily preserved fruit and made jams which she also sold. She'd supplemented her meagre wage from the general store this way.

As the days passed Emily became aware that a lot of men were walking past her house. 'They are railway workers putting in the new siding' Albert had told her.

'What happened to the Chinese shanty just down the road?'

'They left and council knocked it down. It was an eyesore and a health hazard they say.'

'Still, I liked his cooking, and he was cheap. I used to get it sometimes. He fed the men out at the mine on their way to and from.' Emily sighed. She was restless.

Life got back to normal for the people in Damper Creek. All except for Emily. She applied for a pension and got it. As the weeks went passed, she got the backyard sorted and some vegetables put in. Everything was a bit of an effort for her, but she was determined her disability would never define who she was.

She was sitting one day sipping a cup of tea she'd made herself wondering about Tom. Sometimes she could remember his face and other times she could not. There came a knock at her back door which startled her a little.

Putting her cup down she straightened her dress and shuffled to the door. She opened it and there stood a man in dirty work clothes. She smiled politely at him, and he smiled at her. The man was probably in his early fifties and tall, he had grey curly hair and a nice smile. 'Can I help you with something' she asked?

'I'm sorry to bother you miss but I was told I could get pretty good grub around here somewhere. Would that be you Missus? I'd pay.'

Emily stared at the man and thought for a bit. Then she said the words that would change her life forever. 'I suppose I could get you a sandwich. Or a bowl of stew it was freshly made yesterday.'

'I'd take both if you don't mind. So, you are not the one who sells food? It's just that some of my workmates need to buy food to. Lunches… you know.'

Emily turned back slowly to face the man. A thought was dawning on her, a thought which had far reaching implications. Could she? … Dare she? She was largely a cripple. But she would probably only make a couple of lunches a week anyway. She could manage that. 'I am not Mister Wong, and I can't cook Chinese but… If you don't mind ordinary food, I will do my best to supply you with good, wholesome lunches.'

Emily held her breath and then the man smiled and holding out his hand to her he said that he would inform his mates. As he shook hands with Emily he said as an afterthought 'if the prices are right. We are not rich men.' When he laughed Emily told him she would work out a fair price.

There were chairs and a large table on the back veranda and Emily invited him to sit while she got his food.

Back in the kitchen she put a portion of stew in a small earthen bowl and put it on the stove to warm. Then she cut two thick slices of bread and put some cold mutton from a flap that she had boiled and pressed. She added some cheese and pickled onion she'd done last year. She had jars and jars of pickled onions, and she had a pound of cheese from Mrs. Wilson who made it. She cut another two slices of bread for the stew

As she worked, Emily worked out very quickly in her head how much the stew had cost to make then how many portions she'd get and came to a figure for what it would cost to make the portion. She did the same with the sandwich and decided on sixpence. Threepence for the stew and bread and threepence for the sandwich, she would make a profit at that.

The man who told her his name was Harry looked pleased with the price, 'after all it is two lunches. I would think that most of the blokes will love a bit of stew with a couple of slices of bread.'

Emily smiled; she was delighted when he dropped the sixpence into her hand. Her quick mind went immediately to what portion of it would be needed to replenish supplies. She looked over the man's shoulder at the two men at the gate. When they walked up Harry explained to them that Mr. Wong was gone, and that Emily here would make lunches for them.

'You want bread and stew tomorrow? I don't know what I will put it in Maybe my bowls, but I need to get them back to use them again.' She glanced at the bowl of stew in his hand.

Harry nodded then said 'alright Miss. We'll drop them back on our way to and from. If you run out of bowls, we'll just have to go to sandwiches. '

Emily looked at the other men and smiled and they both said at once 'a bowl of stew and a slice of bread.' She charged them threepence each. When she came out, they had sat at her big table and made no move to leave. To Emily's surprise she realised they were going to eat it there. She went inside and got them cold water to drink.

When they were finished Harry knocked on the door and indicating the bowl he smiled. 'That was the best sandwich Missus and so filling, I've decided to keep the stew for my tea. Can we count on you again tomorrow? And these two as well?'

'You can Harry. I will have stew and sandwiches. Were those sandwiches alright?'

'Yes, they were very good thanks, best I've tasted that stew' said one of the two men.

That afternoon after they'd left Emily sat with a cup of tea. She couldn't believe it. She had twelve pence. A shilling. She picked the money up and counted it again. This was Tuesday, by the end of the week she'd have four shillings. She could get flour and Mutton flaps and more cheese for about a shilling. The vegetables for her stew were mostly from her garden. She'd just need onions and potatoes. She had two more shoulders of mutton in the fridge.

When she'd finished her tea, she started to bake bread. She had a loaf, so she'd make three more and start on another stew and cook another shoulder of mutton. She visited the shops over in Mataranka every Thursday morning. She'd stock up.

Emily had another three loaves and the stew going when there came a knock on her door. When she went to see who it could be there stood Harry and four other men. They looked tired.

Emily stepped out on to the wide veranda, 'what is it, Harry?"

'We was just wondering if we could get some more of that stew Missus. And some of that lovely bread to. We'll pay. And could you bring us some tea or coffee to.'

'Of course, Harry. Just give me a minute I wasn't expecting anybody.' Emily smiled at them, and they sat down at the table.

In the kitchen Emily told herself to pull herself together. They looked hungry she thought, and this was probably their tea. She'd have to fill their bowls as full as she could. They were big bowls and probably held as much as a plate. She cut them two slices of bread and made a mug of coffee each.

When she took these things out to them there were another two men sitting there. One of these men was sitting on the step, she didn't have enough chairs. Harry grinned at her and asked for another two plates of stew. Emily got them. When they left, they paid Emily one shilling and ninepence? That was two and nine all up.

After Emily had done the dishes, she went to the stove for some stew. It was mostly gone! What would she do, there were only two loaves of bread left now to?

She sat eating her tea she was hungry. Suddenly Emily remembered the large bag of mince she got from Mister Sutton one of the station owners. She'd make pies for tomorrow. Oh yes, she thought that would be easier anyway. She'd make big pies and give them a slice of cheese to go with it. But she'd have to get busy.

It was nearly ten o'clock when Emily took the last batch of pies out of the oven, she'd made ten and by midday the next day she wished she'd made more. She'd begun to warm the pies at around eleven and by lunch time the aroma had reached the hungry men coming up the road and in her back gate.

Twenty men came for the pies. She had to tell the last ten she ran out. Their looks of disappointment prompted her to promise them pies tomorrow. 'I shall make you sandwiches'

Emily had to get out to mister Suttons place, it was about half a mile out of town. She asked Ned to take her out there and paid him sixpence. Along the way she told him of the men that she was cooking for. 'Well good for you Emily' he said with a grin. 'Yes, I smelled those pies girl. You'd best get stocked up Emily and it's a good idea coming out here. Much cheaper.'

Emily turned to Ned and asked 'would you bring me out twice a week Ned. Are you happy with sixpence? Just until they find somewhere better to eat.'

'Emily, if they find somewhere better to eat, they are fools. I'm so glad you have this, Emily. Those miners will start coming to, you'll see.'

Emily sat in silence the rest of the way, her mind on what she'd need to get to do her until Thursday.

She couldn't help but wonder if she'd bitten off more than she could chew. If it got too much, she'd have to get help. But for now, she settled herself to just see where this venture took her.

Ned was telling her now that he was buying a car, had ordered it and it would be here next week. 'I can take you shopping in style girl' he said with a kindly smile. He admired this young woman.

Chapter 4

Tom came to with a start, he wasn't expecting to see the face which was hovering above him. He moaned loudly and the men standing round him laughed. Tom kept his eyes on Bradly Ellis as he rolled over to get to his feet.

'How are you young Tom?'

Tom shook his head and made for the bathroom. Hell, he was sick, he needed a hair of the dog. He knew one thing; he was in no condition to talk to Bradly fuckin Ellis. How had that bastard got his hands on him so quick?

He relieved himself and swilled his face which was numb and returned to the bedroom to face the music. Bradly rose to his feet and walked towards him stopping a few feet from him. He said softly, 'you don't look too good young Tom.'

'No shit. Thanks to you. Send us off on a cattle drive with a venomous bloody viper in our midst.' Tom was nodding his head vigorously now, his eyes bright. He went on, 'I hope you don't expect me to tell you where she is because I don't know. I am blissfully unaware of where she is, and I would like to stay that way.' Tom sat on the bed and flopped to his side and stretching out he rolled over facing the wall.

He was dragged unceremoniously to his feet and stood in front of Bradly Ellis. After studying Tom for a few seconds, he started to speak, quietly. 'I am sorry for any inconvenience Tom…'

'Inconvenience!' Tom threw off the two men who were holding him only to find they were holding him up. He righted himself and Ellis stepped back. Pulling himself up to his full six feet two he sneered. 'You don't know the half of it. Those of my men who weren't wounded by the bitch were too busy otherwise involved with her to do any bloody work or get too much sense out of. She's a fuckin nightmare.' Tom leaned towards Ellis now and shouted, 'a nightmare.'

'Now hang on Tom, she is my daughter. She hasn't had the benefit of a mother's guidance. She spent so much time in a boarding school because the two of them would have bloody killed each other.' Ellis turned and sat in a chair and put his head in his hands, his mouth was running away from him, and he knew it. He looked up and indicated Tom sit in the other chair. Just as wearily he went on, 'her mother is worse than her. She is a bloody shrew of a woman and has driven me nearly mad over the years. I am afraid of her Tom, afraid of what I might one day do to her. I tell you I'll swing for it.'

Tom shook his head, 'what, may I ask, has this all to do with me? No, don't tell me, this is happy fuckin families, right? Well, I know how happy families ends Ellis, I was in one once. And for your information, it doesn't end well. It never does. So, get out the harps and violins or talk about something else.' Tom turned his head and studied the door wondering what his chances were that he'd make it out through the door and down the stairs and into the bar before the goons got him. God what he'd give for a beer right now. He was getting the shakes.

When Ellis spoke, his voice held a tired resignation. 'Can we have the room please?' His men filed out to wait in the corridor. 'Listen, Tom…'

Tom sat on the edge of his chair. 'What?'

Ellis leaned forward resting his elbows on his knees and fixed his eyes on the floor. 'Tom, did you find that my daughter was holding onto something. Er… that is that she had something, what shall we say, valuable in her possession? Something which you thought might not belong to her?' Ellis held up his hand for Tom to remain silent. 'Now Tom… I am not accusing you of anything. I don't care about your involvement in all this. As you say, that is down to me. But I would like you to tell me what you know.'

'I know fuck all. That's what I know. And I also know that I will never do another bloody job for you as long as I draw sodden breath in case you have any more bloody daughters. And the bonus of say a hundred quid is nowhere near enough. Not to compensate a man for trying to look after that bloody whore.'

Ellis' head came up, 'now see here Tom…'

'No, you see here. Instead of going on about what you already know, why don't you spit out what you really want?'

Ellis' voice held a semblance of a threat now, 'I want these three things Tom. I want my money back; I want to know what you and anybody else may know of it and I want you to marry my daughter.'

Tom sprang to his feet horror stricken. He wanted to tell Ellis where to stick it, but something was happening in his throat and in his chest. Something in his belly. Tom erupted into laughter. He couldn't speak and the laughter was making him dizzy. He knew he ought to stop, knew something else was happening in his belly. But he couldn't stop. He couldn't see for tears as he laughed helplessly at something so horrific as that which he'd just heard from the little fat rat in the chair.

Ellis sat transfixed as if he had seen into his future, and when Tom opened his mouth and spewed all over him, he was unable to avoid it.

Bradly Ellis, for the first time in his life spewed up all the drink he'd consumed the night before as he got to his feet and added it to Toms'.

Tom was flabbergasted as he studied the horrible mess on the floor. He turned to Ellis and called him a dirty pig.

The noise had brought the three men in the corridor in to stand and stare in amazement at the two men standing there shouting at one another about, whose fault it was and who had started it. The three men understood that they were talking about the mess on the floor. The youngest of the three, Billy, rushed forward and added his to the pile.

Tom looked scathingly at them and walked quietly from the room. Marry that bastards' daughter? Marry that bitch? He'd as just as well go home to Emily. Just as well go home and marry that dirty bitch.

As he closed the door, he said softly without turning, 'she's in Darwin but you'd best be quick. She has a plane waiting for her.'

Tom didn't see Ellis hang his head and let a tear fall down his cheek. His money was gone then. Ellis got suddenly to his feet; he had a train to catch. By Jesus he did.

Tom staggered across the bar room floor his tongue practically hanging out of his head. 'Gimme a beer mate and hurry up about it.'

'A hair of the dog son?'

Tom scowled at him but kept his mouth shut. The barman put a beer in front of Tom. He picked it up and downed it slamming the glass back on the bar he slurped the froth from his top lip. He turned and left the bar. He had things to do and getting as far away from that stupid bastard upstairs was at the top of his list. He'd had more sense from bloody billy goats. Marry that bitch, Tom had thought he'd heard everything.

❧

Emily had gotten six pounds of minced beef, two large roasts and six pounds of steak for stewing. She had two lamb shoulders, and two good sized hams. On the way back through town Emily got Ned to call at the store. Here she purchased more flour, eggs, sugar, suet, and some bottles of sauce. She'd put the sauce on the table. When she had everything, she needed she climbed back up beside Ned. She had spent most of her pension cheque.

At last Emily was on her way back to the house. By way of idle chatter, she said 'you know the men eat on my back veranda. Some of them even sit on the floor because I only have five chairs and one table. Some sit on the grass under the trees.'

Ned looked sideways at her, 'well you know that China man's shanty they pulled down. Now he had tables and stools which the council threw out to the dump. Why don't we put your groceries away and take a look?'

'I have to have tea ready for them Ned, but I'd like to get my hands on them. Maybe tomorrow, Ned?'

'Then you go home and start your teas Emily and I'll go look. See if there's anything worth having.'

Ned left Emily in her kitchen and went to the dump. When he came back Emily was delighted to see so many chairs and tables piled high on the cart. She put four of her kitchen chairs with them and all up she had five tables and twenty-four chairs.

Lastly Ned produced a large box which he opened with a flourish, 'look Emily, they just need a wash, and most are not broken. Must have been Mister Wong's' Emily stared wide eyed. There was a stack of plates bowls and mugs, in a smaller box Ned had found all manner of cutlery. 'Oh Ned.' Emily was grinning from ear to ear, and it did Ned's heart good to see it. He couldn't believe how she had met the challenge of living as a partial cripple. How she had turned her life around.

'Come on girl, you need to get busy. I'll give you a bit of a hand. We'll get em cleaned and set up hay?'

Emily had the stew and potatoes cooking and the tables and chairs all nice and clean and set up on the veranda when the men started to roll in.

Harry's eyes lit up when he saw it all and he grinned at Emily. 'My, Emily you've done a fine job girl. Thankyou from all of us, now we have somewhere nice to sit and eat. With good food and good mates. And with you looking after us Emily, we have a home away from home. A place to relax and talk a while.' He stuffed his hands in his pockets and looked about with a smile. Looking back at Emily he said softly, 'I hope you don't mind Emily, but I heard what happened to you. Well sort of. Anyway, may I say how very much I admire you girl. Talk about rising to the challenge and then some. You know, you put most of us to shame Emily.' Harry looked down at his feet, 'and the food you dish up is second to none, dear. Second to none. And I believe those are miners coming in your gate, so I hope you have plenty. I'll take a bowl of stew Emily with two slices of your very excellent bread.'

Harry sat down and Emily noticed how tired he looked. She smiled at him and said, 'I have a wee treat tonight, Harry.'

Harry grinned up at her, 'do you now? Are you going to tell me or is it to be a surprise?'

'Oh, it's just apple pie and fresh cream.'

'Oh lord Emily, my favourite. Oh, we are blessed to have you girl. Just apple pie and fresh cream she says. I can't wait to get my laughing gear round that Emily. And thanks again.'

Twenty-five men turned up for tea that night, miners, and railway men alike and Emily took much pride in the place she had provided for them. As she moved to and fro with her funny shuffle, she noticed the men laughed and talked excitedly. Yes, she told herself she had done something good here. Every chair was full, and one man sat on the veranda step.

That night as she stood at the sink, tired out and she still had the pies to make, she told herself she'd need help. She knew just where to look.

The next day Emily rose early and put the mince on to cook for the pies. She ducked down the road to see Janet who she had been friends with since school. As she walked along, she smiled at the money she'd made last night. She'd made over four pound which was more than her pension. Some of the men had wanted only a sandwich which she had made with ham, cheese, and pickled onions on the side. The apple pie had gone down a treat and for the cost of roughly six shillings she'd made an extra two pounds.

Janet was delighted, to make some money and to have a job was just marvellous. 'Could you start tonight, Janet? I'm alright in the daytime but it's at night. Serving at the tables and cleaning up after is hectic on my own. I will pay you a pound a week when and if I can for a start. Just until I get on my feet. I still have a lot of things to work out.'

Janet's eyes were shining bright, 'a pound a week. By Emily, some of them men don't earn much more than that. It'll do me Emily and get me out of this house. Oh Emily, thank you for thinking of me.'

'I'm glad I did Janet. Now I must get back and see to these pies I only have until one o'clock.'

'Can I come and see what you've done Emily and we'll get those pies done twice as fast.'

Janet clasped her hands in front of her and squealed with delight when she stood looking at what Emily had done with her back veranda. 'Oh Emily, it's lovely. I can't believe it Emily; I thought you would just sit and die in this house. I'm flabbergasted Emily I really am. Oh I'm sorry but most people would have.'

'It's alright Janet. Janet, I don't remember much about the past and I don't really want to.'

'Fair enough Emily, we'll just get on with the future then.'

Over the next few days Emily realised what a Godsend Janet was. She worked hard and was always happy. The men took to her, and Emily noticed that she liked to be around them and listen to their stories of far-off places. Janet's help also allowed Emily to attend to things like ordering and shopping. And Janet had contributed another table and four chairs to the small café growing on Emily's back veranda. Emily didn't know what she'd done without her.

By the end of that week Emily had earned ten pound and so she ordered a large fridge and freezer. In the top of her freezer, she put mince and steak and on the next shelf she had roasts and hams. The roasts she did were a big hit with the men on Thursdays and Sundays. The leftovers she used for sandwiches and cold serves. The extra she could buy thanks to the fridge and freezer cut her shopping trips down to twice a week.

Emily was making and selling about thirty pies a day, sometimes the men would buy an extra pie for his tea. She also made and sold at least fifty sausage rolls each week. She also ordered another stove with a big oven. Emily regularly added apple pie and steamed puddings to the menu.

Every night Emily was exhausted, but she remained excited about her business. Somewhere in the back of Emily's mind she knew she had some atonements to make, some self-respect to earn back. She suspected her accident had been a blessing in disguise. She embraced her new self and felt not a jot of self-pity for herself.

Mavis and Albert helped whenever she needed it, and Albert thoroughly enjoyed the company of the men as he sat with them when they'd finished eating and were talking quietly.

Yes, Emily was happy with herself, and she knew she hadn't always been. Sometimes she realised that she didn't want any more of her memory back. She carried a pain in her heart, one that she tried so hard to ignore. And God willing she told herself one day she would get the chance to apologise to someone she didn't always know what he looked like for something she didn't remember and didn't care to.

Emily got wearily to her feet. She loved how well she slept now, and she also loved that she had little time to sit and feel sorry for herself. Had less time to pine for a face she found she could only remember dimly and was getting dimmer. A beautiful face that she had loved.

She still had nightmares about waking up in the dark in pain and a pool of her own blood. The terror of not being able to go for help and the pain in her head. That awful blackness, a long painful ride to hospital and followed by an awful blankness. Then the pain of physio had been shocking. But she had made it and she was proud of herself.

She woke up in a cold sweat sometimes shrinking from things she didn't fully understand. Woke up begging to be forgiven yet unable to ask and found herself with no understanding of words or meanings. Her lack of use in her left hand was her main draw back. But Emily was glad that mostly the pain was over.

As the weeks went by, she found she was making a lot of money and had started banking. She kept change for sometimes the men gave her a note. Emily knew also that she would need more help. She went to Albert and Mavis with this.

'Well, there's Nellie,' said Albert. 'She's a hard worker and could stay late and do your dishes while you get ready for bed. You are looking a bit-tired girl.'

Mavis nodded her approval all the while. She and her husband had thanked God down on their knees for the turn-around in their girl. And so it was that Nellie joined Emily's little team. And she to, was a Godsend.

In the coming years the three young women were to become firm and lifelong friends.

CHAPTER 5

Tom got another job taking cattle from the Alice to Mataranka. It was three hundred head that one of the big station owners needed to restock his property with.

He'd told Bradly Ellis on parting company at the Katherine stockyards that he would love to marry his whore of a daughter and if he had any more of em at home like her, he'd be willing to consider converting to Islam. 'You know, just so's I could marry the lot of em.' He'd laughed at Ellis and reaffirmed that he would never again work for him. 'You're a bloody jinx ya bastard' he'd finished as he waved goodbye.

Tom did take a moment however to feel sorry for the man as he watched him hurry off, shoulders hunched to catch a train to Darwin to find his daughter and his money.

'We shall see young Tom, we shall see' he'd thrown over his shoulder before disappearing into a carriage and slamming the door behind him.

Tom climbed into the saddle and rode next to his old friend Fred out to join the herd. When they arrived, Ernie was there, and Tom reigned in and hailed the older man. He smiled and said softly, 'haven't seen any women around have you Ernie?'

Ernie smiled and shook his head. Looking up at Tom he said, 'no but Jack is here and so is Cecil. They want to be hired on Tom and you are at least a man down. They're down at the stockyards helping the men with the round up Tom.'

Tom stared off into the distance where the men were getting the herd rounded up and ready to head off. He wanted to clear the stockyards and make camp as far away from town as he could get. He sighed, 'I'll go and see them, Ernie.'

Tom hired the two men and when they pulled out, he felt his heart lift as it always did. The old excitement was back in the pit of his belly. Despite his grog session in Katherine, Tom had deposited most of his earnings for the last trip into the bank. Including his one-hundred-pound bonus for delivering Sue to Katherine as agreed. Tom was pleased with his tidy little nest egg, some of which was in a safety deposit box.

Tom felt good and this was another big job which would pay well. It was a longer trip, but Tom was an old hand and didn't find anything to worry about. And no Sue, which was a bonus.

During his long bouts in the saddle Tom was doing some thinking about his future. He would need to get out of this game one day he'd often mused. Tom had decided he'd save as much money as he could and someday, he told himself he'd buy a block. Start his own herd.

Yes, someday he might even have a son and then… At this point Tom usually told himself he'd need a woman for that. And that part of his dream would evaporate before his eyes.

He sat his saddle quietly; it was a Saturday and he'd been doing some of his musing. Tom suddenly remembered he'd had a dream; it was a nice dream. He had met Emily and they had got friendly… Tom lifted his head and shrugged it off. He had to admit that he sometimes missed her. Missed her very much, more than she bloody deserved he told himself.

A shout from up in front brought his head up. He saw Fred slump forward in his saddle and fall to the ground. Tom galloped to his friend and hit the ground running. He turned Fred over and was horrified at the red stain on the front of his shirt. Fred was unconscious and Tom yelled out to Jack to give him a hand.

'What is it' asked Jack?

'I'm buggered if I know Jack. Give us a hand we'll take him back to Ernie.'

Ernie stood scratching his head, 'did you hear anything Tom? A shot or anything?'

Tom shook his head; an uneasy feeling was making its way into his belly which had nothing to do with last night's curry. He cleared his throat but could find nothing to say.

Ernie knelt by Fred when Jack came up with his medicine chest. 'Help me roll him over.' The three men rolled Fred on to his side. 'There. There it is Tom. An exit wound. Thank God the bullet's passed right through. It's not bleeding a lot from this side, so we'll concentrate on the front for now.'

Ernie went about dressing the wound and he handled Fred with a gentleness that bespoke his love for the big man. The bleeding slowed and Ernie went to the back and dressed that. 'But what knocked him out cold? The fall?' Ernie was scratching his head again. He hunkered down by Fred and inspected his head. 'There' he pointed 'another bloody bullet by the looks. This one only grazed him but hit him hard enough to knock him out. Jesus Tom…?'

Tom was looking at Fred in amazement. 'Shit I'd better get out and about, see if I can find anything. Is he gunna be alright Ernie?"

Ernie shrugged, 'this is a bit beyond me son, but I notice an absence of bubbles in his blood, and I think that's a good sign. I just don't know. If we take him the five days back to Katherine, we may do more damage than good. It's bloody rough going back there a bit Tom. Better we go that way' he pointed to the front.

Tom nodded; he knew of the stretch that Ernie was talking about. 'Alright we need to make him comfortable in the back of the truck. We're only a day and a half maybe from Darlbey Downs homestead. We can get the flying doctor from there.'

The three men lifted Fred gently onto a mattress in the back of the truck and Ernie covered him with a blanket. Tom handed Ernie a handgun and gave Jack a rifle and several magazines. 'You'll ride shotgun' he said.

Jack looked long and hard at the man who had taken him back after his betrayal. He'd never let this man down ever again. Nor would he be cheating on his wife ever again. No Sir, she wasn't as forgiving as Tom.

After Ernie had sorted some stores for the men he climbed into the truck and with Jack set off to deliver Fred to the flying doctor. Tom watched them go as he let the tears rain down his cheeks. He sobbed until the pain in his chest and throat was eased.

Tom swung his horse round and galloped off to where Fred had gone down. He sat his horse in almost the exact spot he'd been when he saw Fred fall. His eyes roved over the horizon, 'the bastard must have been hidden in those rocks up on the hill' he breathed.

Turning his horse, he spurred it on to where the herd was now a half a mile away. He'd need Cecil. While he was there, he told the men what had happened and handed them a side arm or rifle, each. These men were no strangers to danger, they expected it. They'd carry on their day as required.

It took Cecil only moments to take up the trail of two horses. He pointed to the ground behind the rocks, 'that's probably where they fired from. Look Tom there are three shells. They took off that way, they'll be making for the two-mile water hole. They'll probably camp there tonight. They wouldn't wanna stay on the trail Tom. I know a short cut we can be there about an hour before em. If you like Tom.'

Tom grinned and nodded 'my thoughts exactly Cecil. I'd like to meet those bastards. I'm afraid I don't know the short cut though, so I'll need you, Cecil.'

Cecil nodded and swung up into his saddle. The sun was already dropping to the horizon. Tom was amazed at the shortcut. Cecil knew a place where they could ford the river without going miles upstream. It was a bit tricky getting the horses down the high, steep embankment but they managed it.

By sundown they were tucked up in the bushes and boulders near a camp site that had been used the night before. They did a quick scout round and found somewhere to hide, from where Tom hoped he'd hear their conversation.

Tom hoped the camp site was theirs and that they'd use it again tonight. He needed to find out what these two were about and if they acted alone. Why they had shot Fred. Tom and Cecil had tethered their horses in a thicket about half a mile back. 'We'll leave em here and go the rest of the way on foot' he'd said.

Tom had a rifle, and a handgun and Cecil had a handgun. They ran through the bush. Then they settled in to wait at the campsite.

It was almost dark when the men turned up to make their camp at the site. Something had just crawled up Toms pants leg and was wriggling around at his knee. He had to lay still and listen.

Luckily the two men had wood stashed and so they didn't have to go looking for some so never discovered that Tom and Cecil were there. As the two men settled down, they started to talk. It wasn't long before the talk got around to the man they had killed today. Thought they had killed today.

Whatever had crawled up Tom's leg bit it and Tom realised with dread it was a fire ant. He rubbed furiously at his leg his teeth clamped shut. Something else stated wriggling at his ankle. Shit, thought Tom, we could be on a nest of them. He looked at Cecil who had just discovered the same thing. Cecil pointed to the ground and mouthed 'their bloody trail.' They both knew that now they'd been bitten the whole bloody nest would come dark or not.

The smaller of the two men at the fire stated in a whiney voice that he thought killing Fred was a bit drastic. 'I don't understand why we can't just all open fire on em and drive em off and be done with it. All this cloak and dagger shit!'

'No, it's got to look like bushrangers' the other man said. 'And besides it's Tom, that's the boss of this drive. We wouldn't get five miles if we left him at our back. When we get to frost river ford and jeff and Rodney join us we can kill the last of em and make it look like the cattle wandered off. Three of em are gone already so that just leaves five of em. And they haven't got a truck here now. We'll take most of the herd and be across the border in a week and a half if we don't hang about. They did go back to town, didn't they? With the big fulla?'

Alan stared wide eyed at Stew and shrugged his shoulders. Stews face went blank.

Tom felt another bight on his calf and resisted the temptation to jump to his feet. the men at the fire were staring into the flames. Tom grabbed his rifle as he saw Cecil grab at his crutch. A strange, strangulated cry escaped Cecil's lips as he jumped to his feet. Shit there were ants all up his legs. He looked at Tom who appeared to be in the same predicament.

The men at the fire saw Cecil the dark man who'd appeared out of nowhere. He was doing a strange dance, holding his crutch, in a bush making a strange wailing sound his eyes wide and bulging and he was waving a gun around. The men seemed to forget their guns as they cowered at the fire.

Oh, to hell with it thought Tom and he jumped to his feet. The two men saw another man, a white man dancing in the bushes but this one had a rifle trained on them. He danced the same and had the same bulging eyes but this one wasn't wailing. And this was Tom!

The man who recognised Tom, turned, and went for his gun and Tom shot him. The man whose name was Stewart took the bullet in his backside and fell forward adding his screams to the wailing and growling. Tom who had jumped from the bushes and stood near the prostrate man on the ground, let out a blood curdling growl and dropped his pants to his ankles. He rubbed furiously at his thighs the little blighters had reached his sensitive area.

Cecil stopped wailing and dropped his pants to his knees and started rummaging round in his crutch. He was swearing, mostly in English.

The man on the other side of the fire whose name was Alan, fell backwards in a dead faint.

Back at camp the two men who had tried to kill Fred were tied to a tree. They weren't talking. 'Boss' said Cecil in a loud voice, so they'd hear, 'let's take em back and peg em down on those ants. That should loosen their jaw hay.'

'You've been watching too many westerns' grinned Tom, 'how do you imagine we peg them out on an ant's nest without getting bitten to pieces ourselves? Jesus, they hurt the little bastards. Now I bloody know why they call them flaming fire ants.' Tom stopped talking and looked thoughtful.

He stepped closer to Cecil and dropped his voice. 'Why do you think that little skinny bastard fainted?'

Cecil laughed for a time. Tom reached out and grabbed his shirt front. Cecil went serious, looked down at his feet and said 'you had your daks down… You know…'

'Shit! What? No…'

Cecil was laughing again. Tom turned his back on him, 'the things you people laugh at, and you had your daks down to remember? And you were very busy getting yourself out. Hang on, now that I come to think on it, that's when he fainted.' This just brought more laughter from the aboriginal stockman and a chuckle from Tom.

Tom stepped up to the two men drawing his pistol as he went. Everyone was quiet. Alan's eyes looked like they were going to pop right out of his head. Tom's voice was calm when he spoke.

'I have the right to shoot you' he said quietly. 'You shot one of my men and are planning to kill the rest of us and take our cattle. I reserve the right to kill you. What do you say chaps? I mean we all know I have to, don't we?'

'You don't have any such a right' Alan whined.

'Shut up Alan' Stewart spat at him. 'We're good and fucked now.' Stewart was laying on his side. 'Get it over with Tom.'

'Tom…' Cecil started a serious expression on his face now.

Tom replied in a soft voice, 'come on Cecil, how long since we ate well huh?'

Tom walked over to Stewart and hunkering down so the man could see him went on softly, 'how's your arse Stew? I had to plug you. Him' he thumbed at Alan, 'well he was no problem.' Tom chuckled deep in his throat, 'he took a bit of a nap.'

This set Cecil off again as he turned his attention to the cowering Alan. Tom knew what he had to do, and his face was grim. All he wanted was a quiet life. Was it too much to ask? He lifted his handgun and pointed it at the back of Stewart's head. Tom pulled the trigger. Alan screamed and fainted again. Cecil howled with laughter.

❧

Ernie and Jack deposited Fred into the homestead to be cared for by the owner's wife. The woman was gushing with concern and sympathy. She couldn't do enough and even brought them lunch. She was a very pretty woman and both men found they wanted to stay. But leave they must. She had Fred tucked up in bed when she turned to Ernie.

'Please don't worry about your friend, the flying doctor will be here in just over two hours' she said.

Ernie smiled and thanked her, and the two men left the bedroom to go to the truck. Out in the yard the station owner was waiting for them. They thanked the man for his kindness.

'I wanted a word with you away from my missus' he started. 'She tends to panic easily. You men should be careful on your way back there's a band of rustlers about and they don't care if they have to kill. In fact, it's part of their M.O., they kill the drovers and take most of the cattle, leaving a few to make it look like the cattle wandered off. But they are not very bright, and I don't think they've taken on an outfit as big as yours before. There have been a couple of bodies found buried out in the desert and so the police are eager to catch them before they kill again. I've got these four blokes here will accompany you back to the boundary and your outfit should be just about a mile farther on by now.'

Ernie looked at Jack now, 'shit! Tom was going looking for those blokes. We best get going Jack.'

'I hope you don't mind' went on the station owner, 'but I rang the police they will meet you at Italper, the next place over.' The station owner shook hands with them and wished them luck.

'Thanks' said Ernie and he hurried off to the truck with Jack. The four men riding with them were armed to the hilt.

At the boundary to the next property the four men bid them goodbye and wished them luck. Ernie drove the rest of the way to the stock route in silence. Ernie was in a panic himself now. He had to get back, had to make sure Tom was alright. He'd made certain promises to Tom's mother and yet here he was, had never even found the guts to tell the kid his mother was dead. He worried about the conversation that might start. Maybe a conversation about how deep Ernie's love for the woman was. He tried to brush it to the back of his mind.

They turned right at the long paddock and drove for about two miles and Ernie saw the cloud of dust and then the herd came into view. His heart quickened as he counted the men driving them. Five! There were five. He looked for Tom whom he found in his usual position of right flank. Ernie stifled a sob.

He parked the truck up out of the way and almost cried with relief as Tom rode up with a big grin. 'Good to see you, Ernie. Did you get Fred there alive?'

Ernie nodded and got out of the truck while Tom swung down from his horse after signalling the men to halt the herd.

Ernie grinned up at Tom and told him 'We did son. Fred even regained consciousness a couple of times. He is firmly ensconced in the bosom of the very attractive, very good-hearted wife of the station owner. His wish is her command. Yes, son I think he'll be okay.'

'Good on you Ernie, you to Jack.' Tom took both men's hands and shook them. He felt himself relax; he knew Fred just needed a fighting chance. He'd known the man for nearly all his life and there were none tougher, stronger, or bigger of heart. Tom heaved a sigh of relief.

'You want I should put the billy on Tom? Jesus, who the hell is this?' Ernie and Jack were both peering at the two newcomers that the other men brought with them. One of them sat almost sideways in his saddle and Ernie thought he knew why. A slight smile flitted across his face. The other one just looked as though he would die of fright at the least little thing.

Jack noticed the ropes on their wrists and knew they were Tom's prisoners. Must be the bastards who shot Fred he thought. He looked at Ernie and knew that he'd had the same thought.

Tom was talking now. 'Yeah, me and Cecil followed em Ernie. They're part of a ring of rustlers operating in these parts. They thought they'd killed Fred. They had intended to run us all off and take the cattle see they thought they'd got rid of you and Jack and the truck for some days. I finally got it out of them that there are four others. I'm afraid I had to make them believe that me and Cecil needed to make a meal of them because we'd lost our chuck wagon, to get them to talk.'

Cecil who had just walked up started to laugh. 'We had a job to keep skinny one awake. He fall asleep all the time. You should o seen his face when he come to and see his mate on a makeshift spit. He talk good then. He talked a lot, can't shut him up.'

Ernie grinned and said 'Jesus it's good to see your ugly mugs. Listen Tom, the cops will be here any time. They've been looking for this lot. They'll meet us near Italper. They'll be waiting at the stock route where it passes near the homestead. We should be there in a couple of hours.'

Tom nodded, 'good, good, we can hand these bastards over and get on with what we do.' He stepped a little closer to Ernie and said softly, 'Listen Ernie, you got any more of that cream you used on Fred?'

❧

Bradly Ellis climbed down out of the train at Darwin station. He looked about him and noticed a car parked by the fence. When the porter handed him his suitcase, he made for it.

He got in and sat in the front seat. The driver was one of his henchmen. Bradly turned to him and asked quietly. 'So did you find her Colin?'

The man nodded, 'yes, I did. Who is she and how much shit is she in?'

'Mind your own bloody business. Where is she?"

'She's at the hotel Astra. Where do you wanna go Ellis?'

'To the Hotel Astra of course. What did you find out about her?'

The driver was quiet for a while then said 'well we picked up this bloke called Herbert Martin. She had an altercation with him on her arrival at the hotel and knocked him arse up apparently. Could be why she's still here. We dug a little deeper and found he had a plane waiting for him at the airport and no cash to go anywhere. Of course, the little bastard didn't wanna talk so we had to knock him arse up a couple of times ourselves.' The two men laughed.

'Everything alright Ellis? She aint half a looker that…'

'Mind your own business and get me to that hotel. You kept him away from her, so he doesn't tip her off?'

'Course. He's locked up.'

CHAPTER 6

Sue left the small café where she ate breakfast and made her way past the wharf and down the street towards her hotel. It was a lovely morning, but she walked with heavy tread. She had never expected Herbert to be such a cad. Had believed him to be a gentleman. Had thought him the love of her life and had planned to have a family with him. She'd been a fool alright, but she would never be again.

She looked at a rose bush in somebodies' front yard and was taken by its beauty. The deepest shade of red. She looked up to see the rest of the front yard and the house. It was a big three storied house and needed a coat of paint. Sue gaped at it, loved it. The trees and the wide veranda all around it made it look like something from a picture book.

She looked at the for-sale sign on the fence and knew it was providence. She had to have it. Adding to her feelings of fate being at play were two facts. The real estate phone number was on the sign and there was a public phone down on the corner. On an impulse Sue rang the real estate agent and it was arranged for her to see the place just before lunch.

Early that afternoon Sue bought the place. It had been advertised for ten thousand pounds; she got it down to eight thousand five hundred pounds. She'd still have plenty of money to do the place up. Sue had had the forethought to involve a builder and a plumber in the inspection. She wasn't her father's daughter for nothing. They had told her the place was sound and all the renovations would be superficial.

Sue hurried to the furniture shop and bought a big double bed and mattress. After much begging and a little bribing, the man agreed to deliver it as soon as he closed. Sue bought sheets and a blanket then hurried back to her hotel to get her things. She called a taxi and left the hotel. As she climbed into the taxi, she saw her father get out of a big black car and go into the foyer. She gave the taxi driver the address of the house around the corner from her house. She'd have to lay low for a while.

It took Sue two goes to get her things round the corner and into the house. Once she'd done that she waited until six o'clock. The bed was delivered at five fifteen and at ten to six she went to the phone box down the road and dialled the hotel. The young clerk answered, and she told him she wanted to leave a forwarding address for some things she was expecting.

'Yes Miss. Miss there is someone here looking for you. Do you wish to speak with him?'

'No. Now take this address down to send my things on, my father will pay you. The train is about to pull out.' Sue gave the young man the address of her father's station.

Just as she thought the clerk went to Bradly and told him of his conversation with Sue. Bradly left the hotel. He knew he'd missed the train, but he thought he could still catch her before she got home. 'So, she's come to her fucken senses' he told Colin. 'She's gone home.' Ellis wore a smug smile.

Sue went the next morning and chartered the plane at the airport and sent it off with paperwork saying that Herbert was on board. She sent it to Singapore. Let daddy find me there she smiled to herself. She knew when he got home and found he'd been duped he'd be back, and he'd be really mad.

Sue had work to do, she'd have to plan her every move. She intended to make the top story, which was pretty much a loft, of her house into her own private quarters. The first floor would be made into bedrooms for guests, she figured about fifteen rooms and adjoining bathrooms. Lastly the ground floor would be developed into a dining area for guests and public alike. She'd have a private lounge with a bar for her guests and lastly a hall for dances and balls. The end room would need a lot of renovating, but she thought it just might make a nice conference room.

Sue decided she'd start right away. That night she slept soundly with no one troubling her thoughts. Not Herbert nor her father and not Tom. Just her beautiful home and what she was going to do with it.

❧

Emily was doing her midweek washing. She had taken the sheets off the bed and was boiling them. She decided she would sweep and mop her room. She was doing this when she swept an envelope out from under the bed. Slowly Emily bent and picked it up. Her hand shook as she read the writing in the front. It said simply 'Tom and Emily's house money.'

'Oh God' she whispered. The memory these words evoked were like needles in her head. She knew what she had to do. With trembling hands and several thumbs, she opened the envelope. Pulling the notes out she counted five hundred and fifty quid.

Emily collapsed on the edge of the bed. 'Oh Tom' she whispered and made no attempt to stop the tears that rained down her cheeks. She remembered the day he'd left; she remembered Rodney and the punch Rodney had delivered which had done so much damage. 'I'm sorry Tom' she whispered.

As Emily sat and cried herself out, she remembered an address for Tom. It was C/O Post office Mataranka. She had written to him there in the past.

Emily rose from the bed and went to the dresser and got a fresh envelope. On this she wrote the address for Tom. She took her apron off and quickly got tidied up then left the house. At the post office she got a postal order for the five hundred and fifty pounds and sent it registered mail.

As she walked home, she felt her heart break. Instead of going home she went to Albert and Mavis' place. She collapsed in their arms and cried. They knew she'd finally remembered everything and held her tight.

After as she sat at their table with a cup of tea, she told them what she had found and what she had done. They held her hands and told her they were very proud of her.

Mavis sat forward now squeezing her hand, 'it was the right thing love and… you never know love; you just never know.'

Emily tried to smile. 'No Mavis, I remember why he left. Hell, I wouldn't come back to me.'

Mavis wiped her eyes and looked at Albert. He coughed and looked at this young woman who had been a daughter to him for years. 'I agree with Mavis. I am proud of you and if he could see you now, he…'

'But he can't, and I don't want him to. I am too ashamed to face him. I just had to give him his money you understand. Mostly because it was his money and also to show him there are no hard feelings. Now that's that and I have to` get on with life. I have too much to do to sit about crying. Thanks for being there for me as always. I love you both so very dearly and I do not know what I would do without you. I best get home and finish the washing. Maybe I'll see you tonight?' The old couple nodded and sniffed.

Emily walked across the road on shaky legs. Up the road Ned waved to her and sang out 'how goes it Emily love? They keeping you busy huh?'

'Yes, Ned and everything is fine. Tomorrow Ned?'

'I look forward to your shopping days girl. What's on the menu tonight love?'

'Roast beef and Yorkshire pudding Ned and followed by fruit salad.'

'Sounds great. Emily, could you keep that little table for two around the corner for me and my wife? She wants to see how you're doing.'

'Yes of course Ned, that would be lovely. Ned, I want to thank you again for all your help. I remember how kind you were on that night Ned. And I've remembered everything.' Emily put her head down and shook it from side to side, 'oh Ned I don't deserve friends like you.'

Ned jumped the fence and took the distraught girl in his arms 'nonsense little woman. Nonsense. Bloody nonsense!'

❧

Tom had made it back into Mataranka just two months after he'd left. The police had nabbed the rest of the rustlers as they attempted an ambush. Thanks to the conversation that Tom and Cecil had overheard the coppers had lay in wait for them. Tom had gotten a reward which he'd shared among the men. It had come to a hundred each.

After he had paid the men, he'd gone to bank his earnings. With the reward it came to eight hundred pounds. He kept fifty pound to tide him over until he got work again. When Tom was in Mataranka between jobs, he spent his time living in an old hut down by the river. He spent a lot of time down there fishing, he practically lived on the fish he caught.

Tom was dozing under a tree; he hadn't had a bight in the last hour. He heard a footfall and sprang up onto his feet. He heard a familiar laugh as he swung round. It was Fred and he had some bottles of beer with him. He grinned at Tom. 'How are you, Tom?'

Tom held out his hand, 'good to see you, Fred. I owe you some money, I have it in my wallet. How are you, Fred?'

'No hurry lad. Listen I just wanted to have a beer with you. Got a bottle opener?'

When the two men were sitting under the tree Fred cleared his throat. Tom knew it meant he had something to say. 'Listen Tom I don't know whether to tell you this but umm… well… Oh, shit Tom. They took me to hospital, right? And when I came to one night, I heard them all talking about a young girl who … Who had been there some time ago. Anyway, they were talking about this girl as if she was some kind of miracle. Apparently, she'd been brought in more dead than alive weeks before. She'd been beaten up and pretty badly to.'

Fred stopped talking and downed half the bottle he was working on. He looked hard at Tom for a few seconds and cleared his throat again. 'Anyway, the long and short of it is that her head injuries were so bad that she is now partly paralysed down her left side. Apparently, she took weeks to learn to walk and she now has a kind of shuffle. Her left leg doesn't work at all well and nor does her left arm. And they went on to say she now runs a successful business as a diner for miners and railway workers. She serves upwards of forty people a day and they all love her.'

Fred stopped talking and studied his boots as if he was unable to speak, Tom listened as he cleared his throat again. Tom wondered why Fred seemed so emotional. He said softly 'she must have been beaten pretty bad Fred. And it is a bit of a miracle she can work at all let alone be so successful!'

'Well, yes. So, after listening to all this talk, I heard that she was being brought in for her weekly physio appointment the next day and that the chap who was bringing her in was her stepfather, Albert.'

Tom felt something shift in his chest, he swallowed hard. He said quietly 'go on Fred.'

Fred lowered his head, 'it was Emily. And they say the bastard that bashed her was Rodney. Rodney Gaskell.'

Fred kept his eyes on his boots when he heard the muffled sob from Tom. Fred went on, 'I asked how long ago this happened and they gave me the date. I don't know for sure, but I think it was the day we pulled out of Damper Creek to go to Katherine. She almost died because she lay all day bleeding and couldn't move. Somehow, she made it on to the front veranda, no one knows how. There was blood everywhere. Albert found her and got Ned to bring her to hospital that night. I just wanted you to hear it from me lad.' Fred stopped talking and waited.

Tom sniffed and swallowed several times. 'Shit!' Tom couldn't take it all in. 'I wonder why he did that to her.'

'Dunno. My guess is she kicked him out or something there may have been some kind of argument. Must have been hay?'

Tom lifted his head and looked at Fred. 'I best go to her Fred.'

'Well now the thing is she doesn't have much of her memory left, you know, of the past like. Albert forbade anyone talk to her about you. Said she had enough on her plate. Said she was having enough trouble with the little bit of her memory she had left. I don't know what to tell you Tom. Apparently, Albert is searching far and wide for Rodney. God help the low bastard if he gets hold of him. Apparently, Rodney is nowhere to be found.'

Tom picked up his bottle and downed it. 'Why Fred' was all he could say?

Fred put his hand on Tom's arm. 'The only thing I can suggest, and this is for the good of that girl, is that you steer clear for a bit longer Tom. She's working hard and getting on with her life apparently. She has two people working for her now and is very successful. Maybe Albert is right about letting her get better before they tell her anything. To let her regain her memory in her own time. It is thought that she will regain her memory so… I don't know Tom.' Fred polished off his beer. 'If you went to see her, would you want to take up with her again? That's the point here Tom. If not, how much damage are you going to do when you leave her again.'

Tom hung his head for a while and then said quietly, 'so she's okay Fred? She has everything she needs?'

Fred nodded and clapped Tom on the back. 'I think she's doing just the right thing for herself, and she has the whole town behind her from what I can gather. Even the locals go there to eat.' Fred cracked another two bottles and handed one to Tom. 'I would say if you don't care to take her back leave it alone. Figure out what you want first Tom.'

'How did you get so wise Fred'?

Fred laughed. 'So, do you still love her lad?"

'Course I do Fred. She's changed?"

'Sounds like it lad.' Fred smiled at the man he liked and admired above all others. He knew the answer to that before he'd asked. 'Sounds like she does nothing but work. Apparently, the bank in Damper Creek has had somewhat of a lift since she started her business.' Fred smiled.

Tom shook his head, 'well bloody good on her. Oh Jesus Fred. It must have happened after I left. And she lay there all bloody day. Oh Christ…' Tom put his head in his hands.

'No use to beat yourself up young Tom. Give her some time, sort yourself out and then make a decision'

Tom wanted to go to her and take her in his arms and beg her forgiveness. But there was merit in what Fred was saying.

And the next day Tom took home a registered letter to his hut down by the river. When he opened it and saw the five-hundred-and-fifty-pound money order was from Damper Creek a few days ago with Emily's signature and a note saying simply 'the house money', he let the hot tears fall down his face. 'Emily' he whispered into the emptiness of his hut, 'oh Emily my darling.'

Tom hung his head for a time then lifted it to look into space. 'Oh Emily, you remembered me.' He smiled sadly 'you remember'.

Tom had a job the next week to go to a large station near the WA border and pick up a herd to bring back to Darwin. He could hardly bring himself to do it. Tom had sunk into a sort of melancholy and wanted only to berate himself for what he'd let happen to Emily. There was something he had to do before he left, he'd pay a visit to Damper creek.

He got there just after dark and sat in his truck across the road from Emily's house. He noticed what a nice little house it was and wondered for the first time at his need to get a new house for him and Emily. As he sat there pondering the front door opened and a woman came out and shuffled across to the tap.

It was Emily. He watched her though he couldn't see her very clearly. Even though he'd been told of her condition it was a shock to Tom. His hand was on the door handle, he had to talk to her tell her how sorry he was.

She came into the light from the window, and he got a glimpse of her. He hardly recognised her. She was much slimmer, so she looked taller. Her hair was clean and cut short and she wore a very nice outfit, clean and pretty. He let go of the door handle. What would he say to her, this new woman? The last thing he wanted to do was to cause her anymore grief.

He sat still, watching as she turned and went back inside. Every awkward step made him more inclined to want to say to hell with the job tomorrow. He'd go and look for Rodney. Tom remembered the two of them on the bed that day and as always it nearly broke his heart. He realised as he sat there that Fred had been right. He needed to sort himself out. Tom also realised he'd been wrong about what

Emily had done with his money. She had saved it; his Emily had saved the money. And she had given it back to him!

He started the truck and drove away. He'd go and do this job in Western Australia. Maybe when he got back in a few months he would pay Emily a visit. Yes, he told himself, that's what he'd do. There was something he had to do before he left.

❦

Emily sat at the table going over her menu for the next day. There was a pile of mail on her desk that she planned to go through when Nellie had brought her a cup of tea. Nellie was finished the tea dishes and would soon start making pastry for the pies. She always got Emily a nice cup of tea between these two chores.

It was seven o'clock when Emily got her cupper and moved over to the desk to give Nellie the table. Emily looked forward to this time of day. She picked up the pile of letters, she always got a lot of mail. Mostly it was from people who wanted to congratulate her or compliment her on her place, her efforts, or her food.

She had been flattered and touched by the well wishes of people since her accident. She thought of it now as her accident, it was far less upsetting. Emily had had the phone put on in her house and she got the occasional call from a well-wisher. Some people also made reservations to eat there by phone.

Emily couldn't believe how popular her establishment had become. So much so that she had got a builder to extend her veranda several feet at the back. She'd gotten a carpenter to knock up some new tables and chairs.

Her food and her prices however were still geared towards her miners and railwaymen. They would always be her bread and butter. It was to them she owed her loyalty, they who had got her started. Emily would never forget the day that Harry knocked on her door.

Emily flicked through the letters, mostly accounts and some personal letters. Most of the letters were from Damper Creek. Her hands stilled, there was a letter from Mataranka. She wondered if it was a doctor's appointment, she was tired of doctors' appointments.

As well-meaning as they were she resented their pushing and prodding.

She sighed and opened the letter; her hand went to her mouth when she pulled the money from the envelope. There was a note with it, so she opened and read it. It was a short note and said simply

Thank you, Emily. This is your half. I'm sorry to hear what happened to you. Hoping to see you soon. I'll be back in about two months. Regards

Tom

Emily put her arm on the desk and allowed her face to sink into it. She started to cry silently, and her sobs got louder until Janet and Nellie came to her to see what the matter was. Janet rubbed her back and told her nothing was worth all these tears.

Nellie took the note from her hand and read it. She put her hand to her mouth and then handed it to Janet. Janet frowned at Nellie, but she took the note and read it and read it again.

'Oh heavens. Oh, dear me,' said Janet. Janet put her arms around Emily. 'Come on love' she said desperately. 'Come on now it's a nice note. Come on love. Look he says he'll come and see you when he gets back'

'Does he?' Emily lifted her tear-stained face to peer hopefully at Janet through her tears.

'Well, yes. Least ways that's how I read it. Come on.' Janet looked at Nellie, but Nellie had no idea what to say.

Janet put her face down close to Emily's and said quietly, 'would you like me to go and get Albert or Mavis. They will know what to do. Not that there's anything we can do, sounds like he's away. But he says here he will be back in two months. He also says he hopes to see you soon.'

Emily sat up and dried her eyes. 'I know' she said and blew her nose. 'I wasn't expecting to hear from him. Oh, do you think he has forgiven me?"

'Yes', said Janet. 'He says he is sorry… Sorry about what happened to you. Yes, it sounds as though he has forgiven you. Oh love, let's just wait and see. It sounds very hopeful. That's if… He's what you want.'

'Yes. Yes of course, I am being very childish. Alright where are we for tomorrow?' Emily was all business again, but her heart had dared to sing. Dared to hope for a love that had gone down in flames and Emily knew why.

CHAPTER 7

Sue had been in her new home for two months. The renovations were done, the whole place had been repaired and painted. She had made a two-bedroom apartment in the top story for herself, and she loved it.

The first story she had reduced to eleven rooms as she had made them into small suites with bedroom, lounge and ensuite. They all opened onto a veranda and had a small kitchen/dinette. These were designed to house visiting guests or permanent residents.

She already had four of them rented to permanent residents. One of these was merely reserved for a retired cattleman for when he was in town. He came into town quite often to attend appointments concerning his health and to do business. Sue hoped he would be the type to throw his money around.

When she advertised her hotel, she used only the name and address of the hotel and never volunteered her real name. For those who had reason to enquire she was known only as Madam Carmine. She had opened her bank account as Suzette Carmine. The deeds of the house the only thing under Susan Ellis.

On the ground floor Sue had put in a huge kitchen which would service the residents and outside guests. She had a dining room with a bar and dance floor for people to come and enjoy themselves. There was also a ball room which she had great hopes would be hired out for balls and maybe even elegant weddings.

At the end of the building, she had renovated a long spacious room and made it into a conference room. It would seat twenty-four people. Sue walked all over the house and felt a pride in what she'd accomplished. And she still had a few thousand-pound left.

Sue climbed the stair and retired to her room. She sat on her couch by the fire, she was tired. Sue found she slept peacefully now though she suffered a few pangs here and there at having ripped her father off. She was enough of a realist to know it would be a long time before she could pay him back, if ever.

She'd just get on with it and face the music when he eventually caught up with her. For catch up with her he would. Sue wasn't good enough at covering her tracks to stay hidden forever. She missed him, longed to see him. She didn't miss her mother though she hated her.

Sue had a brother who had been sent to law school and she'd always resented that. Why hadn't they sent her to medical school? She'd wanted to be a doctor and he knew it. But her mother had insisted she be sent to finishing school and be married off to a well to do family. Daddy had caved and done her bidding. She hated him for how weak he was. Yes, let him come, just let him come.

Sue had gotten over Herbert except to the fact that it had taught her a valuable lesson. Never again would she be such a fool, such a complete fool. And never again would she be dependent on any man.

She had received a sum total of 500 pounds in the last two weeks being rent for the rooms. Sue knew she was on her way, and nothing was going to stop her. She had also made a few hundred in the bar and dining and she had a conference booked for two months' time.

Sue had a fantastic gala and ball planned for her big opening. She had seating for seventy, all society people, of whom fifty-four had RSVP'd. She would provide dinner in the dining room and then there would be a bar in the ball room. It would be a masquerade ball and Sue would hide behind a mask. She had no idea how long it would take daddy to find her.

She had hired five chefs and fifteen waiting staff. There would be four bartenders and five drink waitresses. The cleaning staff would number twenty. Sue's hotel was fully booked out for the weekend.

After the night when everything went back to normal, she would have one chef and two assistants, three waiters and three cleaners. The bar would be run by two bar staff as it would open only in the late afternoon until ten o'clock.

Sue would wait and see if the staff were adequate if she made it to full capacity and review the situation then.

The ball was tomorrow night and Sue was excited. It was right up her ally this and she loved it. She knew she was damn good at it and looked forward to it eagerly. High society at last, this was what her parents had trained her for.

◈

Tom had two trucks and one-horse float for the horses and all their gear. They would obtain more horses when they got there if they needed to. But they had eight horses with them and one of the trucks was Toms'. The other he had hired for the job; the driver of that truck would get a load of something back.

Tom rode in the front of his truck with Ernie, it was four hundred miles to where they were going. The herd waiting for them was one thousand strong. Tom had hired the usual being Fred, Cecil, Nevil, Jack, Jimmy, Bill, and Ernie. He had also hired an assistant for Ernie a bit of a kid called Sam and one more cowboy called Charlie. Charlie had worked for Tom before; he was a young bloke and very good with cattle. He had a wife and kids back in Katherine and Tom found him to be steady, reliable, and down to earth.

Tom was telling Ernie now that he was pleased with his outfit this trip.

'That's good young Tom. May I ask what is troubling you lad?"

'Am I that bloody transparent Ernie?'

The two men laughed, Ernie said, 'dunno about anyone else mate, but to me you are.' Ernie was considering having that talk with Tom along the way, it was probably a fifteen-hour trip. But he wasn't expecting what he got next.

'I have had news of Emily.'

Ernie clasped the steering wheel a little tighter. 'Wanna tell me son?'

'You don't know Ernie?'

Ernie looked at Toms beloved face noting the anxiety on it and swallowed. He shook his head 'no son'.

'You remember I told you she slept with Rodney Gaskell?' Ernie nodded and Tom went on. 'Well to cut a long story short, the bastard bashed her Ernie. He bashed her to within an inch of her life.'

Ernie felt his heart lurch in his chest, he looked at Tom. 'No Tom! Jesus is she gunna be, okay?'

Tom smiled sadly, 'yes Ernie she is better than okay she is marvellous. He hit her so hard that she is partially paralysed down her left side and is having trouble with her memory. She apparently has had to remember even Albert and Mavis.' Tom looked down at his feet and Ernie wished there were something he could say but words had failed him.

Tom cleared his throat and looked across at Ernie, 'Fred found out when he was in hospital.'

'He never told me son.'

'No well he got the date Ernie, that this happened. It was… It was the day we… Left for Katherine Ernie. Probably just after I left her. She… She lay there all-day bleeding and that night she made it onto her veranda where Albert found her. She had almost bled to death Ernie. That mongrel must have run off and left her there to die. No one knows how she made it to the veranda. Now she walks with a shuffle and her left arm is not much use.'

Ernie looked at Tom and saw the tears running down his cheeks. 'Shit son, I'm sorry to hear it mate I am. I really am. I dunno what to say lad.'

'I know Ernie. Anyways, what I meant when I said she is marvellous is this, Ernie. She has opened an eating establishment in Damper Creek. Fred told me, he said she was serving upwards of forty people a day. Mostly miners and railway workers but some of the locals eat there to. She has two women working for her. Ernie, I went to the house and sat across the road in the dark. I saw her, she has a job to walk…'

Tom went quiet for a while. 'The other day Ernie I received a registered letter from her. It was the money I'd been giving her to save for a house. The last thing I said to her that day was that I reckoned she'd spent it all on her… Herself. It was five hundred and fifty quid.'

Tom slumped back against the seat and stared out the window. Ernie reached across and squeezed his arm. It was quite a story. He found his voice, 'can I ask how you felt when you saw her Tom?'

'Yeah, you can ask Ernie and I wish I could tell you. Fred told me that Albert and Mavis have forbidden anyone to talk to her about me. He said it was because she didn't remember anything about that day, and they don't want her upset. I can understand that Ernie I do. But when I got the letter that went to my address that I gave her I knew she had remembered me. I know it… and I had to see her but then I couldn't get out of the truck. She's changed, everything about her. She's slim and clean and beautiful Ernie. I still love her. All I want to do is go to her and tell her how sorry I am. I mean… I reacted badly because she told me I was just like my father. I'm not like him am I Ernie? I don't remember him too well. Am I like him?'

To Toms utter amazement Ernie was nodding solemnly. 'Don't you see it lad? How much like your father you are?'

Tom stared askance at the man he had thought he loved. He bit back the retort out of respect for him.

Ernie turned and glanced at Tom and smiled sadly. 'Look at me Tom and tell me you don't see it.'

Tom was flabbergasted, he didn't quite know what Ernie was trying to say and yet he did. 'What are you trying to say Ernie' he asked dumbly?

'I'm sorry Tom, I should've told you a long time ago, but I couldn't bear to lose you. I'm your father Tom. Me and your mum… well, we… we umm. Oh, bugger it all Tom. You know what happens when a man loves a woman and… He … and she…'

Tom knew his mouth was hanging open, he started to chuckle. He leaned in and stared at Ernie closely. 'Shit! Now see here old man. I see it Ernie I'll be fucked but I see it. Why didn't you tell me before? Hay, do I call you dad? And one day I might get you to tell me about what happens when a man loves a woman'. Tom laughed.

'Don't be cruel Tom. I have always loved you but I'm a coward. And I didn't wanna tell you about… well about…'

'What? That my mother's dead? I know about that.' Tom sat quiet for a moment then the question that Ernie was bracing himself for. 'Did you love her Ernie?' Toms face was screwed up now.

'Course I do son. I never loved another.'

'Then why did you let her walk out of your life and never seen her again.'

'She never walked out of my life son we just kept it quiet. I held her in my arms as she died.'

Tom sat transfixed as it was Ernie's turn to sniff back the tears. Tom's hand came down on Ernie's shoulder 'sorry to hear that mate, yet I'm glad for her. Why did she leave me behind Ernie? Why did she leave me behind? With that bastard?'

'She wanted to drop out of sight for a little while, she was terrified of him. She knew I was looking out for you. She had always intended to get back into your life but then she got sick. She never recovered Tom. I'm sorry mate.'

'Did she love me, Ernie?"

'Yeah, course she did mate. But when she got sick, and she knew it was the end she didn't want to bring you anymore heart ache.'

'Alright Ernie, I'm sorry. And by the way, I'm way better looking than you mate. I always loved you, old man, but I'm a ton better looking than you.'

Ernie chuckled deep in his throat and Tom did see it. He was so like Ernie that he didn't know why he hadn't seen it before. Life was strange that was for sure. And Tom suddenly realised that he had sorted his feelings for Emily out.

First thing when he got back, he'd go and see her and find out how she felt about him. Then they'd work it out from there. Tom knew he had to forgive her, her indiscretion and forget it. Forget all about it. If only he hadn't walked in on it, hadn't seen it.

Ernie noticed the peace that seemed to settle on Tom, and he knew of Toms decision. He was glad, he couldn't stand to watch this beloved son of his carry around all that pain.

❧

Emily had dished up the last meal and was looking forward to a rest. She sat in the chair at the table, it was lunch time. Janet had just taken the last plates to the table and was filling the sinks to start the dishes. She handed Emily a cup of tea as Nellie didn't work until a bit later.

Emily flicked through her mail, she thought of Tom. It had been a month since she'd got his letter with the money. The money would come in handy, but she was making more money now than she would ever have imagined. Last week she'd banked a hundred pounds, and that was after paying Nellie and Janet a bonus of one pound which they were excited about.

Emily paid both the girls two pound a week now, as much as a lot of men. On and above this she paid them a bonus, usually at least a pound a week.

The two girls were planning a shopping trip to Katherine the following month.

Emily smiled at the memory of the girls faces lighting up when they took from her more money than they had ever seen. She had enlisted the aid of another girl who filled in for the others when they had a day off. Her name was Rose and at twelve years of age she was making two pounds a week. More than her father did.

Emily gasped when she saw the letter with the scrawled writing on it. She knew that writing was Toms. Her heart skipped a beat. Her breathing shifted and tears threatened to fall. She opened the letter carefully as if it was a precious thing and to her it was.

Slowly she slid the paper out of the envelope and opened it out. The writing was only just readable, but it was a letter. From Tom, her Tom. Emily put her hand to her mouth, what if he was telling her he didn't want to see her. She put the paper down on the desk without reading it and drank her cup of tea. She hung her head; how could she blame him? She found it hard to believe she had acted so shamelessly, so carelessly.

'I'm sorry Tom' she whispered as she picked up the single page and straightened it. The letter was short and to the point, which was so typical of Tom.

Dearest Emily,

   I am sorry I wasn't there to find you. I will be back around about the seventeenth of next month. Should take us another three weeks maybe a bit more. I would like to see you. Can I call on you Emily? I sat in the truck one night and watched you walk out to the tap. I lacked the guts to get out. Please Emily. I must go now. Goodbye for now.

Love Tom

Emily held the letter to her and let the tears fall. 'Oh Tom' she cried, 'Tom'. Her heart ached to see him, to hold him.

❧

   Sue's big night had been a success, sixty four of the seventy people she had invited had turned up. Sue had been the perfect hostess and her elderly cattleman had delivered in spades. He'd been attentive to her the whole night. He was a gentleman, still handsome, his manners were impeccable, and he danced beautifully, and she'd felt as though she was floating on air. Yes, he had delivered everything she'd hoped and more.

   By the end of the night Sue was exhausted and climbed the stairs slowly a smile on her lips. Yes, it had been quite a night, she couldn't have hoped for a better turn out. Everybody who was anybody had been there.

   Sue slipped quietly into her apartment and went straight to the lounge. Still with a feeling she was gliding on air she opened the door and sailed in. The shock that went through Sue was almost painful. There standing in front of her fire warming himself was her father.

   Bradly smiled at her; he was dressed in a dinner suit. Had he been there at her ball? All the time? He walked towards her now the smile dying on his lips. He took her hand in his and squeezed it so hard she squirmed. He let go and stepped back a few steps.

   'Didn't you recognise me my dear' he asked lifting his hand with the mask in it? Very aptly he had chosen to wear a bull's face with horns. Sue couldn't drag her eyes away from his. He was talking again in his best smarmy voice that sent chills down her. 'It took me a while to recognise you to daughter. I don't think I have ever seen you so happy.'

A hint of a smile flitted across Sues face. Then she noticed the fury in Bradly's eyes and shrank away a little.

Bradley took a step towards her 'and to most fathers that would be worth every penny of the money, the fortune, he'd had stollen from him.' Bradly shouted now the spittle flying from his mouth. 'But not me you dirty little bitch. And I had to listen to what a whore you are from that Tom Cooper. Now in payment of your loan you will sign over half of your profits from this place. Then after you are married to Tom you can sign the whole place over to me.'

Sue was stung, so much so that she found the backbone to talk back to her father. 'Well, you know what Daddy you can get fucked.' Sue felt satisfied at the look of horror on her father's face.

Bradley stepped back and peered at the foreign creature taking shape before him. He almost felt a certain pride. 'Well, I see all that money we spent on finishing school in Adelaide was well spent...'

His eyes opened wider as his daughter flew at him again. 'Yes Daddy. I got sent to finishing school. I wanted to go to medical school to become a doctor, but you denied me. Mainly because you never had the guts to stand up to your wife. John got what he wanted, he got sent to law school, the useless good for nothing that he is. But me, I got finishing school. I hope you are very happy with the results.' Sue took a step towards him now. Waving her hand around she shouted, 'all this dad, this is all I know how to do. This is what I learned from that stinking finishing school you sent me to. And what do you think us girls learned from the Dean there Dad, the fine upstanding pillar of the community that he wasn't? How to shut our mouths and open our legs. First thing a lady must learn he'd say. And he would laugh Daddy. He was laughing at you not us. All you loving fathers that dropped their daughters off in such a place. Keeping him in comfort, money, and young girls huh.'

Bradley collapsed into a chair. He put his hands to his face. Surely not! He dropped his hands and sat up straight as she went on now, 'that's right father dear. We learned to be good little whores. We learned how that man liked to be rubbed and kissed and sucked and smacked. Oh, he liked his arse smacked daddy. Did I get an A for that dad? You bet your sweet arse I did. That's where all my fucking A's came from.' Sue took a deep breath and let it out, her eyes were shining, she leaned towards him. 'Don't you fuckin dare come in here trying to shame me you mongrel. You did that when you dropped me in that place and left me there. I hate you. Do you hear me, Dad? I hate you. Now get the hell out and don't ever darken my doors again. I will never pay you a penny, you bloody owe me this. What are you gunna do? And I will never speak to you again. I have no farther use for you Daddy dear.'

Now Sue collapsed into a chair, she sat breathless, glaring at her father. The tears were streaming down his face. He was wagging his head from side to side, 'is that all true Sue?' He stared at his daughter and somewhere in his tortured mind he wished his son had half her guts. She'd been right about him… but this other…?

Sue nodded and leaned forwards, putting her elbows on her knees she stared at the floor. The clock on the wall ticked away the minutes. They sat there like weary combatants, exhausted, breathing hard.

The knock on the door brought them both upright in their chairs and Bradley stood up. Sue watched him walk to the door and open it; Bradly Ellis swung the door wide. Sue and her father and the visitor all stood gaping at one another.

Herbert's smile died an ugly death on his now paling face. His eyes darted from one to the other. Sue and Bradley were both staring at him in disbelief. He squirmed visibly.

Bradley came to first, 'you, you mongrel. Did you put her up to it you louse? I'll have you thrown in bloody jail you…'

'Yes, go on Daddy and they can lock me up with him. I gave up expecting you to care many years ago. And you are a great one to be calling anybody a louse.'

Bradley turned to look at his daughter. Herbert, sensing a shift in power sidled into the room. Hell, he had nowhere to go anyway. He brought his eyes to rest on Sue and stood drinking in the beauty of her.

How could he have been such a fool? Herbert had had a bit of a look around on his way up the stairs. Yes, this would do him nicely, he'd be comfortable here. For a while, at least until the heat cleared. And he was experiencing all sorts of feelings looking at her. And didn't he know just how to work this woman?

But Bradly Ellis and his daughter were standing staring at each other, and he'd best pay attention. He slid across to stand beside Sue, she turned and delivered such a slap to his face he staggered back and fell over a chair. He watched the rest of the exchange from the floor.

Bradly spoke softly now, 'I didn't know baby girl. I'll kill the mongrel. Forgive me I have been a selfish, weak-minded fool.' Bradly held his arms out to his daughter.

Sue turned back to Herbert ignoring her father. 'What the hell are you doing here you nasty little weasel. You get out of my house. Go on get.'

Herbert turned on her, his best sincere look from where he lay with one leg over the upturned chair. 'But I can't leave you when you are so upset.

Bradly snorted and walked to the door. He opened it slowly and stepped out into the corridor. He had no idea how to deal with it all. She didn't want him had turned away from his embrace. Nothing in his life had prepared him for this.

He found his way down the stairs though the tears in his eyes had him blinded. Bradly decided to go to his hotel room and wait until morning. He'd come back in the morning and try and talk to her. All he hoped now was that she'd be happy enough with this place. Shit, he owed her this much. He only hoped she had enough sense to throw that bludging little mongrel out.

Back in Sues lounge room Herbert was getting to his feet. He held his arms out to her and she walked into them and kneed him in the groin. 'Now get out Herbert before I use you as my punching bag.'

Herbert sidled around the room and at the door he turned beseeching eyes on her. She pointed at the door. Herbert went to the guest lounge on the first floor to sleep and got tossed out the next morning.

CHAPTER 8

Tom pulled his horse up under a tree and swung down out of the saddle. Fred was sitting in the shade leaning against a tree and Tom suspected he was asleep. His hat was pulled down over his eyes as Fred was wont to do when he wanted to sleep. His hat brim was like a bedroom door to the big man. Tom suspected he'd slept outside for most of his life.

Tom sat down beside him, and Fred grunted himself awake. He smiled at Tom. 'What's going on young Tom?'

Tom stared out at the hills and the heat shimmers that danced along their tops and handed Fred the lunch he'd brought back for him. 'Fred, I want to talk to you about a couple of things.'

'Sounds very deep young Tom. Tell me.'

Fred poked half a sandwich into his mouth. Tom smiled at this man who he loved every bit as much as he loved Ernie. 'Well,' he started, 'did you know that Ernie is my father?'

Fred choked on some crust. Between coughs he shook his head. He got the crust back up and, red in the face, he smiled. 'Probably should have Tom' he looked Tom square in the eyes 'yeah probably should have mate. That's a great piece of news. How long have you known?'

'Not long Fred.'

'Now what's the other thing my boy?' Fred sensed he'd just gotten the good news.

Tom looked thoughtfully down at his boots. 'Well, I got a letter from Emily before we left. She sent me the money I'd given her to save for a house. Five hundred and fifty quid.'

'Well, that's mighty fine of her Tom' Fred said sincerely around his mouth full. Fred's lovely manners ended with his elocution.

Tom looked at the older man who was only about fifteen years older than himself. 'I went to see her Fred. All I had the guts to do was watch from my truck in the dark. She came out and shuffled across the yard to the tap with a bucket. It nearly broke my heart. Though I hardly recognised her Fred, she's slim and looks taller and she's cut her hair. She's beautiful. I want her back; I do still love her. I just need to stop seeing... Seeing... That... you know...'

'Yeah' said Fred. He knew alright.

'Well anyway' went on Tom, 'I sent her a letter asking her if I can call on her. But I have to forget that...'

Fred studied the younger man's face for a time and drew a long breath and let it out again. 'I dunno mate. Try replacing the memory of it with something else.'

'Well, like what?'

'Did you ever watch her undress, Tom? Ever watch her take it all off?'

'Yeah' a half smiled crossed Toms face and his eyes took on a faraway look.

Fred smiled now, 'There you go young Tom. That'll do nicely wont it?'

Tom nodded the silly grin still all over his face, 'You know Fred I believe you're right.' Tom shook his head and looked at Fred. The big man so often amazed him.

'How long you reckon Fred, till we get back?'

Fred smiled knowingly, 'I'd guess about two weeks. We've been lucky this trip Tom.'

'Fred did you know that Bradly Ellis tried to order me to marry that bloody daughter of his.' Tom noticed that Fred said nothing and sat there eating and studying his boots. Shit, he thought, he'd hoped the big man was passed all that. Funny, he thought how life worked out. Who'd have thought that poor bloody Fred would lose his heart to such a demon. Dear old sensible, all knowing, wise old owl Fred.

Salt of the earth was Fred. Tom got an ache in his chest, he hated those. He'd had his fair share of those lately.

'Well anyway, I let him know how I felt about that. Wonder where she got to Fred?' Tom wished he'd just shut up and leave Fred alone.

Fred tossed his last bit of crust away and got to his feet and shrugged. 'Well come on young Tom, let's get this show on the road. Won't get you home to your lady love sitting here under a tree all day that probably won't drop an apple on us.' The big man smiled; he had a lovely smile thought Tom. Had good teeth, even white teeth.

Both men swung up in their saddle, nodded to each other and went off in opposite directions. Both left to their own thoughts.

Tom took up his position at the front and settled down to concentrate on thinking about Emily getting undressed. He was sure that with enough practice he'd get the hang of it. Jesus he'd loved that woman. He'd had a few women in his time but none of em knew how to take it all off like she did. Yes, he mused, good old Fred. Two weeks!

Later that day the herd skirted the small hamlet of Dawson. There was a shop and a pub there. Ernie had gone off in the truck to get a few things he needed and see if any mail waited for them.

When Tom caught up with Ernie that evening the old man handed him a letter. He was smiling and Tom knew at once it was from Emily. He found a tree by himself, sat under it, and read his letter. It was short and to the point. She wrote,

Dear Tom,

your letter was most welcome. I would be glad to have you call on me. You have absolutely nothing to be sorry for Tom. Unlike myself. I am appalled at my behaviour, the shame of it stops me from sleeping sometimes. I am sorry and I hope one day you can forgive me. I am glad for what happened to me Tom, it is my retribution, I am a different person now and I like this Emily a lot better. Please be safe and I will see you when you return. I remain,

Yours faithfully.
Love Emily.

Tom let the tears fall down his cheeks, for the first time he just let them fall. Emily not only forgave him, but she had never blamed him. And she was sorry for what she had done and learned a lesson from it. He heard Fred sit by him and put his arm across his shoulders and he was grateful.

He handed Fred the letter and Fred smiled as he handed it back. 'There you are Tom, she's sorry. Sounds like she has changed. She certainly sounds like she's one mighty fine woman Tom. And going by your face today, one mighty fine stripper offer.' Fred laughed and Tom joined in.

Ernie lifted his head from the fire and gazed over at them. Sounds like good news he thought. Thank God. The girl had done him wrong, but she was young. He was young and not without fault. This time apart appeared to have shown them what they had thrown away. Ernie was also glad that Tom had formed a bond with Fred. Fred was a bit of a wild card but a good bloke all the same. Salt of the earth was Fred.

Ernie went about getting the evening meal with a much lighter heart, anything that eased his sons' pain was alright with him. He smiled inwardly at how good it felt to think of Tom as his son now. And the young man loved him. Yes, life could be pretty damn good sometimes.

Emily was putting the finishing touches on the cakes she had made for sweets. She had two hours before the tea rush, just enough time to go down to the river and see a very old friend of hers. Whenever Emily visited Eric the trapper, she took him enough food to do him for days. She had spent a lot of time with Eric down at the river fishing as a young girl. It had been the thing she looked forward to all week at school.

When Emily approached his hut, she called out to him. She waited for his dog Bluey to run out to greet her, but he didn't. For eighteen years that dog had run to meet her. A feeling of dread settled on her.

Emily walked to the door of his hut and peeped in. She saw him sitting hunched over in his chair. 'Eric! Where's Bluey' she asked hardly daring to walk up to him? When Eric turned his face to her it was tear stained and red from crying. 'No! No Eric' was all she could say.

'He died in his sleep Emily. Found him the other morning. Buried him down by the fishing hole. You remember Emily?'

'Yes Eric' Emily put the hamper she'd brought on the table. 'Course I remember. We haven't fished for so long Eric, and I miss it. What about next Sunday Eric. You wanna do some fishing Sunday?'

Eric shook his head. Emily went on 'do you still have your accordion Eric?'

The old man nodded and looked down at his feet. Emily had had an idea and now, seeing him the way he was it seemed even more important. Imperative even. She took a deep breath, 'Eric I have come to ask a favour.' She sat down next to him and put her arm about his shoulders. 'You know I have opened a sort of eatery Eric?"

He nodded. 'Yes, I know girl and I'm most proud of you. What's the favour girlie?'

'Eric most of the men who eat at my place are away from their families Eric, and they get a bit tired and lonely and a bit forlorn.' She stopped and Eric nodded and looked at her with a puzzled expression on his face. She hurried on, 'well Eric I came here today to ask you if you would come on Saturday dinner time and play your accordion. A bit of a treat for them. You know?' Emily knew she had to succeed in giving Eric something to get him out of his doldrums.

He sat looking doubtful. Emily edged forward in her seat and touched his hand. 'Please Eric. Even just for an hour or so. I would appreciate it if you could start this Saturday. I'll come and get you and I will pay you.'

A smile made its way slowly across Eric's face and Emily breathed a sigh of relief. 'Alright girlie, I'll start practicing today.'

Emily brought her hands together. 'Oh, thank you Eric. Can you start now so I can listen for a little while? Please?'

Emily sat and listened to her lifelong, old friend play and as usual it was hauntingly beautiful. Other tunes he played were lively and uplifting, just what the lonely men from the gangs needed. Before she left him that day, she went with him to visit Blueys grave. She cried with Eric, and he comforted her. Emily knew it did him good to forget his own pain at losing the dog to bring her some comfort.

Leaving him at the door of his hut he promised her that he would practice every day. 'How are you, Emily? You still can't walk properly and your poor arm. I can't believe what you have achieved since your accident. I have heard all about it. People are talking about the mighty effort you've put in.'

Emily smiled 'I'm okay thanks Eric. I feel better now knowing you and I will work together some. Any way Eric, today is Wednesday, I'll come for you at about five o'clock on Saturday. I will give you dinner Eric so don't eat. And you just give me what you can. If you get tired, you stop playing. Alright Eric?'

Emily walked slowly on the way back, she hoped playing for the crew would draw Eric out of his grief a little. She thought the company would be good for him.

When Saturday evening came Emily went to collect Eric, she didn't think he'd come on his own. she was surprised when he met her halfway. He was smiling and he had his accordion over his shoulder.

That night was an even bigger success than Emily could have dreamed. Eric played and some people got to their feet and danced. Eric played into the night until around midnight. The sound of the beautiful music and laughter and Eric were as a tonic to Emily. young Dan danced with Nellie and when the night was done, he walked her home. Emily worried about losing Nellie to the tall handsome miner. She worried for nothing.

The Saturday night music was repeated the next week and some people came just to sit and listen. Eric seemed to enjoy the company of the men and sat with them from time to time to talk and listen. Emily had so many people come to eat there that she had to organise them into several sittings so sitting on the lawn was a common occurrence. The music provided a nice distraction for the people who were waiting also.

It was a Sunday; Eric had spent the second Saturday night playing for Emily. She approached Eric's hut quietly, she was nervous. At the doorway she called out to him. He came to the door and his eyes fixed on the young blue heeler dog she had on a string. It was skin and bone and covered in wounds. A tear slid down Erics face at the sight of the emaciated creature. Then he smiled, 'what is this, Emily?'

'I found him laying at the side of my house and I fed him for a bit, but I can't keep him there. I wondered if he could hang out here with you and I could come and see him and feed him Eric. Would you mind?"

Eric looked at the poor animal as it gazed steadily back at him. 'I suppose he can hang around Emily. Yes, he'll be alright here. That's if he'll stay.'

'I have food to put down for him and a water bowl. I hope he does, I'd hate to see him go back to where he was. See those people have been out looking for him and I don't want them to find him.'

'Oh no. Oh no Emily dear. I'll keep him inside with me for a while. Just till he's used to the place and no one's looking for him hay?'

Emily smiled as the dog got up and walked inside the hut and lay down beside Eric's bed. Seems he's home she thought as she watched him stretch out on the mat on the floor and go to sleep.

She went to the kitchen of the small one roomed hut and took out some food. There was curry and rice and some stew and bread for Eric and raw meat and bones for the dog. She turned to Eric who was edging towards the sleeping dog.

'Eric, he doesn't have a name. It's important to have a good name, isn't it?'

The old man nodded and looked thoughtful. 'I'll think on it girl. It was nice to sit and talk with Albert and Mavis last night. They love you, Emily. They told me about Tom, I was heart sorry to hear about that. Do you think you and he…'

Emily smiled sadly, 'I got a letter from him saying he wants to call on me Eric.'

'Oh, that's good love. Do you still love him?'

Emily nodded and a grin came over the old man's face. He looked back at the dog and smiled thoughtfully. 'I think I'll call him Drover. What do you think dear?"

'Oh Eric, I think it's perfect. Like Rover with a D in front to make it drover. Yes, I like it. I let everyone down you know Eric, I did. I have some atoning to do.'

'Oh, Emily love, not to me you don't. You have been the bright spot in my world for a very long time, so long that I don't remember a time when you weren't. I hope you get everything you want. And I hope I'm there to see it.'

~

Fred sat his horse and ran his eyes over the landscape. Normally he loved this land but the last couple of trips he found he was getting more and more tired. Fred knew he wasn't getting any younger and soon he'd need to hang up his saddle and bridle and his boots. He figured he might have a couple more years in him if that. He didn't know why he felt so tired. By his reckoning he was a bit shy of forty, probably thirty-eight maybe. a little bit less.

He was brought up out of his musing by a shout from Tom up in front. He and Jimmy were coming towards him. Fred liked Jimmy he was part Afghan and had a friendly disposition and a beaming grin.

Tom pulled up and leaned towards him now, 'there's been a change of plan Fred. We are to take this lot to Darwin docks. Ernie picked up a letter from those blokes who went through this morning from the station.'

'Okay Tom, that puts another week on our job. I wouldn't mind a few weeks in Darwin you know. Wash some of this dust out of my throat mate. Might get good and drunk young Tom hay.' Fred gave Tom one of his dazzling grins and winked, 'maybe a woman or two.'

Jimmy laughed and Tom looked serious. He thought the man was suffering more than he'd imagined. Fred never spoke thus about women. Tom had never known him to be much interested in them. Though Fred was a classically handsome man, he was big and dark with a good physique and women always gave him a second look at least.

Tom decided to keep an eye on him for a while. He'd never heard the man plan to get drunk either. He liked a drink, and he could certainly hold his liquor, but Tom had never seen him drunk. He'd try to take him back to Damper Creek with him.

Fred saw the look and pulled his hat farther down over his eyes. People had told him before that he wore what he was feeling in them. Fred had never experienced depression before, but he was low right now. He knew that.

'Righto Tom' he said in his best dismissive tone.

Tom searched his friends face and the look in his eyes threatened to bring Fred undone. He studied his saddle horn as Fred was wont to do when he felt awkward.

After another few weeks Tom and his crew brought the herd in to Darwin. Once they had been deposited in the stockyards Tom went off to the Commonwealth bank to withdraw funds to pay the men. Most of the men went to the Darwin hotel. Fred booked into a room immediately. He'd stick around a few days at least. Jimmy, Bill, Nevil, and Jack lined up at the bar. Cecil went down to the river. The others were with Tom.

By the time Tom got back to the pub the men had downed a couple of pints. Their horses had been stabled near the yards. Most of them would sleep in the stable next to their horse. But not Fred. He had women on his mind. And he didn't want to smell like no horse for his lady. That's if he got one, he wasn't going to pay one. He didn't mind if she was a bit loose, but he drew the line there.

So, when Tom came back into the pub and handed him half his wages he was miffed. He stared hard at Tom. 'What is this, Tom? Do I have to ask for the rest of it?'

Tom stood looking at him, 'I don't want you to lose it or get it stollen. You said you were planning to cut loose Fred.'

'So, what are you? My mother? Jesus Tom, you got so little faith in me?'

'Fred, you know I've got more faith in you than I do in me…'

'So, what's this' Fred shook his money at Tom?

'Just the way you were talking the other week Fred, I never heard you talk that way about drinking and women.' Tom blushed his embarrassment. He forgot his embarrassment when Fred grabbed his shirt and hoisted him almost off his feet.

Fred put his face close to Toms. 'I'm not gunna ask you Tom. I have faith in you that the rest of my money will appear in front of me as if by magic. I am tired Tom. I'm tired and dirty and hungry. I am thirsty and I have need of some comfort. Am I so different to other men?'

Tom shook his head, but he stood his ground, 'that's a lot of money I just handed you Fred. If I have to, I will stay here until you are ready to come home with me. I can't not worry about you Fred; I don't know how. What would you do if it was me? You go and get into the drink and the women and whatever else you want but I'll be here Fred. And when you run out of money the rest of it will appear in front of you back at Mataranka.'

Fred let go of Tom. To Tom's relief Fred smiled at him so he relaxed a little. 'Righto Tom. You take the other half of my money to Mataranka, and I'll see you there. In about a week or two. Go home Tom, see to that lovely woman of yours.'

Fred peeled off a fiver putting it on the bar and carefully put the rest in his pocket. He turned back to the bar and ordered a drink. Tom slid down the bar a bit and ordered a beer. 'So, aren't I good enough for you to drink with now young Tom?'

Tom spent the night with Fred until the big man found some female company then said goodnight and went to sleep with his horse. The next morning, he saddled his horse and rode to the station where he put the horse on the train. Tom left Darwin by train; he had things to do back at home.

When Fred came to the next morning his head hurt and he felt sick to his stomach. He turned over on his back and almost knocked the woman next to him clear out of bed. She objected and Fred told her to get dressed. Under protest she got dressed, 'Now go on home woman and leave me in some semblance of bloody peace.'

His companion swore at him and left. Fred felt worse than he ever had. He thought back over the night and to his dismay he remembered everything. He shook his head, God he wished he hadn't. He had gleaned a great knowledge of women over his lifetime, and he had made that woman squeal and moan until nigh on dawn. But Fred found none of the promise in it, none of the pleasure in it that he used to. It had only been a release.

He rolled out of bed and bathed, shaved, and put on his new duds. He needed a drink, Christ he needed a drink. He combed his straight black hair, donned his hat, and left the hotel. He walked to the end of the street and turned right and found his way into a small café. He ate there when he was in Darwin.

He walked to the counter and asked for a sizeable breakfast. He knew it would be the only food he would eat that day, he planned to be good and drunk by noon. He sat at a table and his mind went back to the night before, even Fred didn't know why he felt so bad about it. He'd certainly pleased his companion. He lowered his head into his hand. It ached like shit.

'Hello Fred.'

Fred spun around and looked up into the face of the most beautiful woman he'd ever seen and got the shock of his life. 'Oh, hello Sue. How are you?'

'I'm good thanks Fred. It's good to see you. I think' she added and smiled.

Fred laughed, 'are you coming or going?'

'Oh, I've just come in for some breakfast. The food is good here. Well, I like it. Alright Fred… I'll just be…'

'Well sit-down woman and eat with me. It's good to see you looking so well. What are you doing here? I heard you were leaving in an aeroplane. Did things not work out with you and Herbert?'

'Oh please' Sue laughed as she sat down opposite Fred. 'I found out what a skunk he was on my arrival at the hotel around the corner. I'm afraid I knocked him down in the foyer with my suitcase.' She giggled and Fred laughed heartily. She went on 'I bought a place around the corner a big three-story place. I have converted it into a hotel and function rooms. That sort of thing.' She turned to order a breakfast of bacon and eggs.

Fred studied her. She was the most fascinating creature he had ever seen. Just sitting looking at her was enough for him. He thought it would have to be and all. And had she done all this that she talked about by herself. Herself and daddy's money. The waitress put his meal in front of him. He looked down at it but didn't pick up his knife and fork. 'Did your father catch up with you?' He heard himself ask. He grinned his most dazzling at her to take the edge off his words. Fred was good at that, and he knew it.

Sue dropped her eyes, something about his smile made her heart positively flutter. 'Yes.' She said simply and smiled. She'd noticed how well Fred scrubbed up. He was clean shaven and neat and tidy. He smelled good to.

'And how did the reunion go, is he well pleased with what you have achieved?' Fred was choosing his words very carefully now.

To his surprise she laughed 'I don't know, and I don't care. He showed up and tried to tell me what my future held so I showed him the door.'

Fred had picked up his fork, but he let it drop and laughed. He laughed again and pulling himself together he eyed this strangest of women. He was afraid his admiration may be showing. He looked at his plate.

'And what happened to poor old Herbert? Did he make it out of town pretty lady?' Fred was sitting still, smiling at her.

Sue's face was serious now, 'he did leave but then the stupid man came back.'

Fred looked suitably shocked a twinkle in his eye. He waited for a moment and said, 'did he leave town again?"

'No'.

'Oh, come on woman, you have to tell me. Don't leave me hanging here like this.'

Sue laughed heartily now and said quietly. 'Well, he's in the hospital.'

Fred spluttered his laughter and put his hand to his mouth to try and contain it. It was no good, so he just laughed, and she laughed with him. God, it felt good, God she looked good, and she smelled good. Now if he'd been with her last… Oh fuck it he thought. He started to eat; the food was turning to cardboard in his mouth.

'Where are you staying Fred?' she asked.

Fred decided carefully on his lie. 'Well nowhere yet I slept at the stables last night, but I'll get somewhere today sometime.' He lifted a small amount of food to his mouth. The silence shouted 'liar' at him

'You must come and stay at my hotel Fred. It will be lovely to have a friendly face around for a while.'

Fred tried not to ask but he knew he had to. It was now or never, do or die. 'Did your father's future for you include Tom at all pretty lady?'

He'd spoken softly and Sue found it seductive. A shiver passed through her. She had no idea what it was about this man that she found so fascinating. She nodded slowly. 'Yes, it did. Tom and I, Fred. Imagine that?'

She laughed and Fred breathed a sigh of relief and laughed with her. 'How much?"

'What?"

'For a room at your establishment woman. How much.'

'Fred!'

Fred kept his eyes on his plate as he shrugged a shoulder. 'Well, if it's as classy a joint as I think, I may have to end up working it off.'

'Fred!'

He glanced up, she was smiling. 'I wouldn't charge you Fred. Not you.'

Fred felt something he hadn't felt in a long time. In fact, the last time he felt something this good he'd got stung by a bloody wasp and this woman wasn't far off.

When Bradly Ellis had gone back to see his daughter to try and make amends, she had thrown him out again. In light of what she'd told him, he didn't blame her. He had let her down in the worst possible way. He had no intentions of going to see the Dean of that girl's school either, that had been an empty threat. But he had just made arrangements for someone else to. He'd paid for two broken legs a broken nose and a good kicking. And Bradly intended to make it the bastard's big yearly event. Revenge was a dish best served anyway you could manage it.

Sue had told him she never wanted to see him again and it broke his heart. Before she slammed the door, he told her he wanted none of the money back. He also told her that she would forgive him one day. 'And I will return here every so often until you do.'

Sue closed the door and let the tears flow down her face. She shouldn't have told him she hated him, she didn't.

Bradly Ellis walked into a pub and downed several whiskeys. He'd get the train home in the morning. He hated going home, home to the bloody shrew. He knew of course that she hated him coming home.

One day, he promised himself once again, he'd divorce the bitch. But what then of his fortune? Bradly started thinking, he'd have to spirit money away, so she didn't know he had it. That's what the seventy thousand had been for, his ticket out of his hellish life.

But Bradly realised that his hellish life paled in comparison to that of his daughter. The poor little bugger he thought again and felt the hot tears. He knew in his heart he'd never get over what he'd heard.

A very attractive woman sidled up to him and Bradly asked for a room. Yes, this would do nicely. He bought her a drink.

After he'd drank a few more he invited the pretty woman to dine with him. He liked her. She was funny and entertaining, and his mind went to later in his room.

But later in his room the lady turned out to be just that. She gave Bradly a run for his money. Bradly sat and listened politely to her chatter. He looked at the clock and was shocked to find it was almost twelve o'clock. He found that he'd been enthralled by her story, but he had an urgent need. He was forty-seven and he still had certain urges. And this lady was tantalizing to say the least.

Bradly got out of his chair and turned the radio on. He found a station with just the right music. He held out his hand to her, 'will you dance with me Lilly?' He smiled his most gallant at her. The odd thing was that he felt like smiling.

She smiled shyly, another thing he found he liked about her. The only thing that bothered him was how young she was. She stood up and stepped into his arms. Bradly held her and danced with her. By the end of that dance Bradly Ellis was in love. Bradly Ellis was in trouble, and he liked it. At the end of the dance Bradly Ellis took her home to her place. Then he rang the railway and postponed his trip home to the next week.

CHAPTER 9

Tom alighted from the train at Mataranka, collected his horse and made his way to the hotel. Ernie was bringing the truck and some of the blokes down.

Tom was tired and hungry. He would get lunch and a drink, but he wouldn't be getting drunk. Emily had stung him with her comment about him being the same as his father. She'd been right though he'd had to admit. He would never take her for granted like that again. No Tom had seen the error of his ways also and he would tell her that.

Before the vision of Emily and Rodney made its way across his mind, he saw there a picture of Emily. A rerun so to speak of his Emily undressing for him, his practice was paying off he thought as a smile made its way onto his face. As soon as he got his food and drink down, he went home to his hut. He'd get ready for his trip to Damper Creek the next day.

Tom had banked his money from the trip, which was a massive nine hundred pounds with the money Emily had sent him. He had enough for a house, a very nice house. He was in a dilemma, he wanted enough to put a deposit, a sizeable deposit on a piece of land. A sizeable piece of land. Tom wanted his own place where he could spend the rest of his life raising cows and kids. Fred had helped him with that to. 'A man has to have a dream' he'd told Tom.

Tom's sleep was nice and peaceful that night though he worried about Fred. He worried that the big fellow had lost his heart to a no-good woman whom he would never have. Poor bloody Fred. He hoped his old friend would get laid and get over it.

He woke at around two in the morning and found his stomach was churning. What if Emily no longer loved him? What if she took one look at him and asked him to leave. Shit, he thought I should've got a haircut. He'd bath and shave and wear the new clothes he'd bought for the occasion.

Tom looked at himself in the mirror now. His hair would do he thought. He looked at his watch. He couldn't leave here too early he told himself, else he'd get to Damper Creek at breakfast. He had a few hours to kill. He knew that Emily did lunches and aimed to get there around two. She should be finished by then.

It was ten miles to Damper Creek, so Tom gave himself an hour. Ernie had dropped the truck off the night before. He'd wished Tom all the best and for the first time ever he'd put his arms around Tom, hugged him to him and turned and got on his horse and left.

Tom had a change of heart and changed his plans accordingly.

Emily had just sent Janet home for a couple of hours to return again at about four to get ready for the tea rush. All the men were gone, and the tables cleaned ready for the next meal the girls had assured her as they left.

She rose from her seat and went to inspect things as she always did. She'd make sure the tables were clean and set and that the floors were swept and clean and the chairs were pushed in neat and tidy. She opened the back door and her heart all but stopped. A man sat at the table farthest away. He had a very familiar hunch to his shoulders.

Emily knew her heart was racing; she could almost hear it. Her hand went to her mouth as the man slowly turned. 'Tom' was all she could say. She stared at him, mesmerised by the lovely smile that slowly crossed his beautiful face.

Tom looked at Emily, this woman he had loved for a long time. He'd never loved anyone else but her. He looked at her standing in the doorway. She had let her hair go back to a dark brown and she wore it collar length. She was slim and wore a dress that showed off her figure. His eyes travelled over her tiny waistline and her small perky breasts. Her eyes were clear, and she wore a little make up. God she's beautiful he thought as he smiled at her.

Tom stood up slowly never taking his eyes from hers. 'Will you join me Emily' he asked politely? When she smiled it took his breath away. Clean, white even teeth, surely, she'd had some work done on them.

He'd witnessed the lunch rush and knew she could probably afford it. Then she walked towards him, and the struggle almost brought him undone. Her left arm she kept tucked up at her waist. She shuffled towards him, and he was unable to move. Her left leg she had to sort of drag behind her then she could stand on it to take another step. Christ, he thought, how did she manage all this?

'Hello Tom' she said quietly, 'when did you get back?' She sounded matter of fact and he smiled.

'Yesterday, Emily. I didn't go and get drunk, I knew when you said that, that you had a right to. I'm sorry Emily that I treated you so badly that you had to look for some love elsewhere and look what bloody happened to you.' Tom shut his mouth suddenly. He'd gone on too far, said too much. He hadn't meant to. 'Oh, Emily I'm sorry. I shouldn't have said that. Don't cry love.'

Emily took the few steps towards him; he held out his arms. She walked right into them and fell against him. She cried and cried. Toms' shirt was wet, but he held her to him. He knew enough to let her cry it out. The tears she had kept back, been too afraid to release. He held her and rocked her gently. 'Oh Emily' he whispered, 'my Emily.'

When the sobs started to subside, he cupped her chin in his hand and lifted her face to look at him. 'I love you woman; I bloody love you.'

He let go of her and pulled out a chair. 'You wanna have a talk, Emily? Wanna sit a while and tell me all about it? Please Emme.' He helped her into a chair and pulled a chair up so he could hold her hand. Gazing into her eyes he sat like that, and she told him the whole horrific story. By the time she had finished she was wiping his eyes with a table napkin. At last, she got onto her starting the business here and told him about Harry and the girls. Her face brightened and she was smiling, even laughed occasionally. She was transformed he thought tenderly, his Emily. A businesswoman. Smart and clever and beautiful.

Eventually she told him how she had found the money under the bed and her memory had hit her with full force. She told him of her shame and degradation. Her humiliation and heart break. Her face brightened again when she mentioned getting his letters. 'And when I got that last one, I was at peace again Tom. I knew I'd see you again and have a chance to beg your forgiveness. And here I am, and I want to do just that, but I don't know where to start or how. I can't offer you an explanation Tom, the woman that I was is a mystery to me. So, I'll just say this, please forgive me Tom. I need you to forgive me. Just that Tom, just forgive me.'

'Oh, you are forgiven woman. I blamed myself Emily. Eventually' he grinned now. 'I was a bit stung at first, but when I thought about it, I knew I'd been a bloody fool Emme. I'll find that fuckin Rodney one day woman I promise you that and we'll see how he likes it.'

'No Tom, he did me a favour. I was a selfish girl, thought only of myself. And you know, when I came to in that hospital, I had no recollection of what happened. No memory of you but I knew I had done a lot of harm. It became clear over the next few months as I fought to walk and talk again that I had hurt someone and lost someone that I would never get over. Isn't that weird Tom? I couldn't remember you in my head, but in my heart I knew.'

Tom dropped his head and nodded. He swallowed and looked at Emily. 'Emily, I have something for you.'

'Oh Tom, a present. Oh, darling you shouldn't have…'

Emily stopped talking as Tom slid off his chair and knelt before her. His hand came out of his pocket and in it was a small box. 'Emily, my dear Emily, will you be my wife Emme? You don't have to say…'

'Oh yes Tom Oh yes. I love you, Tom. I have never loved another. No Tom, never.'

Tom stood up and took his woman into his arms and carried her through the house to the bedroom. Vaguely he realised that the house was clean and tidy. It was a nice little house.

Tom lay her gently on the bed and easing himself down beside her he kissed her on the lips. 'Oh Emily, I have missed you. Missed this.'

As he took her in his arms, he realised with a start how thin she was. He made love to her, and she responded eagerly. Emily had forgotten what a joy he was. 'I have missed you, Tom. I will never hurt you again.'

Tom chuckled and said quietly, 'that's quite a promise my love.'

It was three thirty when Emily turned and looked at the clock. She turned to Tom and smiled. 'I never knew anything could be so wonderful Tom. Oh God that felt good. I have to get up and go now darling we have the tea rush in a couple of hours. Will I see you again Tom? Will you stay and see me after?'

'Course I will my love. Course I will. Just try and get rid of me. I have plans Emme, I'd like to talk to you about them later. Can I help you with anything?'

'Oh yes Tom. You may be sorry you said that. Come on dear, you are about to find out how hard we work for our money here, us girls.'

Tom was overjoyed. He loved this new Emily even more than the old one. This new one was a woman. A smart mature sophisticated woman. Least ways he thought so. And she had loved him like never before.

As Tom worked beside Emily, he was amazed at how she coped. She never got flustered no matter what, never lost her temper, she was cool and calm and collected. He was proud of her. Maybe the accident had made her he thought. Had changed her thinking. He had never been loved like that back in the bedroom. Now there was a thought, he'd practice that one to.

This thought brought his mind back to Fred as he washed the big pots. He was deep in thought when he heard a cheer go up and the soft tones of a piano accordion, he knew it was Eric.

When Tom walked out onto the veranda, he was nothing short of amazed as people got to their feet and danced to the music. He'd dance with Emily. Then he spotted her shuffling towards him. The smile died; he'd have to ask her about that. Oh God look what he was responsible for. He should have bloody turfed Rodney fuckin Gaskill out and given him a hiding. But instead, he'd run off like a coward. And his beautiful woman was maimed.

Emily had seen it, saw the smile die on his lips and she knew why. She and Tom had often gone to dances. She walked up and took his face in her hands. 'It's alright my dear.' She said softly. 'We'll get it back.' The sunny smile she gave him almost convinced him it would be so. He looked around him and realised, if his Emily could do all this she'd probably dance again. And he'd help her instead of feeling sorry for her. He owed her a bit bloody more than pity.

And later that night he told Emily of his plans to own a cattle station. Told her he almost had enough for a sizeable deposit. He talked of marriage and children, making a home together and growing old together. 'You'll see Emme, I will never let you down again woman.'

Emily smiled in the darkness, she knew he would, and she'd forgive him. But she didn't know where her business figured into all these plans. It worried her. But when Tom took her in his arms and set about loving her, she forgot all about her business. As she scaled the heights of pure pleasure with Tom, she knew she'd do whatever she had to do.

Ernie went back to Katherine arriving just on dark and let himself in his little house. The last thing he remembered was putting his hand out to switch the light on. Ernie lay unconscious on the floor for that night and most of the next day. When he came to, he knew he had to try and get to his feet and get outside. He opened his eyes, but the brightness hurt so he closed them. A man's voice made him jump. He thought he knew the voice.

'Well look who's awake. Righto old man, I have come for what you owe me.'

Ernie sneered; it was Wally Cooper. He hadn't seen that bastard since he'd run him off for beating Tom who was just twelve at the time. He turned his head and looked at the man he so despised. Thank God he'd told Tom this mongrel wasn't his father.

'What is it that you imagine I owe you, you fat pathetic excuse for a…'

Ernie was winded by a kick to his midriff. Wally stepped back, 'you stole my wife and my son.'

'Neither is true. I saved your missus and gave her a son. You beat her up and I took her away. Tom is my son and I told him so last…'

Ernie was feeling a bit faint from the kick to the head, he'd stop talking for a while. He knew he couldn't take too many of those. Wally was an ox of a man.

Wally knelt down beside him now, 'I have your pay packet you piece of wife stealing shit. That will do for a first instalment.'

Ernie looked around at him and sure enough he had the brown envelope with his pay in it. 'You never cared for her you arsehole.'

'Never cared about him neither. Never liked the little bastard and now I know why.'

Wally laughed and Ernie could only lay there and look on. Ernie kept his voice even as he said 'so what now Wal? I take it you'll be back for more money.'

'Too fuckin right' Wally stepped closer and leaned towards Ernie. 'I never fuckin liked you. Always had your big nose stuck in other people's affairs. Never in your own though Ernie. Should have kept a bit of an eye on your own affairs. Especially the ones with other men's wives. You're a piece of work alright Ernie. Judy died not long after she run off with you. You must o been worse n me ya bastard.' Wally took a pound note from his envelope and threw it on him where he lay on the floor. 'Have one on me ya prick, oh yes and I got what was in the tea caddy' Wally laughed. 'Fuckin old woman' he mumbled as he was leaving.

He opened the front door and let himself out. He had an accomplice because a car started up outside before the front door was shut. Of course, thought Ernie, Wally would never have the guts to do this on his own. Ernie smiled at the thought of what Wally would say if he knew the fortune Ernie had hidden in the flour bin.

Ernie had more immediate problems. His feet had been bound tightly and he couldn't feel them. His hands were still tied behind him, so he'd have to get those free in a hurry. He tried to get to his feet, but he couldn't stand on them.

He heard someone walking past in the street. He knew all the neighbours, so he yelled for help. It was Jack from down the road, 'is that you Ernie' he called as he opened the door? 'You, okay?' Jack came to a halt when he saw Ernie laying on the floor, trussed up like he was someone's Christmas dinner. 'Jesus Ernie.' He ran to the kitchen and came back with a sharp knife. 'Who did this to you Ernie. Do you know?'

'Yeah, I know who it was Jack. Get these cords off my legs Jack I can't feel my feet.'

Jack cut the bindings away and rubbed Ernie's feet. 'Shit, how long you been here Ernie? Like this?'

'Since last night I think Jack.'

'Did the bastards rob you mate?'

Ernie nodded. He was in considerable pain now as the circulation returned to his limbs. As soon as he could move them Ernie started kicking his legs back and forth. He eventually got to his feet. 'Thanks Jack. I was hoping someone would come by.'

'Do you need to go to the hospital Ernie?'

'I don't think so Jack. He gave me a couple of good kicks. Jesus I'm thirsty.'

'Do you want me to call somebody Ernie? Tom maybe?'

'No! I don't thanks Jack. I'd rather he didn't know about this. Let's just keep it to ourselves hay?'

Later that day Ernie went to the hospital, he was sure his nose was broken, and he had concussion. He was right on both counts and already his eyes were black and swollen.

Fred walked home from the dance hall with Sue, it was chilly, and he took his jacket off and put it round her shoulders. It was a new jacket he'd bought yesterday. 'Oh, that's lovely Fred. It's so warm and it smells good.' Sue looked down at her feet.

Fred glanced at her and smiled she'd embarrassed herself. He stopped halfway home in the darkness under a tree and grabbing her hand he pulled her to a stop. She looked up at him. She couldn't see his face very well under the brim of his hat.

Fred had dined and danced with her until she'd complained about being tired. He stood now in front of her and slipped his arms around her waist. She quivered and he felt it go right through him. Fred was in love, and he knew it. He'd been in love with her since that fuckin wasp stung him right on it. He smiled.

Fred knew that he had to play his cards just right if he was to have a chance with this woman. She was the woman of his dreams, though she was young. This was the woman he'd waited for, for so long. Had given up on. Yes, he would play his cards right. He knew she felt it to, he could see it, feel it, hell he could taste it.

Fred dropped his lips on hers and kissed her softly. He left his lips on hers and moved his hands slowly up and down her back. She melted against him and kissed him back. He lifted his head and smiled down at her. Turning he took her hand and walked the rest of the way to her hotel.

Along the way Fred mused about the last couple of days he'd spent with this woman. He was almost sure she had strong feelings for him, but he also remembered what she was like out along the trail with the other blokes. Yes, Fred was no fool, but his heart was.

At the front door he took the key from her and unlocked the front door. He looked back at Sue as he opened it wide for her. He saw the look of horror on her face and spun round his fists coming up in readiness. He dropped them.

Herbert stood there looking pathetic. He looked at Fred. 'Who are you?'

Sue pushed passed Fred. 'Didn't I tell you never to come back here. If you don't leave at once I shall call the police.' She went to grab him, but Fred restrained her.

Fred spoke, he sounded amused. So, this was Herbert. He was about as old as Fred and much less spectacular. 'What do you want here my friend?' Fred was smiling down at the man. He'd need to keep his cool, he knew that. With a woman like Sue, he'd have to be able to keep calm as men tried to take her away from him.

'Well, I am not your friend I'm hers. Now I asked you who you are?'

Fred took the much smaller man gently by the shoulder and guided him out onto the path. Herbert struggled and Fred let him go. But Herbert wasn't finished. He swung at Fred and the punch caught the big man by surprise as it bounced off his chin. He grinned at Herbert and said softly, 'what was that Herbert? You wouldn't be trying to hurt me, would you? Just when I thought we were hitting it off to.'

Herbert produced a knife and as quick as a flash he'd stuck it in Fred's left arm above the wrist. Fred reached up and pulled it out. Before he could stop it, Sue was standing beside him, and she hit Herbert with an uppercut to his jaw which sent Herbert sprawling across the footpath. Fred tried to grab her but was too busy watching Herbert as he struggled to his feet.

Fred stared at Sue open mouthed, he held his left arm to stem the flow of blood. Sue turned to him and to his amazement she had tears in her eyes. 'Oh, Fred I'm sorry. I'll go and call the police.'

Fred reached out and stopped her 'no, just let it go honey, I'm okay.' He grinned at her now and pulled her into his arms. He turned his head to look at the now standing Herbert. 'You better go Herbert.' He spoke softly. He could see the man did actually love the woman. Well, he knew what that was like.

'I have nowhere to go. I came back for you' he looked now at Sue. Beseeching her with his eyes.

'Yeah, I realise that mate,' said Fred. 'Go down to the stock yards and you'll find the stables. Go to the third stall in on your left and you'll find my stall. There'll be a big bay mare in there a white blaze down her face. In the corner on a shelf, you'll find my swag. Use it. Come back tomorrow we'll sort something out.' Fred was glad he'd only gotten half his money from Tom now else that would have been in his swag.

Fred smiled inwardly now at the memory of Tom giving him half his money. Unbeknownst to Tom Fred had a lot of money sitting in the Commonwealth bank. He'd been saving to buy himself a couple of acres at Katherine and build a small dwelling on it. He'd run chickens he decided, he'd had enough of bloody cattle and droving.

Fred noticed that Herbert didn't look at all pleased with the notion of sleeping in a barn. He walked away from Sue and grabbing Herbert by the arm dragged him away a bit. With their backs to the woman Fred slid a pound into Herbert's hand and spoke in a soft voice. 'Here, now fuck off mate. Come back tomorrow or you could go find yourself a bloody job. They're looking for people at the stockyards and I think they are probably just desperate enough to hire you. Now go on… Git.' Fred's words were harsh, but his voice and his eyes were full of compassion.

Once inside the hotel Sue inspected Fred's arm. 'I'll clean it and bandage it for you' she said.

But Fred had already calculated his response. 'It'll be fine. I need to bath so I'll clean it and put a plaster on it. You go on up to bed and I'll see you in the morning. Go on now. You got work tomorrow I don't.

At her door Fred took her key and opened the door for her. He handed her back her key and pulled her gently into his arms. He kissed her long and tenderly and deeply on the mouth. All the love he felt for her was in that kiss. Fred hoped it would do the trick. It did.

Fred disengaged himself from the now trembling woman. He smiled down at her and turned and walked to the stairs. He looked back as he disappeared from view. She was watching him, her hand to her lips. He smiled his most dazzling.

As Fred let himself into his suite, he let himself fall apart. He had an erection from Hell, and he knew bloody well she had felt it between them. Where was that bloody wasp now? Well, he'd deal with that in a moment or two. He got bathed and cleaned his wound. It was deep, Fred couldn't believe that little ferret had actually stabbed him. He couldn't believe either, that Sue had knocked him arse up. He smiled at the memory. He found that he was starting to feel sorry for Herbert.

The bleeding had stopped though he had lost a lot of blood. He got a plaster from his bag and stuck it over the gash. Fred went to the bed, now he'd take care of his main problem. It was taking too much to control his need of that woman. And control it he must.

❧

CHAPTER 10

Bradly Ellis sat in the bar of the hotel Darwin until 9.30pm. He was disappointed because Lilly hadn't turned up. They had agreed to meet in the saloon bar at eight. He had dressed up in a nice suit, his dark hair slicked back waiting for his girl. He looked down at himself and shook his head. His girl? Ellis put his drink down and left the pub.

He walked the few blocks to her house and wondered all the while if he should. Well, he told himself he had to. Had to see her. Jesus, he shook his head, he had it bad and he knew it. He was a forty-seven-year-old married man. He shuddered and kept doggedly on to her door.

He knocked on the big ornate door and waited. He knocked again and waited for a minute or two. The house appeared to be in darkness.

He looked down at his feet, maybe she was in bed asleep, he wouldn't knock again. He turned on his heel and heard a tiny voice. He went to the door and put his ear against it, 'Lilly' he said and listened.

'Help' he heard from inside He stood not knowing if he'd actually heard that. Then it came again, 'help... Bradly...'

Bradly didn't think about it he took a step back and threw his shoulder at the door. Bradly Ellis, though he was only five six in his socks, was a very thick set stocky man as strong as an ox. The door didn't budge, but it did hurt. 'Shit' he said out loud, 'doesn't hurt those bastards in the movies, just flies right on opened.' He took a few steps back and gritting his teeth in anticipation he threw himself once more at the door. The door flew opened as he made contact with it and, he realised why, as he rode the bloke who opened it to the floor.

Bradly had no way of knowing what went on here, so he made it back onto his feet in a flash. He even surprised the small skinny man now looking up at him from the floor with wide eyes. He looked over at the couch and was astounded to see Lilly there trussed up like a turkey.

'What goes on here?' He asked as he looked back at the man getting to his knees.

'Well, that'll be none of your damn business so you can fuck off.'

Ellis turned towards Lilly. Taking a skinning knife from his belt he cut the ropes from her. He sat next to her and put his arms around her. 'Lilly, for the love of God what is this?'

Lilly buried her head in his chest and cried. Bradly's shirt was dripping wet with her tears and snot. After a minute or two he took both her arms and lifted her off him. He said as softly as he could, 'Lilly? Tell me about it. Why the hell were you tied up and who the fuck is this?' Bradly turned to look at the man now standing in the middle of the room.

The man replied. 'Not that it's any of your damn business but I'm her father. And she's a little slut. She was out until all hours last night at that bloody pub. Barman told me she'd been up in some bastard's room for quite some time. She aint leaving the house again.' He turned beady eyes on her now, 'I'll stop you, you little trollop… I'll whip the fuckin hide off ya. Your nothing but…'

Bradly Ellis wasn't a fighting man, but he bounced up from the couch and with one punch he knocked the man flying. Lilly's father slammed up against the wall and slid down it. He sat in a daze, blood dribbling down his chin.

Bradly was having trouble believing what he'd just done but he yelled at the man. 'She was in my room last night and I can assure you she is no trollop. Nor did I treat her like one.' He turned to Lilly dropping his voice. 'Where's your mother' he asked Lilly gently?

Lilly wiped her nose on the hanky Ellis had given her. 'She left years ago.'

'Yeah well', Bradly swung his arms around for a bit then, 'go and get your things. All of them.'

'Where am I going?'

'With me' Bradly walked over to the couch and helped her to her feet. 'Come on Lilly I'll look after you.' A little voice inside his head was asking him how he planned to do that. He told it to shut up.

Lilly hesitated and he went on softly. 'Come on woman you can't stay here.' He stood in front of her and put his hand gently to her face, he went on tenderly now. 'You like me don't you Lilly? I don't mean I want… I want to sleep together but I will look after you. And… well, I'll wait for as long as it takes… for you.'

'Well, isn't this fuckin touching'.

'Alright' said Lilly. Bradly Ellis stared wide eyed at her. His heart was beating fast, he was dumbfounded, this beautiful woman could have anybody.

'Now just a bloody minute' her father put in. 'You can't come in here and take her… just take her like that ya bloody mongrel. Who the hell do you think you are? She's mine. She's, my daughter. Go on get out of my house. Lilly, go in the kitchen and start dinner. You're acting like a… a…'

Lilly turned on him now, 'you know what father, Bradly's right. He didn't treat me like a slut, he treated me like a lady. He was a gentleman and I liked it.' She looked now at Bradly and her cheeks went red as she said, 'yes, I do like you Bradly, very much. I only have my clothes, and some make up. That is all I have in the world Bradly.'

'Go ahead and get them girl. Don't hurry my dear, your dad and I will have a little chat.' Bradly settled himself on the couch pulling his jacket around him.

Lilly ran to her bedroom. Her father said, 'Christ man, she's twenty-four. You're old enough to be her father. You are making a… a… fool of yourself and a whore out of my daughter. What you gunna do with her, is she to be a kept woman is she? Your bloody…'

Bradly leaned back on couch and put his finger to his lips 'for the older man to keep quiet, he did realise he was about the same age as her father. Bradly himself was in a bit of a daze that he'd struck a man so violently and all over a woman he'd known for about a day.

He knew also with certainty he would do it again and again for her. He'd take on the world for her, he might bloody well have to.

A picture of his wife's face flashed before him. He shrugged it off, she hadn't slept with him since the day she'd announced she was pregnant with their twenty-four-year-old son. He knew she didn't want him but just how pleased she'd be that somebody else did, only time would tell.

Bradly and his wife had never actually been lovers. She had visited his bed to have the two kids. His son was just like her. Well fuck him and his mother. How he hated her. He'd have to spirit money away a bloody sight quicker now. Bradly's thoughts were all tumbling around in his head.

Presently Lilly came out with a suitcase and her bag. She was wearing a hat and a nice blue and white dress with a red belt at the waist and black high heels. Bradly knew with absolute certainty he loved her. Was in love with her, wanted her. He smiled and saw her visibly relax. His heart melted, but what was he to do?

He couldn't sleep with her and not… And what would she think if he tried it on and her all upset. Shit, he was not good at this he realised. His own miserable marriage had all been arranged and that had been nothing but a disaster. He heaved a sigh; he couldn't do any worse than that could he? And he told himself, he actually liked this woman, enjoyed her company. Yes, everything would be okay, he was sure of it.

Bradly got up off the couch and took her case. He'd head back to the hotel and try to get another room. Then again maybe he should sleep with her and be of some comfort to her. After all he was dragging the poor girl from her home. Although how happy she'd been here was another thing, he thought as he looked around at the place. And she had been bloody tied up when he arrived and had to throw himself at the door.

He closed the front door behind him and knew a moments panic. He looked at Lilly and the panic ebbed away and left only a delirious happiness in its wake. Shit I'm in trouble he thought. A grin appeared momentarily on his face.

On the way back to the hotel it occurred to him to wonder what that fuckin barman was doing talking about who he had in his room.

He'd get to the bottom of that to. He held Lilly's hand tightly. Bradly had never hit anyone before, but that mongrel was asking for it and it felt good.

As he walked along beside her, he turned and asked her what she wanted him to do. 'You want a room of your own or do you wanna sleep with me?' He stopped and turned her to face him. Putting his hand to her cheek he said softly, 'I don't think I can sleep all night next to you and not try it on darlin.' He shrugged.

She looked back at him for a while her face looked thoughtful, and Bradly's heart sank. He started to turn back to the front when he heard her sob. 'Oh Bradly… Bradly'.

He swung back to look at her and in his forty-seven years on the planet he had never had a woman look at him like that. The desire he saw straight away, then the need, the love. He dropped the suitcase and threw his arms around her. She did the same and they both toppled against a wall. She was the same height as Bradly in her heels.

He kissed her long and deep, with a passion that only thirty odd years of loneliness can breed. When they separated, they were both breathless. Bradly pulled back from her, he had got an erection and a powerful need to go with it, but he had his answer. He held her hand and hurried her back to the pub.

Rushing up the stairs with his woman and the heavy suitcase he thought of that bloody barman. Well, he'd keep until the morning. Bradly was dizzy, breathless when they got to the top of the stairs. The woman he had with him had filled him with a wonder he would never have believed possible for someone like him.

When at last Bradly lay down beside her, he was so overcome he had to let the tears fall. The woman wiped them from his face and smiled softly as she pulled him close.

Herbert walked the few blocks to the hotel the pound note still in his hand. It stung him, burned into his flesh. That he'd taken a pound from one of his girl's roots. Herbert was not blind to what she was, but he'd been using her. And then he'd been asked by the big ugly bastard to fuck off. He'd keep the fucking pound note and go sleep in the barn with the bastard's bloody horse and all the horse shit. Tomorrow he'd see what he was to do. He'd have to do something he knew.

Herbert had no trouble finding the stable. There was a long shelf on the wall about shoulder height. He could hear snoring coming from the next stall and when he investigated, he saw that the man was laying on that shelf. Herbert decided he'd do that to, up out of the shit and Christ knows what else. Probably wouldn't get stomped or pissed on up there either.

He found what he hoped was Fred's swag, he didn't need another belting this day by Christ. He couldn't believe Sue, what had got into her? To knock him arse up in front of the new boyfriend? He finally lay down to sleep, the place stunk something awful. That bastard would be in bed with his bloody woman by now. It was too much, he tossed and turned for hours.

Herbert opened his eyes. The sun was coming up and he couldn't believe he'd actually got some sleep. It had to be the worst day of his life the worst night of his life. He'd just slept in a room full of horse dung and he had a pound note to his name.

He sat up and swung his legs over the edge and jumped down from the shelf. As he was rolling Fred's swag up, he noticed a bag of coins in the foot of it. He opened it and counted two pounds. He took ten shillings put it in his pocket and left the stall as he found it.

Herbert didn't bother with breakfast; he'd have to ration himself. He asked a boy mucking out the stalls to point him to the boss of the yards. He'd get a job in the yards; he'd show that bastard. Desperate hay? Well, Herbert thought wryly, I should bloody well hope they are. He found an old soft drink bottle and filled it at the tap. The place he was going, he figured it would probably be thirsty work.

The man he found was Bill Wilson and after shaking hands with Herbert, he looked him up and down. 'Jesus', he said softly, scratched his head and looked him up and down again. He grabbed one of Herbert's hands and said 'you got any gloves there Herbert? The skin on these is gunna come right off mate.' Bill liked the hungry look in Herbert's face. He could also see that he'd lived a life of privilege, but he was down on his luck. Bill was no stranger to being down on his luck himself.

Herbert shook his head and Bill stopped a very dirty looking man walking passed them. 'Find some bloody gloves for Bert here will ya Pete and put him on opening and closing the gates for today and tomorrow. Matter of fact he can do that for the rest of the week. Show him the ropes, will you?'

'Gordon's not gunna like it boss.'

'Well, I don't give much of a fuck what Gordon likes or dislikes Pete. Last time I fuckin looked I was the boss here. You go and get him and bring him to me and I'll ask him real nice like if he wouldn't fuckin mind. How about that?'

And so, Herbert, who everybody now called Bert, was hired on. He went to sleep in the stall until somebody told him there were rooms for them to sleep in. Despite the gloves Herbert's hands blistered, skun and blistered again several times. He had never felt such pain in his life. He ate with the men and gradually got used to their language and their teasing.

One of the ladies who worked in the office had been in the kitchen with him one day. She'd noticed his hands and had dressed them and applied an ointment to them. Gradually they got better.

Herbert found it hard going at first, but it got easier as the days passed. It amazed him how he picked it up, was able to see the pattern emerging. Herbert hadn't realised when he'd asked for the job, but he was a wharfie now. On the livestock side of it but still a wharfie.

He opened and closed gates and helped with moving the stock around. The ones being brought in by the drovers and the ones being loaded on the big ships, some were off to other stations or the abattoirs. In and out of the yards they went all day long.

It was hot, dusty blistering work but he loved it. He would never again depend on a woman for everything, he was in Hell now and it wasn't so bad. When the woman tossed you out you had nothing. He did realise though that he hadn't been much of a man.

At the end of the next week Herbert still had the ten shillings and he'd got his pay. It was nine pounds and Herbert couldn't believe it. He was sleeping better to he was that bloody tired at night. The first thing he did was to go and put the ten shillings back in Fred's swag. It was gone!

'Shit' Herbert had to give that money back and the pound. He'd just have to go and see him. He'd front the bastard and then he'd be able to hold his head up. It was about five o'clock in the afternoon and he'd just knocked off work.

He'd gone into the shops a couple days back and got himself some denims and a pair of boots. He'd got socks and a blue checked shirt which he was wearing now with the sleeves rolled up. Herbert noticed that for the first time his forearms were tanned. He looked in the mirror and his face was tanned and looked healthy. He liked what he saw for the first time ever. He'd also bought himself a good hat and he put that on his head. Yeah, he'd go and see Fred, man to man.

Herbert got a look at himself in the full-length mirror on the back of his wardrobe door. For the first time he could remember he thought he didn't look shabby and worn.

He set off on the long walk to Sue's hotel with a spring in his step. The cheek of that bitch knocking him arse up like that. Well fuck the pair of them. He knocked and walked into the foyer just as the happy couple were heading into the dining room.

'Excuse me' he said and watched them turn.

Sue took a step towards him a nasty expression on her face. 'What the hell are you doing here? What did I tell you?' She stopped and he saw her expression change to one of interest when she actually noticed him. She looked puzzled and this pleased Herbert, let her look.

Herbert lifted his hand for silence (a thing he never would have done before) and looking at Fred now he walked boldly towards him. He said, 'It is Fred I've come to see. Fred, I took you up on your invitation to spend the night in your stall. I didn't get into your swag, but I slept on top of it. And I did take something that didn't belong to me.' He handed Fred the ten shillings and he could see the big man was surprised and impressed as he looked down at it in his hand. Herbert put a pound note on top of it and said, 'I thank you for your generosity my friend and I humbly ask your forgiveness.'

Fred put his hand out and shook hands with Herbert, 'you have it Herbert and thank you.'

Fred looked puzzled and Herbert smiled, 'I got a job at the yards.' Herbert's smile turned to a grin and spread all over his face.

'Oh really' said Fred a grin lighting up his own face. 'Bill Wilson?' He watched Herbert straighten. Fred knew that Bill Wilson was a good bloke, one of the best and he found he was glad that Herbert had found him. He knew Bill was just the bloke to straighten a crooked pin like Herbert out. He could already see the results. And if Bill saw something in Herbert, then Herbert was worth a second chance for sure.

'The same' said Herbert proudly, he still hadn't looked at Sue. Fuck Sue, but he found he liked Fred. He was the same stamp as Bill.

'What's he got you doing?'

'Well, I'm opening and closing gates. It took a bit of keeping up at first, but I can run a bit faster now. And my, but some of those cows can run like hairy goats, they can. The gates don't seem so heavy now either.' Herbert smiled ruefully and went on 'I'm getting used to the dust and the stink also. I do find I like it there Fred, I'm glad you suggested it, just as I am glad, they were indeed desperate. Anyway, I just wanted to repay you for your kindness. Stealing from you was pretty low you know?' Herbert studied his feet for a few seconds. 'I suppose you know the boys are all going to the pub later. If I see you there, I'd like to buy you a drink. Anyway, be seeing you Fred and thanks again. And I am sorry for how I repaid your kindness before.'

Herbert turned on his heel and walked quietly from the room. 'I might take you up on that drink a bit later mate' Fred called out after him. He shook his head in amazement as he watched Herbert walk to the door his back straight his shoulders back. And Fred hadn't even realised that he'd taken the ten shillings. Well, well he thought.

Herbert looked back and smiled, he flicked his eyes and nodded very briefly at Sue. She had a dumb look on her face.

He couldn't figure out the emotion, but he found he no longer cared, he was done with women. Especially her, and all the other Sues he'd been wasting his time on. No fuck it he thought and grinned. Fred wouldn't be down the pub tonight if he knew anything about women. And he did. Yes, Herbert was a bit of a bloody expert, for all the good it had done him.

❧

Fred was hoeing into his steak like a man possessed, he had to get out of this fuckin house. He had bedded down with Sue a week ago and the woman had never let him out of her sight. He needed a drink badly. Sue hadn't spoken to him since Herbert's visit and wore a strained expression. The woman was cold.

'So, you are planning to go to the pub tonight?' Her voice was flat. Fred nodded his head and kept eating. Her tone rankled him.

Sue said in a venomous voice now, 'well if you go to the pub you can sleep in the lounge. I have rented your room to someone else. You didn't consult me Fred, didn't bother yourself with how I'd like it.'

Fed swallowed his mouthful. 'Sue, I don't mean to hurt your feelings my dear, but I don't really care how you feel, I'm going to the pub. And I will have a couple of beers with Herbert. The man is trying. Then I'll probably come home. I find my work down the pub. I have to sit in the pub and the drover boss's find me there it's how we all do it. Soon, I have to go see Tom in Mataranka. And then I will sit in the Mataranka pub until closing. If no one contacts me, I 'll be there the next night and so on. See? I need to get work.'

'So that's how you want it Fred' Sue was using her best hurt voice and it wasn't lost on Fred. He softened a little.

'It's not a question of how I want it darling, that's just how it is.'

'And when you get work what? You'll be away droving for weeks or even months.'

'Yes Sue, that is because I am a drover. At the moment I need to work. Knowing Tom, he'll be teeing up another drive by now so I need to be where he can contact me by phone. If he can't find me, he'll hire someone else.'

'He can contact you here, give him this number Fred.'

Fred sighed and put his knife and fork down. He was sick of chewing on cardboard and walking on eggshells. 'Have you finished your tea, Sue?'

'No!' She practically shouted at him now.

'Alright Sue. I'll get out of your hair for a few days. I'll go see Tom I have some business with him, and I'll come see you before I go on a drive.'

'Oh, just go Fred.' Sue flicked her hand at him, and Fred was stung. He got up and left the room.

Up in their room where Fred had thought they'd be happy he threw his things in his bag. With heavy heart he looked around the room, he hadn't been happy with Sue and yet he'd thought all his dreams had come true. He found her to be a spoiled brat and was sick of her constant whining and nit picking. When he made love to her, she seemed to suffer him more than anything. That fuckin Herbert, no wonder he was grinning like a Cheshire cat.

He bounded down the stairs and out of the hotel. As he walked to the pub, he took deep breaths. The deep sweet breath of freedom. He'd had enough of women. He suddenly felt that he had a few years of droving left in him after all. Tom had been right he thought as he looked at the footpath. He shrugged his shoulders and quickened his step.

Fred pushed the door of the pub open and stepped in, he breathed the smell of the liquor and tobacco into his lungs as if he had been holding his breath for the last ten long days. He spotted Herbert at the same time as Herbert spotted him.

Herbert left the bar and walked over to Fred. 'She let you out mate.'

Fred laughed, 'not exactly Bert. I think I was wise to bring my swag and bag with me put it that way.' After he threw his bag and swag on the floor in the corner, Fred leaned on the bar Herbert beside him. The smaller man bought two beers and after taking a swig Fred said, 'no mate, I think I'm for the stables tonight somehow.'

'I didn't mind it in the stable Fred, at least I was free and that pound you gave me was all I had. I didn't like the stink but I'm getting used to it.' Herbert smiled up at the big man he'd come to like and respect, 'you alright Fred?' Fred lifted his beer and downed it in one go. 'Guess not' said Herbert in a quiet respectful voice.

Fred smiled at him, 'I'm alright now Herbert. You sit on that one mate I'll get another. I'm a bit thirsty.'

Herbert looked at the plaster on Fred's arm, 'I'm sorry about your arm to Fred, dunno what got into me.'

Fred laughed as the barman put another beer in front of him, 'I do' he said.

Herbert nodded and smiled ruefully. Yeah, he liked this life liked it a lot. He also liked Bill and this man standing beside him drinking with him at the bar and him with his own money. Who would have thought? Herbert had left more than half his money back in his room in one of the bed legs. Bill had given him some damn good advice lately. He owed that man a lot to. Bill had even shown an interest in where abouts in England he came from.

At around nine o'clock that night the barman called Fred to the bar and handed him the phone. It was Tom with a job. 'Thank Christ for that Tom. I'll be back tomorrow. Hay listen is Ernie coming down?'

'I dunno,' said Tom. 'I haven't been able to get in touch with him. You couldn't call in there could you Fred? The job doesn't start for another two weeks. But I mean it's Saturday night he's always in the pub Saturday nights.'

'Yeah, okay Tom I'll go see him. And are you in Damper Tom? Everything okay?'

'Yeah, I'm in Damper now. Yeah, everything's okay Fred. I'll go home to Mataranka in the next week or so and get preparing, so I'll probably see you there. A long one this time Fred we pick up a herd of about nine hundred head at Angel Downs and we take em the five hundred miles to Alice Springs. I'll need everybody Fred. It'll take a bit under two months. You up for it Fred?"

'Course I am Tom, I'll be there. I'll go see Ernie'.

Fred put the phone down and went back to his beer. Now that he'd quenched his thirst, he wasn't so happy about walking out on Sue. But he didn't think he'd ever revisit her. She needed somebody like Herbert or at least like Herbert used to be. Fred was astounded at the change in him. He found he liked the man, though he had a ways to go yet.

'You get a job Fred?"

Fred nodded and downed his beer. 'Yep, in two weeks we take a herd to Alice Springs.'

'Wish I was coming with you. What's the pay like?'

Fred smiled at him. 'Just stick with what you are doing until next season Bert. The pay is better than where you are but you're not quite there yet mate. And anyway, the wharf is good steady work that pays pretty bloody well. Ask me again next year Bert if you're still inclined.'

Herbert lowered his head and stared at his beer. His shoulders sagged a bit, so Fred brought his hand down on one of them. He smiled, 'I can hardly believe you're the same scrawny pasty-faced little bloke that tried to kill me a couple of weeks ago. You stick at it mate, stick with Bill, he'll see you right.'

Herbert smiled at the praise from the big man. 'Thanks Fred'.

Fred smiled back and said seriously, 'sorry about your girl Herbert.'

'No sir' said Herbert wagging his head from side to side. 'Not a problem there Fred... honest. Not a problem at all, no siree.' Herbert picked his beer up and downed it. Jesus no he thought, he remembered wearing the same look the big fellow was wearing now. She took a bit of getting over he had to give her that. But over her he was, and he wanted nothing more than to stay that way. He looked at Fred and said softly, 'I am in a state of over Sue, now Fred.'

Just then Fred spotted young Charlie farther up the bar. He leaned out across the bar and sang out to him. Charlie came straight down to see him.

'How's it going Fred' he said amiably?

Fred introduced him to Herbert and after the two shook hands he told Charlie about the job. 'You in Charlie' he asked?

'Yeah, mate I'm in. Need the money.'

'You seen any of the others about?'

'I know where Cecil and Jimmy are. I can go see em if you like.' Charlie, though he hadn't been at it for as long as the others, was a drover down to his bootstraps. He loved the life and right now he was excited. Domesticity was all very nice for a while.

Bradly Ellis had just seen Lilly upstairs to their room, they'd been out for a meal and Ellis felt like a drink and a look see. He spotted Fred at the bar sinking a half a glass of beer and made his way over. 'Fred' he said smiling and holding his hand out to the big man. He'd met Fred a few times and had always liked him.

Fred looked up and smiled and shook Bradly's hand. 'How's it going Ellis' he asked?

'Good mate' Ellis signalled the barman over, this was the bastard he wanted to see. The barman came over and waited a sullen look on his face he wasn't trying to hide. Ellis looked at him for a minute, Fred and Herbert waited in silence, sensing something was up.

Ellis's voice bore this out now. 'So, is it you who has been interested in the comings and goings in my room?'

'Dunno what you mean. What do you want to drink?' The barman wore an insolent expression, and his voice was quite rude.

'You told a young lady's father that she'd been in my room for quite some time did you not? About a week ago or there abouts.'

Fred looked at Herbert, both men were surprised but smiling.

Ellis went on, 'you caused a lot of trouble you prick.'

The barman shrugged and went to turn away. Ellis had forgotten the other two men were listening, he was losing his temper. 'Just a minute' said Ellis, 'I want your name. I'll have your fuckin job you little bastard. Who do you think you are? The who's in who's room fuckin police.'

'I never told anybody anything…'

'You fuckin did, now what's your name or should I just go and get your boss down here now. He'd be in a good mood about that right?'

The barman, belligerent himself now, leaned across the bar. 'You go and get fucked ya little bas…'

Elis's hand flashed out and punched the barman in the face, the barman slammed up against the fridges and blood ran from his nose. He stood glaring at Ellis though he was obviously a bit dazed.

Fred grabbed Ellis and pulled him back from the bar but to Fred's surprise Ellis shrugged him off as if he was nothing. He was glaring at the barman now, but he lowered his voice some. 'What the fuck business is it of yours who I have in my room?'

'It's John' the barman spat at Ellis through a mouth full of blood spraying some of it all on Ellis. He jumped back and was wiping furiously at his jacket with his hanky.

'Out of curiosity then John, what business is it of yours?'

'I'm her brother.'

'Oh well, just the same mind your business in future. I'll let the matter drop now if there's no more interfering.'

Ellis turned and looked at the men he was about to have a beer with. He looked at Herbert and his face registered disbelief. 'Fuck! Is that you Herbert?' Ellis looked him up and down and smiled 'what's going on?"

'Nothing' said Fred. 'But we could ask you the same question.'

'True' grunted Ellis and he downed half his beer. He looked at the two men who stood waiting, expectant expressions on their faces.

'Oh, for Christ's sake' said Ellis a hint of a smile on his face. 'I have a woman in my room. End of story.'

'No … no,' cried Fred. 'Tell us about it.'

'Nothing to tell' mumbled Ellis down his front. 'She's a nice lady and I am fond of her.' He looked Herbert up and down again and pointed at him, 'now… what's going on here? This little bastard looks like a regular bloke now. What gives?' They all laughed, and Fred bought the next round.

When Bradly Ellis walked into their room that night, he was singing to himself. Lilly smiled and put down the magazine she'd been reading. She held her arms out to him as she stood up.

'What is it, Bradly? Have you had too much to drink you naughty boy?"

'Oh, am I Lilly? Am I your naughty boy?' He took Lilly into his arms and kissed her hungrily. He couldn't seem to get enough of her.

Bradly stepped back from the woman now and his face sobering he pulled her down next to him on the couch. Taking both her hands in his he began to talk. 'Lilly, you know that I love you don't you woman?' Lilly was nodding she could see he was troubled. 'And you know I will always look after you. But I just ran into your brother down in the bar. It was him told your father you were up here.' Ellis nodded.

Lilly sat up and went to withdraw her hands from his, but he clasped them tighter. 'It's alright my love, I didn't hurt him very much. But here's the thing honey. I must take you with me to Katherine. I cannot leave you here knowing how he feels about this… About us. Knowing he will conspire with your father. You will have to come with me. It will get around fairly quickly who you are and what we are in Katherine. Do you understand my beautiful princess?'

She nodded and he stared at her, he couldn't give her up. And who knew what that pair would do anyway. It was all down to him that she was in danger in the first place. Bradly studied his boots as if he'd find an answer there.

He looked up suddenly, his mind made up. 'I have to go out tomorrow honey, I'll be away all day. I have to find somewhere for us in Katherine and set things up. I'll give you some money and you can go shopping for whatever you want. You might want to look at getting some crockery or cutlery or whatever and some linen and get them to ship it to Katherine to the depot. Do you want me Lilly, do you want to live with me? Eventually I want to marry you woman but as things are… Well, I've got a lot to do. I will need to get a divorce.'

Lilly took her hands from his, her eyes never leaving his or the pleading in them. 'I don't want to come in between you and your wife. Don't want to hurt anyone.'

Lilly was looking down when Bradly let out a bellow of a laugh and so she jumped. He stopped laughing and pulled her to him. 'Oh, my girl, my sweet girl. Hurt one of us? We have hated each other for over twenty years. You are a breath of fresh air to me. And her? All she'll do is run off to a solicitor to see how much she'll get. So, I have to move fast now. So, I will be out most of the day for the next week. I want you to be very careful Lilly. If your father or brother get hold of you, they might… You'll be alright Lilly.' He'd decided to put a tail on her.

Lilly nodded. 'For twenty years Bradly? Oh Bradly.'

Bradly sighed and got to his feet. He pulled her to her feet now and led her to the bedroom. He had a powerful need. No, he told himself honestly, he couldn't lose this woman now. She'd shown him what love is, this selfless woman who cared only about him. He wanted the rest of his life to be just like that.

❧

Emily and Tom were planning for a wedding early in the new year. Tom had said that there was no reason why they couldn't live in Emily's house for a while. Though Tom was very adamant that he wanted a place of his own, a station.

He drove the ten miles to Mataranka where he hoped Fred would be waiting with Ernie. Tom was beginning to worry about Ernie. As he drove the short distance, he made up his mind he would ring the hospital in Katherine when he got back to Mataranka if there was still no sign of Ernie. If that failed, he'd go to Katherine and begin a search maybe even report him as a missing person. He had an uneasy feeling in his gut about it, something wasn't right.

Tom pulled into the post office come general store. Jeanie usually knew who was about the place. She greeted him as he walked in the shop and said, 'Tom I've been trying to get hold of you since last night.'

'What is it Jeanie, is it Ernie?'

Jeanie nodded slowly and Tom felt as if he'd be sick. 'He's in hospital in Katherine Tom. The police said that he'd been badly beaten and had a broken nose and a smashed cheek bone. He had concussion and a hair line fracture in his skull. He was in a coma for a week Tom, but he woke up yesterday morning and is demanding to be let go. He has something wrong with his leg the police weren't clear on it except that… Except he was tied up. What do you make of it, Tom? Who would tie Ernie up, and they robbed him, Tom. Fred's with him, it was him who rang. Fred says Ernie was adamant that no one was to ring Tom and tell him. Apparently, this all took place in his own home Tom.' Jeanie sniffed back tears. 'I'm sorry Tom but I sent a telegram in the mail first thing this morning. I believe from what Fred said that he's on the mend.'

'It's alright Jeanie and thanks anyway. I'd best get up there. Could you ring Emily please and tell her I'll be in Katherine for a bit. Thanks.'

Tom walked out and got in his truck and headed for Katherine. His first and foremost thought was who would do this to Ernie. Bash him, tie him up and rob him. Tom thought it was probably personal which only made it more of a mystery. No one hated Ernie not that he could think of.

Tom arrived at the hospital and hurried down to the ward to see Ernie. Ernie was eating his breakfast and smiled when he looked up and saw Tom. 'They have brekkie late here Tom. Fred tells me we got another job on young fulla.'

Tom smiled down at Ernie, 'I don't think so Ernie. You can stay behind on this one old man. Seems you really can't fight your way out of a wet paper bag huh.'

Ernie laughed, 'I'll be there Tom, I aint staying behind. The mongrel bashed me before I even seen him.'

'But Ernie...'

'And what if the bastards come back Tom. What then?'

Tom studied Ernie real close, 'I believe the correct term for that, old man is emotional blackmail.' Tom smiled and went on, 'so you know who did it'. It was a statement not a question.

Ernie nodded his head slightly, 'I will not tell you Tom. Now when do we pull out?'

'Is there any use arguing with you? Bloody pig-headed old goat. Bloody...'

'Shut up Tom. I'd hate to have to put you over my knee. In front of all these nurses to.' One of the nurses smiled at Tom. 'This is my son, Tom.' Ernie was beaming.

Tom laughed out loud; he could see Ernie was going to be okay. He could also see the old man was coming with them. And there was some merit in what he said about the mongrel coming back. He leaned against the wall and studied his father, 'well I'll be fucked' he said very softly, a sneer on his face. Pushing himself off the wall and leaning down to Ernie. 'Where did that mongrel Wally get the balls to do this?' Tom put his face down closer to Ernie's now, 'bet he wasn't alone.' Tom shook his head as he straightened up.

Ernie looked up into Tom's beloved face. 'Let's just concentrate on getting out of town mate hay? You know getting the job done. He's, mine Tom.'

'Like hell he is.'

CHAPTER 11

Sue had gone straight to bed after Fred had left and found he'd taken all of his stuff. She was distraught, but Sue wasn't the sort to let anything get her down for long. A few days after Fred left town her rich cattleman came back to town.

Sue soon found herself happening along to breakfast when she knew he was there. He always asked her to join him which she did. It was a Saturday night; he'd been back in town for four days. Sue sat opposite him at dinner, and he ate in silence.

'Is anything wrong Richard' she asked sweetly? She had dressed to the nines, and she knew she looked good, damn good.

He looked up and smiled faintly at her, 'I had something on my mind when I came here Sue. But I have heard some disturbing news since I got here, from Mrs. Williams in the suite next to me.

'Of course,' Sue said. Mrs. Williams had her eye on Mr. Richard Waters. Mrs. Williams was an interfering old biddy and Sue thought she knew what was coming.

'Well, tell me what had you in mind Richard?' Sue looked nothing but concerned.

'Well Sue I have done some thinking about us while I was away. We seemed to get on alright and you are a charming hostess. I feel something for you, and I was thinking you feel the same. I went to the jewellers and bought a ring to propose to you. But then Mrs. Williams tried to tell me that your bed is still warm from a big handsome man whose name is Fred? Could this be true Sue? And he's a drover she said.'

Sue cleared her throat; she'd have to tell him the truth and make up the rest. 'Richard, Fred had asked me to marry him before' She lied. 'When he came here, he took a suite in the hotel. Well, I had a regular coming to town and needed that suite, so Fred kindly offered to sleep on my couch. It turned out that I had a date with Fred and had agreed to meet him at the hotel. When I arrived there, I found him… with… a woman. He was kissing her' Sue dropped her eyes to the table and squeezed a tear out of them. She looked up eagerly at the man who sat opposite her, 'it is certainly lovely that you thought of me like that. I do like you Richard, but I felt I had to honour a prior arrangement.'

Richard reached across and took her hand. 'Of course, you did, oh my dear I am sorry. I didn't mean to distress you. Oh, do forgive me my dear.'

Sue took out a hanky and dabbed at her cheeks and looked at Richard through tortured eyes, 'You see Richard, I will need a little more time. I think, it would be most unfair to you to accept your proposal straight away. I would rather wait a little while so I can give you my answer whole heartedly. Do you understand Richard? Oh, please say you understand dear Richard.' Sue grave a great sob and shut her eyes tight.

'Please dear lady, do not distress yourself any farther. What say we play it this way. You know I want to marry you, so you just let me know when you are ready. All you need to do is pick up the phone, call my number and ask me when I am coming into town next. Alright my love? And I will know what you mean, and I shall return post haste and get down on my knee and ask for your hand in marriage.'

'Oh, Richard I don't deserve anyone as good as you.'

'Oh, nonsense my dear. Now I have a meeting of the cattleman's association to attend. I will see you to your room if you like.'

At Sue's door Richard slipped his arms around her waist and kissed her gently on the lips. 'I will see you in the morning at breakfast my dear.'

They were both brought about abruptly by the sound of a man clearing his throat. 'Oh Daddy' Sue said sweetly. This is…'

'Yeah. I know Richard' Bradly Ellis shook hands with him and stood back politely and stared at the man.

Richard looked decidedly embarrassed, he said 'How are you, Ellis? Are you attending the meeting tonight?' Bradly shook his head. Turning to Sue now Richard said politely 'until tomorrow then.' He nodded to Bradly and beat a hasty retreat to the stairs.

Sue opened the door, let them both in and closed it again. She turned on her father now, 'what the hell do you want?'

'I came to tell you I'm leaving for Katherine in a couple of days. Are you seeing that man Sue?'

Sue sighed, 'well what is wrong with that?'

'Well, he's old enough to be your bloody father.'

'So?' Sue sat down I on the couch. ''But he is richer than my father and you know that don't you daddy?'

'Well, I can't talk I suppose…'

Sue looked up at her father as he sat tiredly on a chair. 'What does that mean?'

'I am seeing a woman, Sue.'

'Oh daddy, and she's old enough to be my mother?'

Bradly put his head back and laughed, it was like the bursting of a dam and Bradly laughed again. He pulled himself together and went to get up. Sue's voice stayed him.

'Oh no you don't dad, I think you have something to tell me.'

'Maybe we'll just leave it at that Sue. I wanted to you tell before it gets around. I'm taking her to Katherine I purchased a flat there. So of course, your mother will be off to her solicitor I expect, and this will be all around the district before you know it.'

'It's serious dad?' Sues face was screwed up. When Bradly nodded, she went on, 'so how old is she. What is she younger than you?'

Bradly nodded dumbly again and looked at his shoes. 'Dad!'

He looked up at his daughter and said quietly, 'about your age. Well, she is twenty-four, same as your brother.'

'Dad' Sue's eyes were like saucers. Suddenly she smiled and said, 'Dad, you can't take her to Katherine. They'll crucify her there. What about mum, what about the station? See daddy this is just a bit sudden. Do you love her dad?'

The smile that crossed her father's face told her everything. Bradly was wagging his head from side to side. 'Oh, I do Sue and the amazing thing is she loves me. Me! She loves me! And she has shown me what love is. Oh God, I love her, and I cannot be without her. Now there is another problem. When her father and her brother got wind that we had been on a date they tied her up to stop her from seeing me. I can't leave her here. Who knows what they would do. But it hasn't given me time to get some money out to live on. Your mother will take me for everything I have.'

Sue looked thoughtful, 'how much time do you think you'd need dad?'

'Oh, I don't know at least three months. I got some out over the last few days, About twenty thousand pounds. I went to the races and lost some big money so I can blame the exit of money from the account on that. I don't know Sue; I can't give her up.'

'No dad. I have a vacant suite if that's any help. You'd pay for it of course.' Sue smiled at her father; he didn't look like the old man anymore. He looked younger, at peace and happy. He looked happy and he was nice looking!

'Alright Sue, if, you're sure. I could get money out and then get it squared away with your mother. She hates me anyway, you do know that Sue?'

'Yeah, I know dad. Alright then. I'm glad you're happy. I hate mum, I do. I'm sorry I said I hated you, I don't dad.'

Bradly stood up and held his arms out and his daughter walked into them. Could life be any more perfect he wondered? He hugged his daughter to him and wished he could make it all go away. All the bad things that had happened to her.

'I know you didn't mean it love. Did you feel any better getting it out and all?"

Sue smiled, 'I don't blame you for it dad, if anyone's to blame its mum. Oh, I hate her. I'm glad you're getting out. I'm on your side.' Sue grinned sheepishly now. 'And I owe you dad. Okay you can have the suite for free. Bring her here when you are ready. I won't let her go out on her own dad.'

Bradly told Lilly back at the hotel about Sue's offer, Lilly looked worried. 'I don't know your daughter Bradly and you've only just started speaking again. No, I don't want to be a problem you have to park somewhere. Anyway, I got offered a job yesterday and I can get a room by myself.'

Bradly just stared at her until his legs gave out and he sank onto the couch.

'Alright then fuck it. We'll both go to Katherine as planned.' Bradly got up and went to the bathroom undressing as he went. He was stung by her attitude, to his amazement he felt tears in his eyes.

Lilly didn't follow him into the shower as usual. He poked his head round the corner and saw her sitting on the couch staring into space. He put a towel round him and came and sat down with her. 'Come on then love let's have it. What's going round and round in that very pretty little head of yours.'

Lilly turned slowly towards him a tear tumbled down her cheek. He went to wipe it away, but she stopped him. 'Please Bradly, I love you more than I have ever loved anyone or anything. More than life itself. But I can't go with you and make problems for you. And I won't be parked with your daughter. This is all about money, how much you'll get, how much your wife will get. Why can't you just come right out with it. Make a clean breast of it and we'll take our chances. You bought a flat, we have somewhere to live. Did you manage to get some money out?'

Bradly nodded; he was dumbfounded. He took her hand in his and said 'yes, I managed to get twenty thousand pounds. The flat is in your name so she can't get her hands on that. I need to know you'll be safe, you know, taken care of.'

'And where is the twenty thousand pounds Bradly? That is a fortune!'

'It's in a bank account or some of it is. The rest, about ten thousand is in my suitcase.'

'What do you think the courts will do Bradly. Would getting half each be so bad? We can make a clean start, a fresh start with that.'

Bradly looked down at the floor and shook his head absently, 'no. No it wouldn't be so bad.' He lifted his eyes to hers. they were full of wonder.

❧

Tom stayed with Ernie until he was on his feet, he was home from the hospital. 'I've got to get back Ernie, we are due to pull out in a week. We'll have to leave in about five days, and I've got things to organise. I'll go and stay with Emily so you can have my hut if you want.'

'Okay son. Might do some fishing hay.'

'Ernie are you well enough to organiser the food before we leave? I can do it.'

'I've organised it all son. We can pick it up from the store tomorrow morning at six. Or did you want to leave it until we get to the Alice. I intended to get the perishables there anyway.'

'No Ernie you do it the way you would normally. So can we leave in the morning?'

'Of course, lad.'

'I put the word out that I'm looking for Wally fuckin Cooper to.'

'Well, I already know where he is, you leave him to me.'

'No can-do old man. I know what I'm doing.'

'Well, hell yeah you know what you're doing. You just put him on notice you're coming. He'll hide Tom, behind all his cronies to. He didn't give me a chance, did he? Just jumped me and robbed me like the thug that he bloody is.'

'Did he get all your money old man?'

Ernie laughed now, 'hell no. but he thinks he did. I told him he wasn't your father that I was. That's when he decided to kick me in the head.'

'Are you well enough to be on this drive Ernie? Can you give me your word on that?'

Ernie nodded, 'yeah, course I am son.'

Fred had listened to this conversation. He was anxious to get back to Mataranka. He'd been in Katherine for a few days now and he'd decided when the time came, he'd look for a place at Mataranka. He looked at Tom now, 'I'd like to be here when Bradly Ellis gets back. I ran into him having a row with a barman in the Darwin hotel. Seems Ellis is shacked up with this barman's sister. Not only that but he's bringing her here with him to Katherine and he's gunna ask his missus for a divorce. Unless I miss my guess, the man is very much in love. The barman got a bit argumentative about it all and Ellis hauls off and hits him. One punch and he almost knocked that barman clean out. Not a little lad either.'

Ernie and Tom stared open mouthed at Fred for some moments as he went about rolling his swag up. He wasn't the type to give voice to mere rumours. Tom and Ernie looked at each other. 'Holy Hell' said Ernie shaking his head. 'Mind you I'm glad for the man. That wife of his is beyond bitch. She's a fuckin demon. Bloody good on him. I'd like to be a fly on the wall when she finds out that's for sure.'

When the three men left town, they had Charlie and Jack with them. Cecil and Jimmy, they picked up at a roadside stop just out of Katherine. The rest were waiting in Mataranka. Most of these men camped out at Toms place and spent their next few days before the drive fishing and drinking.

Tom had bought a car for all of his running around; he preferred his horse, but it was too slow. He bought a dodge almost new for fifty pounds.

It was decided that Tom would take the car to Damper Creek and Ernie and the rest of the boys would follow in a week in the truck. Fred asked Tom if it would be alright to turn up at Emily's eatery for tea on Saturday night. Tom grinned and said it would be great.

'Well Ernie wants to go' said Fred as Tom was leaving, 'and don't worry we will all be solid and sober.'

'Well Ernie better be he's driving, and I need that truck. Okay I'll see you there. Bring all your stuff we'll leave from there.' Tom smiled at Ernie.

'She's all packed up and ready to roll Tom, all except the stuff I gotta pick up in Alice Springs.'

Tom got in the car and left. He wanted to get back to Damper Creek to spend as much time with Emily as he could. He found this new Emily was very different to the old Emily and it took a bit of dealing with. She reacted differently to just about everything. He liked it though; she was much more loving. A smile played around Toms lips now, and she was much more adventurous.

❧

Ernie and Fred jumped in the front of the truck and the rest of the men climbed in the back. They had six horses in the truck they would pick up more at Alice Springs. They towed a trailer behind the truck with all their saddles and swags in it. All of Ernie's stores were in that trailer and more were at the front of the truck. The men were clean, and They were all dressed in their Sunday best. And more importantly they were all sober.

Each and every one of them knew the story of Tom and Emily and they all knew the work and the guts the young woman had put in. How close to death she had come, had lost everything even her memories. And they knew how she had turned it around. How she had chosen to fight rather than sit down and give up. And they knew she had built something out of nothing into the bargain. Yes, Emily was a bit of a hero to the boys, and they all loved Tom. Yeah they were all sober.

When they arrived at Emily's eatery, they were in high spirits, but they were trying to hold it in. Fred, Charlie, Jack and Jimmy had never met Emily, but they knew her by reputation.

The eight men filed into Emily's veranda; they all knew even if they knew her that they would be introduced to her again. Ernie led and Fred followed him. They were followed by Jack, Jimmy, Cecil, Charlie Bill and Nevil. Tom stood at Emily's side and Ernie could see how very proud he was of her. Tom reintroduced her to Ernie first.

Ernie smiled his best and shook her hand saying as he did so how very glad, he was that they should meet again. Emily smiled at the big man whom she knew was Tom's father. 'How are you Ernie, I heard you weren't well?'

'Oh, I'm okay thanks Emily. A bit of open air will do me a power of good.' Ernie smiled and stepped aside.

Next, she was introduced to Fred, he scrutinised her in his way. He had a friendly way about him, but Emily almost faltered under his open and frank gaze, but she regained her composure. It was not lost on Fred, and he took her hand and smiled his most dazzling, he noticed the young woman relax and he was glad. 'Nice to meet you at last Miss Emily. You have done a wonderful job here. May I say how very sorry I was to hear of what happened to you; we all were.'

'Thank you, Fred. I appreciate that.' Emily smiled at him.

Fred smiled again and stepped aside, and he decided that Tom was a lucky man. Very lucky.

Jack took her hand and nodded, 'How are you Emily, I've heard all good things about your tucker, and it sounds like it might be even better than Ernie's here,' The men all laughed, and Jack stood aside.

Charlie shook hands with Emily and said, 'something smells mighty good Miss, can't wait to get my laughing gear round whatever that is.' Emily laughed and was glad of his easy boisterous manner which eased the tension.

Emily said she hoped he enjoyed his meal. Jimmy shook hands with her and gave her his biggest grin. It did the trick, Emily relaxed. Cecil hardly touched hands with her as was his way but the smile he bestowed on her made her heart quicken.

Bill grinned at Emily, and so did Nevil. They'd met Emily before and like Ernie they couldn't get over the change in her. 'Nice to meet you,' said Nevil. Bill commented on what a nice place she had. 'And I can't wait to sample some of that food either' he laughed.

Emily said now 'I am so glad I have met you all. I won't worry about Tom so much now I know he is in such good and capable hands.' She turned and said 'this is your table just here' she indicated the table next to them. 'When everyone has gone and we clean away, you can throw your swags down here if that would be acceptable.' She glanced at Tom. 'What me to?' he asked playfully

'No not you' her face reddened, and the men laughed.

Fred sat down first saying as he did so, 'yeah this will do nicely thanks.' The men all said thank you. Fred went on softly 'bit bloody better than the gibber flats Ernie usually spreads us out on.' There was much agreement and laughter, some of them even rubbed their backs.

Ernie smiled good naturedly as was his way, 'well I have sense enough to sleep in the truck,'

'In the horse shit' put in Tom.

Emily said, 'if you'll excuse me, I have meals to get out.'

The men nodded and smiled. Every one of them watched from the corner of his eyes how she shuffled away. Each one of them looked about at what she'd accomplished and were amazed. They'd heard but seeing it was different. Seeing was believing. There were tables and chairs, and the tables were set with tablecloths. Everything was clean and homely, even the floor was scrubbed clean.

The next surprise was the amount of people who came through the back gate and when the tables were full, they waited on the lawn for a table or got a plate and ate on the lawn. Some got containers and took their food away with them.

Fred was amazed at what this woman had achieved, he'd thought Sue was good. Jesus, he thought for the umpteenth time since he'd left Darwin, what had he seen in her? He just hoped Herbert had sense enough to stay away.

Emily served roast beef and vegetables with Yorkshire pudding and gravy. She accompanied this with pastries, sausage rolls and pies and fresh bread she'd made especially.

For dessert she served apple pie and fresh whipped cream and fruit salad. She put plates of small cakes and freshly made biscuits on the tables and on the side tables. This was Saturday night and she'd gone all out. The men were speechless and tucked into their food. They could see now what all the fuss was about. There were pitchers of freshly made lemonade also on the tables as well as fresh coffee.

The next big surprise of the night came when Eric walked in with his piano accordion. The girls waited on the tables in a very professional manner. The oldest of the girls, Janet, had caught Fred's eye. She seemed to like him as she joked with him and didn't pull back when he flirted with her.

When the tables were cleared away and the girls and Tom were doing the last of the dishes Eric began to play. As usual he started with some hauntingly beautiful tunes and got livelier as the set went on. He finished with a couple of polkas. Eric put his accordion down and talked with the men for a little while. It caused quite a stir when Erics blue heeler ran in and jumped in his lap.

Gently the old man put his dog on the floor and played another set of tunes. The men who sat on the lawn to listen drank bottles of beer they had stashed there. Some people sat at tables. The end of the veranda was cleared, and people started to get to their feet and dance.

Everyone was sat at their table including Tom and Emily. Eric was playing a lively waltz and Fred jumped to his feet and pulling Janet after him he made for the dance floor.

Fred knew the minute Janet put her arms around him and he relaxed in them, he needed her. He found himself laughing and joking with her and what was more amazing he was talking about himself. He told her of his plans, how he intended to buy a place at Mataranka with a few acres.

'I think I'll raise some chickens' he finished.

'Chickens' Janet sounded surprised.

'Yes', said Fred. 'I am sick of cattle. If I never have to look at cows' backsides through a haze of dust and flies and breath in the stink of their shit it'll be too soon for me. It's the shit that gets to you.'

Fred nodded down at her and she laughed as he swung her around and around. She laughed with Fred until she snorted, and Fred knew he was in love. Hopelessly and helplessly in love. Eric played a slower waltz and Fred pulled Janet in close and held her tight. She didn't try to pull away and he danced with her like that for the rest of the night just relaxing into each other. Fred had got aroused but she didn't seem to mind.

Eric announced the last set and Fred looked up and found that Nellie was dancing with young Nevil and there were other couples on the floor. Ernie was in a deep conversation with Tom and Emily. When the set ended Fred bent and thanked Janet for the dance. As he led her back to the table, he held her hand. He bent towards her now and told her he had thoroughly enjoyed the night. 'I like you, Janet.' He smiled his best at her, and he could see it did the trick.

She stopped and looked up at him her face becoming serious she said softly, 'I like you to Fred.' Janet did realise that Fred was a good bit older, but no other man had ever set her heart to fluttering and her mind to wandering the way he did. And, most surprising to Janet was where it wandered to.

When Fred got into his swag that night, he drifted off into a peaceful sleep the like of which he'd never known. He'd never experienced this kind of peace ever before. He dreamed only of her and was certain in the knowledge that she dreamed only of him.

The little team of drovers left at first light the next day. Emily was there to see them off and Tom had pulled her aside to say goodbye. Fred was overjoyed when Janet and Nellie rocked up. He had hoped against hope she would care enough to come and see him off. Not only that they brought baskets of food with them for the men to eat on the road.

As the other blokes climbed into the back of the truck, Fred walked away a few steps with Janet and leaning towards her he spoke softly. 'I hope I 'm not embarrassing you.' She shook her head, and he went on.

'I would like to see you when I get back, would that be to your liking woman?'

Janet smiled 'it would Fred, it surely would.'

'Oh, to hell with it' he murmured and bent and kissed her on the cheek then briefly on the lips. He smiled his most dazzling as he straightened up, 'I intend to marry you.'

'And I intend to hold you to that.'

He said now, 'you're on the phone here aren't you' Janet nodded. 'Tell me the number, I won't forget it.' After she told him he said 'you never know when we might be near a phone. I'll see you when I get back.' Another quick kiss and Fred climbed into the back of the truck. He sat on the cabin and smiled down at the women, he liked them, they were brave. All three of them.

Some of the neighbours turned up to wave them off. Fred waved to Janet and for the first time in his life he didn't want to go. But go he must, he had work to do and there wasn't a doubt in his mind that Janet was his. He thought of her as his. He'd need to build a bit bigger dwelling on those few acres.

Fred looked over at Nevil and was surprised to find the man looked as though someone had hit him over the head with a cricket bat. 'Well, well' he whispered to himself and smiled.

Tom sat in the front with Ernie and the two men chatted. 'I can't believe what that young woman has achieved Tom,' said Ernie. 'I mean when you hear about it it's pretty spectacular but when you go there and see it. I see now why you sat in your truck. She's awesome mate.'

Tom smiled 'she finds it hard to get everything in her day done but she pushes herself. You know what she told me Ernie. She told me it's like an atonement. She is desperate to be forgiven. '

'Does she remember Tom? You know any of that last day when she was injured. I'd like to get my hands on that bastard, he must o known she was badly injured. And he just runs off and, leaves her there. She could've died.'

'I know' said Tom and hung his head. 'Yeah, she remembers Ernie.'

Ernie put his hand on the younger man's shoulder and said softly, 'you weren't to know. It would've been quite traumatising for you to young Tom. Main thing is you two are getting hitched. Is she still gunna run that eatery Tom? After you're married?"

Tom shrugged. That question had been on his mind to.

Ernie shrugged now and said to Tom as matter-of-factly as he could 'Good little money spinner Tom. And it'd certainly give her something to occupy her time while you are away Tom.'

Tom smiled; he hadn't thought of it like that now, had he?

Chapter 12

The boys got into Alice Springs around lunch time the next day. After Ernie had gotten his perishables from the store they headed for the outskirts of town to camp. Bill helped Ernie get the meal as he often did. Bill spent probably half his time in camp helping Ernie. He was handy to have as a spare as he could turn his hand to just about anything droving. And he could cook.

When they'd eaten and the camp was set up for the night Fred said, 'is it okay if we go for a beer or two Tom?'

Tom nodded 'I'll come with you and see if there are any messages at the pub for me. Might call home to while I'm there. The girls 'll be finished be time we had a beer or two' he winked at Fred.

'My thoughts exactly Tom.' Fred said in his most posh tone and set the men to laughing.

'Well don't hog the phone' whined Jimmy, 'I want to phone home to.'

Ernie smiled, 'Ooh? What do you wanna phone home for? You got a Missus somewhere we don't know about?'

'Two' said Jimmy casually. He slanted his eyes at Ernie.

The men stood in total silence waiting for the joke, waiting for the punchline. It didn't come, Jimmy pulled his jacket on and went about pulling the sleeves down as if it was the most important thing he'd ever done. His face had healed nicely, and the scar only added to his appeal.

'Are you fuckin joking Jimmy' asked Ernie?

'Nope, got six kids to. Are we walking Ernie?'

'Yes, we are but I Can understand you wanting to conserve your strength young Jimmy.' Ernie sighed and grinned at the little Afghan. He liked Jimmy, he suspected everybody liked Jimmy. But he hadn't seen that coming.

At eight o'clock most of the men went back to the truck to get in the swag. All except Fred and Bill and Nevil.

'Who'd a thought about Jimmy,' said Nevil.

Bill smiled at the younger man, 'you hoping to catch up with him young Nevil?'

'No bloody way. Is he Muslim or something?'

'Yeah probably,' said Fred. 'I'm just going out to rinse the prince.'

'Yeah' said Nevil. 'you're going out to ring your girly friend and make kissy noises like I heard you was doing before. It's not rinsing it, what you're gunna do is it?' Nevil's voice was loud the drink starting to show up in it, and he giggled hysterically.

The withering look Fred bestowed on Nevil made Bill burst out laughing. Fred grinned good naturedly and left. Well hell he was going to ring his girly friend and if he made kissy noises, it was nobody's business but his own. And he'd take fine care no bastard heard him this time.

They got good and drunk and were back in their swags by ten o'clock. They had an early start the next day but an easy day though all the same. It would take them all of the day tomorrow and probably half the next sitting in the truck, to get to Angel Downs. Nice easy day thought Fred as he drifted off to sleep. 'Janet' he whispered and smiled.

Bradly turned up at Mable Downs wondering what sort of reception he'd get if the dragon had heard. If she'd heard, he was happy. Him screwing another Sheila wouldn't phase her at all but if he was happy, now that was different. And just wait until he told her he wanted her out. He'd realised he'd have to sell the place to settle with her.

He'd not only got most of his money out of the bank, spending a lot at the racetrack to make it appear that he had a gambling problem. But he'd managed to borrow heavily against the station.

If she wanted to, she was welcome to stay there until the bailiffs came to throw her off, he told her now. He had never seen her so livid, she let out a screech that didn't sound human. All of a sudden, a nasty smile crossed her face Bradly didn't know which one scared him most. She hissed at him now, 'nice try you weedy little rat but I don't buy it. You wouldn't…' She stopped talking and looked at him now. There was something different about him, something she couldn't quite put her finger on.

He pulled two papers from his pocket and held one in each hand. 'This on my right is a cheque to buy you out of what's left of the station and this on my left is the deeds to the place. If you tighten your fucking belt' he said as he put them back in his pocket, 'and run the place efficiently you can probably save it. But you will do it by yourself because I am leaving you. You horror of a woman and I should have done it years ago. Go on Victoria, phone the solicitor. You'll see.'

Victoria stared at him, 'where do you get the balls? I'll…' Bradly heard her sniff to see if he was drunk.

He cut in, 'From Lilly. Lilly is my girlfriend. I love her and she loves me, and we are living happily in a flat in Katherine, she can't get enough of me you know. And she is helping me with my little gambling problem dear.' He grinned at her; he was enjoying this. If he got nothing else, he'd have this. He'd struck the bitch where it hurt. Pow, right in the bank account.

By this time Victoria was starting to buy it and she was also starting to panic. Her life flashed before her eyes. Her very comfortable and lavish life. She watched on as it turned to shit before her eyes, turned to this little toad in front of her eyes. The bile was rising in her throat almost strangling her. She made a choking noise in her throat.

Bradly spotted it and decided not to stick around for the clothes and personal items he was going to get. When Victoria ran towards the kitchen, he made a run for it. He'd pushed a bit hard he thought now. He jumped in his car and started the motor. Screaming like a banshee now, her eyes wide and bulging, Victoria ran with astounding speed towards the car. It was a frightening sight and Bradly's fingers had gone stiff.

Bradly pushed the car into gear and taking his foot off the clutch he tramped his foot down on the accelerator. Victoria had reached the car and shoved the knife in his chest as he left. Bradly felt it go in and he was pretty sure all she'd got was flesh.

Having some idea about treating wounds he left the knife where it was and drove the fifty miles to town leaning on the steering wheel. He went straight to the police station. He had what he needed, a knife in the chest with his wife's prints on it. He'd show that bitch!

When Ernie and Tom and the boys got to Angel downs it was late. the manager strode out to meet them. His name was Andy, and he shook hands with the men and asked if they wanted some tea.

But Ernie was already setting up the camp, so they thanked the man and declined. Andy talked about the herd, and he mentioned the way to Tom, and began to give him directions. Tom took a deep breath and said he wanted to use the route through Devils canyon. There followed a silence.

Andy looked awkward for a few moments and cleared his throat. 'Yes, but you see… There is a very good reason why they call it Devils canyon. Cattle and indeed even people have disappeared… My predecessors claim they have put up that fencing to keep the cattle out. I haven't been here long but…'

Tom smiled and the men gathered realising that this was why they were specifically asked, by Tom to attend this meeting. Tom was saying now in his best know all manner, 'I have heard about these grannies' tales, but it is shorter that way. It would cut off about fifty miles or near enough. And then there's an abundance of water and feed along that route.'

Oh, an abundance thought Fred as he stood transfixed. An abundance! What sort of bloody cod's waddle was this? He'd heard it dribble out of the best assholes but this… Well, this was something. He'd heard these grannies' tales to, and they were the stuff of legend.

But Tom assured the nice man there was nothing to worry about. He droned on, something about staking his reputation and that was when Fred decided he'd heard enough.

Fred turned and sauntered over to the fence and leaned on it and rolled a smoke. He looked at Cecil who wore the same mask of disbelief on his face as Fred. But poor old Cecil would follow Tom through the gates of hell. Or Devils Canyon, it was pretty much of a muchness really. And Fred knew with the same certainty that he also would follow the man through the very same gates no matter the cost. But he didn't have to like it.

Fred watched Tom shake hands with Andy and Andy's nervous smile. Tom had assured him his cattle were in good hands and Fred didn't have an argument about that. As far as driving cattle from point A to point B these men were the very best, their reputation was second to none. But Tom didn't believe in old wives' tales. So, it was off to Hells gates and the Devil waiting there.

The next morning, they got the herd moving by six o'clock and the owner came down to wish them the very best of luck. He looked at them all in turn as if he would have only this to remember them by. He leaned against a fence post and watched them go. Fred looked back twenty minutes away and he was still there, Fred shivered in the warm sun.

For three weeks they moved steadily across the spinifex covered plains towards the hills off in the distance and Devils Gates. At last, they reached the fence and the gate to Devils Canyon. As Ernie got tea ready Tom and Fred took time to enter the gates and climbed to the top of the canyon.

Fred felt a shiver pass through him as he looked down into the misty valley. This was it he thought. He looked at Tom but for once he couldn't read the man's face. Or didn't want to.

Well, the next morning they would drive that herd into the canyon and hope to God on high that they would drive em out the other side. Some said the dingos didn't even go in there. Fred pulled his hat down over his eyes.

And at six the next morning they rounded the herd and moved them slowly into the canyon. The cattle were skittish and some broke ranks and ran away wildly. The dogs had a busy morning and so did the men. Once in the canyon the cattle settled down a bit and so did Fred though he watched as Tom shut the gate behind them.

❧

Ernie had gone all out and made curry and rice for tea. Nobody ever remembered anyone complaining about Ernie's curry before except maybe, for the occasional belly ache afterwards. Fred loved his curry but better still, for some reason Ernie always made a cake for after. And this one was iced!

Fred sat munching his huge wedge of cake, savouring every bite. He couldn't explain it, but he was on edge. Cecil's behaviour didn't help, he was positively jumping out of his skin. Fred had an instinct about Cecil, and he knew the man was terrified of something. He suspected something real and not the usual heebie-jeebies.

The men sat around talking quietly, they all felt it. They were finishing their coffee and handed the mugs back to Ernie. They had all noticed Cecil, most of them put it down to his nervous disposition. But then the cattle started lowing and stamping. Some of them were walking around and around and waving their heads from side to side in despair.

The men were all tired as usual and when Fred got up to roll his swag out, they all got the same idea and followed suit. Cecil made no move to join them but sat with his legs crossed staring out into the darkness. He could have been made of stone.

There was a glow in the eastern sky as the moon came up behind the hills silhouetting the rocky scraggy outline of the ancient skyline. The horses were awake, but they were closer to the comforting glow of the fire. They started stomping. The terror in the first loud neigh sent a chill down Tom's back and he was pretty sure they all felt it. As one they felt it. The fear was insidious.

Every man at the fire noticed that Ernie sat close to Cecil. He tried to draw Cecil into a conversation but to no avail. Fred was on the far side of the fire getting into his swag when they heard it. It was a scream so terrible that Fred got back out of his swag at lightning speed and stood stock still. He stood crouched on the far side of the fire like a combatant waiting for an attack.

The most terrible thing about the scream was that it had a surreal quality. An unworldly, unholy quality and it wasn't in the least bit a fearful scream. It made their blood run cold. The fear seeped in through their eyes and ears, through their skin.

The scream was followed by a low droning roar, also surreal. It pulsated and moved up and down the valley like the low droning of thunder off in the distance. Only this wasn't off in the distance it seemed it was just across the valley. Maybe in the hills or the trees.

It seemed to draw close to the men and engulf them in its energy, almost closing their throats, only to fade away again quickly. It was akin to the didgeridoo yet was not. Fred decided it was akin to nothing he'd ever heard as for the first time in his life he felt his legs shake.

They waited, not knowing what to do. The mist was gathering, and it weighed heavily on them. They couldn't avoid the doom in the gloom, it was real, and brought a sense of foreboding that they could've cut with a knife.

The men stood now at the edge of the firelight none of them daring to move outside of it. Fearing the darkness and what came in it. Tom called out to Bill who was taking first watch of the cattle.

Bill hollered back that he was okay. 'Come in' Tom sang out and Bill fairly ran into the fire light glad to be out of the dark. But Bill was a man who stayed where he was sent.

Tom knew in his belly that whatever was out there was a threat. He'd try to close ranks and worry about the cattle when they got it figured out. He looked at Fred, Fred was always his gauge. The look on the man's face now told Tom that he was right in his thinking. They were in trouble, big trouble, the big man didn't scare easily.

The noise droned on and on pulsating and growing to a crescendo and fading to almost nothing. It was hypnotic and when Fred looked up the moon was up. How long had they been listening to this most ancient rhythm? Had it hypnotised him? What could be making such a noise? Tom turned to look at Cecil.

When Tom yelled Cecil's name everyman there almost jumped out of his skin. 'Cecil… Cecil…' he roared as he rushed to the edge of darkness his eyes wide. Fred grabbed him and stopped him from going any farther. The men all looked around; Cecil was nowhere to be seen. He'd vanished from their midst without a sound, without a trace.

'He's gone Tom,' shouted Fred as he held Tom in his arms. 'If you go out there you might be gone to. We need to stick together now mate. Christ only knows what that is out there. We'll look for Cecil later. It can't be helped Tom; it can't be helped' Tom nodded dumbly, and Fred let him go.

'Look' shouted Bill. They looked and Bill was pointing towards the hills on the far side of the canyon. There was a full moon risen behind the hills giving the whole scene an eerie quality. Then they saw it. Fred was hardly breathing as he watched the strange light dancing along the hills bobbing up and down as it went. Always in the shadow of the hills but always above the mist. It was tantalising and yet held a warning. He breathed in and out, he'd heard about these min min lights of the Australian bush but had taken it with a pinch of salt.

One of the horses screamed and everyone jumped, their muscle taught with fear. The fear was palpable, Tom knew it. He swore later he could taste it, could smell it. The rhythm and the pulsing effect of the noise began to play with his mind, he couldn't think. The screaming of the horse broke through to him and he ran to it.

The horses were stomping now and pulling at the ropes that had them tied as they screamed. All of the men went to his own horse as they tried and tried to rear in terror. They were snorting now, and their eyes were wide and unseeing. Tom worried. The dogs, all but one, broke free of their chains and ran off barking and growling as they went.

Tom yelled as he went to get more ropes that they needed to tie them down. They'd need to hobble them he shouted unable to keep the fear from his voice. But they had to abandon that idea for fear of serious injury by the horses' kicking hooves.

Another of those terrible screams rang out and they quickly tied a second rope to the other side of the horses' halters and tethered it to the line. Ernie checked the tether line and thought it would hold; it was designed to hold panic-stricken animals. Big, strong panic-stricken animals.

Another scream, this one quite close, rang out and was followed by a cow bellowing in terror. A growling noise came to them the like of which none of them had ever heard and a cow gurgled its last death rattle to the moon.

All eyes turned towards the sound in the valley that was fast filling up with mist. At first Tom thought it was smoke, but it was a thick mist rolling in from the north.

Ernie sidled up to Tom and poked a pistol into his hand and a rifle in the other. 'Six rounds in each' he shouted. Tom looked at him, he noticed that Ernie had and armful of guns and breathed a sigh of relief that at least somebody was thinking straight. He nodded to the old man and put the pistol in his trouser pocket. Tom was comforted by the feel of his rifle in his hands.

With the horses tied and somewhat quieted by their closeness Tom called to the men to regroup in the fire light. Ernie was by his side again and told him he had the keys in the truck ready for take-off. Tom looked around at the frightened faces. The fear looked like pain on their faces, so Tom gave them a choice, he had to.

'Do we get in the truck and run, or do we stay and fight?"

'What are you doing Tom' asked Fred?

'Fight' said Tom. 'I fight.'

'Me to' said Fred, 'the bastard's already got one cow. M…maybe they go now hay?'

Ernie gave him a rifle. Fred was their best shot and about the strongest and bravest man he'd ever known. He gave him a pistol and a spare magazine for the rifle. 'Eighteen rounds' he shouted to the big man. Fred nodded. 'One in the barrel, safety on' Ernie told him tapping the rifle barrel and he went on to the next man who'd said stay.

It was Bill. Ernie gave him a rifle; he'd been a sniper in the army. Bill nodded, he understood that he may be staying to his death. He thought that, even if he got in the truck and made a run for it, he probably wouldn't make it. No, he'd stay put and fight it out along with the others. Whatever was out there was feeding.

Tom spoke loudly, 'whoever elects to make a run for it know this. You can take your weapon and some ammo and no hard feelings. If you make it out, remember to send help.'

'Who else' shouted Ernie and every man put his hand up. Every man was armed, and Ernie broke out the strong box which had bullets and magazines ready to use. There in the firelight surrounded by mist and moonlight and a danger the like of which they'd never known and probably wouldn't know again, these eight men dug in.

All went quiet and the rhythmic roar was almost inaudible. The minutes ticked by. Another noise of doubtless unpleasant origin was coming to their ears. It was the sound of an animal feasting and growling while it did so. They looked at each other. The cow! They could hear whatever it was tearing and gnashing at its hide and flesh. They heard it shaking the cow's carcass around as if it were a rabbit. Tom shuddered.

Tom made up his mind, he stepped out from behind the rough barricade they'd made from drums and boxes and swags.

'Where you going' asked Fred fearful for his best friend?

'I've got to take a look mate. You wait here Fred and shoot the first thing that comes out of that darkness that aint me.'

Ernie stood up, 'I'm coming with you son.' Tom shook his head; Ernie took no notice. He stared defiantly back at his son and Tom found himself comforted by the lack of fear in his father's face.

Bill, Jimmy, and Nevil stood up and Fred stepped out in front of them. 'Just try and stop us' he said with a crooked grin. Charlie stepped out and Ernie sighed, 'might as well stick together.'

They swung around to look at Jack. He was staring back at them with bared teeth and wide eyes and an expression on his face they'd never seen. All seven men started to feel that uneasy shiver in their spine take hold, what now?

'What' barked Bill, fear growing in his belly. 'What the fuck' he barked again?

Jack shuffled his feet as if coming out of a trance, 'well see… I think I need a shit.'

Tom had a small sack of onions in his hand he'd picked up off a drum and he gave into an impulse and threw it at Jack. As Jacks took the onions in the face and the men chuckled nervously, his bowls opened up and it was decided he'd stay in camp and mind the tucker the truck and the horses.

Tom said to him 'shoot anything that's not us.'

'Bullshit' barked Jack, 'I'm not staying here by meself. No fuckin way. No fuck that Tom, I'm coming.'

Ernie lifted his eyebrows at Tom. He wouldn't want to stay behind either and his bowls had nearly done the same as Jack's a few times in the last hours. Vaguely it struck Ernie as odd that he had no idea whatsoever how many hours, he looked at the moon, it was high now. Ernie suspected it maybe that only the blokes who'd emptied their bowels recently wouldn't end up shitting themselves this night.

'Alright' said Tom softly, he had to admit to himself he'd come close himself. Might still happen to he thought sardonically. He nodded to the man and turned and one by one they left the firelight and stepped into darkness. Stepped into the mist.

Just beyond the firelight these eight bushies, some of them old soldiers, stopped a few seconds to let their eyes adjust to the dark. The moonlight was reasonably bright, but the sky had clouded over. The mist had a stink to it that had nothing to do with Jacks pants. It had a sweetish musty smell, a toxic smell.

Tom led the way with Fred, they skirted the herd sneaking as quietly as they could. They were all seasoned hunters, and they were quiet but moved quickly. Tom noticed the herd had quieted down since they drew near and wondered if that would give them away. This was a hunter they were stalking he was sure of that and probably a very good one.

Tom threw his hand out and Fred stopped in his tracks his heart skipped a beat then took off wildly. It pounded in his ears as the other six men lined up with them. There in the moonlight was a huge shape, a bit like a huge bull, eating the cow which looked as if it was already about half gone. It was hunched over the carcass ripping it to pieces and swallowing. There was a clump of very large bushes just off to its right. Fred had thought he'd seen everything in this country, but he couldn't make this thing out. 'A lion maybe, or a panther.' He whispered. 'Like a freak or something?'

'A bear?' from Tom.

Ernie was shaking his head, something wasn't right. It was sitting not hunching. He said this now and Tom was almost frozen with fear. He had to know what this was that they were dealing with, but he really didn't want to. All the men without exception lifted their rifle to their shoulder or aimed their pistols. Four had rifles four had handguns.

The animal that was eating, was sat behind the half-eaten cow and they could really only see it from a bit lower than waste up. They stood there, eyes straining into the darkness, hearts pounding in their ears.

With a blood curdling growl the thing stood up on two legs and screamed. The bushes to the right, two of them, sprang up onto legs and started to run away. But not the big one doing the eating. That leaped over the cow's body and rushed at them. On two legs.

The eight guns opened up and the thing stopped and staggered for a bit and fell down. The men lifted their weapons and fired at the shapes running on two legs towards the north and in seconds were swallowed up in the mist. The droning noise began again only this time it was louder and had an aggressive note to it. It had a thumping noise within it that sounded remarkably like a heartbeat.

'Shit' shouted Jimmy. The eight men backed away to the tree line and stood in the darkness there. As they watched, one of the other shapes, a smaller one crept back and stole the remains of the cow's carcass. Then it ran off into the mist and disappeared. All eyes reverted to the huge shape which resembled a bull that lay unmoving on the ground.

'Back to camp,' said Tom. They all walked back to camp, each trying to make sense of what they'd just seen. Back at the truck they sent Jack to clean himself up. When they all sat at the fire Tom suggested they try and get some rest. The valley was quiet, and the animals had settled.

Tom spoke in a quiet steady voice now. 'We'll take it in turns to sit watch. Ernie and I will take the first watch. Then Fred and Nevil, then Bill and Jimmy and then Jack and Charlie. We'll take two hourly watches then start again. Righto keep your weapons with you men and keep em close. Hug em if you like.' Tom smiled confidently and the men were comforted by that.

'Reckon we got him Tom' asked Jimmy?

Tom nodded and smiled, 'got the big bastard anyway.'

'What the fuck is it' asked Jack?

'We'll know in the morning we'll go and have a good look at him.' Tom sat on his swag leaning against a wheel of the truck to stand watch. He didn't want to talk about it right now. No one else did either.

The men all climbed out of their swags at first light. 'Let's go' said Bill eager to see what this thing was. But Ernie had other ideas 'a coffee first boys' he cautioned.

As soon as the coffee was downed, they set off for the herd. Tom was pleased to notice that most of the herd had relaxed enough to eat. They were grazing quietly, and the horses were eating the hay they'd been given. All in all, a very good sign.

They walked around the herd and then walked around again. Bill who had saddled his horse already ran and got it. He came back and split the herd up looking for the thing, but there was no sign of it. They looked for tracks and found none. It was as if they had imagined it. The men were uneasy, that thing must have been stunned and had got up while they slept and gone. Not just gone but disappeared without trace just like Cecil.

'Cecil' cried Nevil turning to Tom. 'We should go and look for him.'

Tom spoke firmly now, 'I want everyone to get the camp packed and get these cows the hell out of here. Keep an eye out for him as you go everybody. I'll take a quick scout round the canyon back this way and catch up to you.'

'No' the desperation was evident in Ernie's voice.

'I'll just be a couple of hours at most dad, don't worry.'

Ernie choked up, his throat closed, and his eyes misted. His son had called him dad. He gazed lovingly at this son of his and Tom smiled softly. 'I'll catch up in a couple of hours don't worry. Go on now git. The lot of you, get these bloody cows the hell out of this.' He looked around at the canyon 'ancient hell hole with its demonic fuckin inhabitants. I'll get going, this place gives me the creeps.'

Bill handed the reins of his horse to Tom and muttered to him to be careful. As he swung up in the saddle Tom said in a loud voice, 'keep them movin boys, just keep em movin.'

He cast a last grin at Ernie and Fred, nodded his thanks to Bill and left at a trot. And the boys didn't have to be told again to get moving. Yep, thought Fred he'd keep pushing them up and out of this... what Tom had called it.

Tom back tracked along the canyon for about half a mile and crossed to the other side. He carried on until he spotted a ledge, he thought might be able to climb right up to the top. He'd get a good view from up there.

He made it to the top though he had to lead his horse for a bit at the very top. It was a long way to the valley floor and Tom could make out the herd up ahead. The boys had already got them moving he smiled bleakly to himself. He looked up at another jump up which took you right up to the tree line. Even in the daylight it looked dark and foreboding up there. He shivered and got back in the saddle.

He walked his horse for about half a mile and then felt as though something blew on the back of his neck, the hair stood up. He walked slowly and after a while he got down from the horse and walked. He was almost level with last night's camp sight across the canyon now. His heart quickened. The herd was up in front, the boys were pushing them hard.

He stopped when he saw what looked like Cecil's tracks cross the ledge he was on. He straightened, the icy hand of fear gripping his belly. He filled with dread as he turned his head and made his eyes follow the tracks.

Tom's gasp was audible as he saw the tracks went over the cliff. Leaving his horse where it was, he inched slowly towards the edge. He looked over the side and tears sprang to his eyes as he looked down on Cecil's twisted lifeless body. He said a prayer for his lifelong friend and apologised for not being able to retrieve his body. Promising to come back he swung up onto his horse and sadly turned away.

Rather than risk finding another ledge down to the valley floor he went back to the one he'd climbed up on. Once down on the flat ground he spurred his horse into a gallop, this place gave him the creeps. He kept up the pace glad he had Bill's horse underneath him. He knew the speed and stamina of this animal, Bill refused to use another. Bill had realised he might need it and Tom smiled.

Tom kept up the pace until he caught sight of the herd up ahead and he relaxed a little. He was glad when he noticed the ever-watchful Fred turn his head and see him. Fred waved them on and broke ranks and came trotting back to Tom.

'Thank God Tom. I should never have let you go back by your fuckin self; I could've lost you. We could've lost you. You find him T...' Fred stopped talking.

The look that crossed his friends face told him. Tom shook his head and swallowed a couple of times and spoke. 'He's back there dead but he's down on a ledge, looks like he fell. I couldn't get down to him. I saw his tracks Fred...' Tom paused for a while. Then, 'he just ran right over the edge. He was there Fred...he was there. I felt him, he showed me the tracks.'

Fred turned his horse and fell in alongside his mate. He clapped Tom on the back and that small act of deep caring almost brought Tom undone. They rode back to the herd in silence. Jimmy was coming to ask if Tom had found Cecil and thought better of it when he saw Tom's face. He nodded to Tom and rode back the way he'd come his head held low.

At lunch time when they caught up with Ernie the old man ran to Tom and hugged him tight against his chest. 'You found him son?"

Tom nodded and met Ernie's eyes. Ernie pulled the big man back in his arms and held him. Tom cried like a baby. He cried for his friend laying on a ledge in the middle of this terrible valley.

Fred climbed up on a rocky outcrop and looked down. He saw across the valley the mist rolling in and dark shadows that moved around in it. He ran down. 'Come on you bastards' he screamed, 'we got about three hours and we're out. Let's get moving and move these animals as fast as they'll go.' As he left Tom, he said why don't you go with Ernie Tom. We'll get em there.'

The men including Tom jumped on their horses some with their lunch in their hands and spurred them on. Tom thanked Fred for his thoughtfulness, but he said he'd got em into it so...

Fred nodded and rode off to do his job. He loved his friend, and his heart broke for him. Even he felt the weight of leaving one of their number in this valley. This awful God forsaken valley. This Devils fuckin Canyon. He shivered in the hot afternoon sun and yelled at the cattle.

Three hours later and the finish line seemed to have moved. 'Keep em moving' Tom screamed. He reckoned no more than another hour. It'd be dark in about four. They pushed on and Tom worried. They all worried about pushing tired frightened cows so hard.

An hour passed and the finish line was still about half a mile. 'Slow' Tom signalled, he couldn't keep pushing them till they fell in their tracks, they needed a bit of a breather. He felt his heart quicken when he heard the sound. When he turned his horse around to look back the valley was almost out of view. The mist was rolling in. The howl that stood the hairs on the backs of their necks on end was almost human. It reverberated around the valley, wild and unhinged.

Tom swung around to the front and there was the gate, about five hundred meters away. Fred wasn't wasting any time and he'd already gone ahead to open it. They had no trouble getting the cattle through it this time and Fred took a deep breath when he'd closed it behind him. He looked back and to his horror a strange two-legged giant of an animal stood on two legs watching him, only just visible in the mist. He blinked and the thing disappeared back into the mist.

'Get em moving' bellowed Fred as he swung up into the saddle, 'we can do another mile.' Tom didn't object, he'd seen it.

The men turned and eyes to the front they pushed these tired cows another mile and a half. It was slow going and nearly dark, but they did it. They were well out of the canyon and onto the plains.

The valley was out of sight and with tired, aching limbs they made camp. With the horses tethered and the cows grazing and drinking in a meadow the bone-weary men collapsed in their swags. In the horse shit in the back of the truck. Ernie slept at the wheel, they seemed to have decided unanimously and without a word spoken that tonight, we run.

None saw the dark troubled eyes watching them from a tree as they slept.

❧

Herbert had been working at the stockyards for eight weeks now and had learned the job thoroughly. He turned up for work every day on time and Bill Wilson was pleased with him. He had told Herbert how pleased he was with his progress and told him that he'd be considered for any promotions that came up.

Today, Herbert had been sent for and he felt a little nervous as he walked into the boss's office. He hoped he hadn't done anything wrong. He sat when Bill told him to.

Bill looked across his desk at the man he'd staked his reputation on and who had come through for him and smiled. Herbert relaxed.

'Herbert, I wanted to see you to ask you about whether you'd be interested in taking on another job. It's a bit less physical work and I know you have the head for it. There's a position for a tallyman opening in the next month. Are you interested Herbert? I know it's a bit quick, but I need someone in that position, and you could go with Dusty and start to learn now.'

'But what about the other blokes?'

Bill smiled; he had been right about Herbert. The man would worry about upsetting the others he was desperate to fit in and Bill liked that quality also. 'There aren't any others so suited to the job Herbert. I've seen firsthand what a head you have for figures. So yes or no Bert?' Bert was hesitating, Bill put in, 'I can square it away with the men Bert. See most of em don't want the job because the numbers side of it frightens em off. Some of em can't even read so you see Bert, you're it.'

Herbert grinned and said, 'and the pay?"

'Better' Bill nodded. 'An extra pound a week. You can go and find Dusty and he'll start to train you right now. I told him to expect you.' Bill shifted papers round his desk. 'We've only got three weeks Bert.'

'Righto' said Bert, 'I'd best get cracking.'

Bill laughed, he liked Bert, he'd heard what a fiasco he'd been with the ladies since he got here. Bill didn't tend to judge men on that score, he himself was fifty and still single. He waved his hand at him now, 'go find Dusty he's over by the loading sheds.'

With a dizzy head and desperately trying to pull himself together, Herbert went off to find Dusty. With an extra pound a week he could get a real nice house. With the thirty pound he'd saved for a deposit he could buy a house.

Yeah, Herbert dreamed, and Betty. He could marry Betty who worked in the office. Salt of the earth was Betty. He smiled to himself; he was picking up this local lingo alright.

He owed Bill a lot and Fred. He wondered how Fred was doing and hoped he'd see him again one day. Yeah, he owed these two men a hell of a lot. They had literally picked him up out of the gutter and trusted him and helped him when no one else would. And it was for sure he hoped Fred stayed away from Sue. he'd heard that Fred left town and she was on with a rich cattleman. He was glad, glad for Fred. He had to admit he was glad for Sue.

❧

Sue had bidden her cattleman goodbye the day before. Richard had vowed he'd be back soon and 'til then he'd told her, he was just on the other end of the phone. You call me if you want to know when I'm coming into town. He had smiled and kissed her, a soft lingering kiss.

Sue had come to like Richard. She actually liked him. But Sue knew well enough she had liked other men until she had slept with them. She looked at him as he reached for her to kiss her goodbye. As she stepped into his arms she felt at peace. It made her happy that she felt that.

Maybe in time she could learn to love him in that way. And then he had kissed her again, had dropped his mouth on hers and really kissed her, long and deep and with a passion she felt herself meet. Oh yes, she thought she could learn to like this. Her head swam. There was a softness about Richard, a sophistication. But there was a hardness to. She thought now that he was perfect.

And now this morning she got word that her father was in hospital with a stab wound. He'd been transferred from Katherine to Darwin Base Hospital early hours of this morning. She hurried along to see him.

Sue couldn't understand it. Had Lilly done it or her bloody mother? Her mother she'd wager, he must have told her she guessed.

She hurried down the corridor to the ward the nurse had told her he was in. She came to an abrupt halt at the door and stood looking in at her father. He was asleep, his face was pale. He looked small.

She tiptoed to the bed, and he opened his eyes. He smiled up at her and she sighed her relief. She bent and kissed his forehead. 'Are you alright Dad' she asked?

Bradly nodded 'course I am Sue. They took the knife out at about five this morning. I guess it had been in there so long that when it was out, I just relaxed.' He put his head down and swallowed.

'Dad who? Who did this?'

'Victoria. She didn't take kindly to me leaving her. I told her she could stay on at the station, but she'd have to do it herself and she'd need to tighten her belt. Do you have any idea how many times over the last quarter century I had to move heaven and earth to keep that bloody station. Had to drag us out the shit because she couldn't control her spending. Always had to have the best of everything. If anyone in the whole of the bloody territory remodelled their sodden house, she had to. If they got a new car, we had to have a better one. It's been a bloody nightmare. Now you're out and Johns too busy gambling, drinking, and bedding loose women to pass any exams. Well, he's twenty fuckin four. I'll give him ten thousand pounds and tell him he's on his own. He can man up and look after himself, I sent him a letter to that effect. Told him I'd help him as much as I can if he decides to do something with his life. Of course, I won't need to give you any money, will I?'

They both laughed and, on an impulse, she took her father in her arms and held him. 'I'm sorry dad… I'll…'

'You're not gunna make promises to your old man you don't intend to keep are ya love? Mum's sitting in jail but I'll tell her that if she leaves and goes to her parents' estate in Adelaide, I'll drop the charges. And she can take her no good son with her. If not, she'll go to prison. If I'm going to drop the charges, she'll need to sign the station over to me and I'll give her an allowance to live on.'

'Do you think she'll do it?' Sue couldn't believe what her parents had done.

'Course she will, she'd die before she'd go to jail.' Sue nodded. Bradly went on 'listen love can you take me to Katherine? Lilly will be out of her mind with worry. I got the cops to go round and fill her in.' They both jumped as the phone beside the bed rang. Sue picked it up and passed it to Bradly. She watched as his face relaxed when he heard who it was and smiled.

'Oh, Lilly thank God it's you. I've been worried about you. She stabbed me, Lilly. But at least she is in jail, so you have nothing to worry about.'

Lilly's voice was strained as she answered him, 'are you alright darling?'

Sue saw he father's face soften. He said into the phone 'course I am sweetheart. I'll be home soon it's just a flesh wound. I left the knife in the wound so it wouldn't bleed too much, and I went straight to the cop shop.'

When Bradly had assured her, he was fine, and he'd stay until tomorrow he said goodbye and hung up the phone.

'You love her dad, don't you?' Sue was smiling softly.

'Yeah, I do. I will marry her as soon as I can. Who would ever have thought that a woman like her would look at me. But she loves me, Sue.' He picked up Sue's hand, 'well I won't need a ride now love I'll get to Katherine tomorrow.

'Well, I don't blame you dad, you deserve to be happy at last. I have made up my mind to marry Richard. He's the only man that I like, and I like it when he touches me.'

'I hope you'll be happy Sue. He's a bit older but he's a good man love. I hope it works out.'

When Bradly got back to Katherine, he went straight to the police station and was shown through to Victoria's cell. He sat on a stool just outside of the bars. 'Hello Victoria' he said softly.

'I hope you are happy' she snapped. 'You know Bradly, I actually hate you, have done for a while.'

Bradly lowered his head 'I know' he said softly. 'Well, you are free of me now and maybe you will find happiness yet. Victoria, I don't want to see you go through a trial and then to jail. If you agree to leave the station and relinquish all claim to it in writing and go and live on your parents' estate, I will give you an allowance. Can we agree on that do you think?' Victoria nodded and Bradly went on, 'I would appreciate it if you took your son with you. He doesn't like me any more than you do.'

Victoria agreed. 'Can I get out now?"

Bradly shook his head 'as soon as you sign an agreement to all this. I'll send a solicitor along.' Bradly stood up 'You can never come back to the station Victoria; I will have a restraining order in place by tomorrow.'

Victoria showed no emotion as she nodded her head in agreement. But the hatred was there, and Bradley felt it.

When Bradly left the police station he was singing. He stopped to buy flowers and went home. Lilly threw her arms around him, and all of these troubles melted away.

'We can go home now Lilly, to the station.'

Lilly shook her head and smiled softly at him. 'I'm sorry love' she said softly, 'I can't go there to live. Anywhere but the place you spent so long in misery. We need to make a fresh start my darling.'

Bradly nodded, 'alright Lilly, we'll sell the place and buy another place.' He shrugged and smiled apologetically. 'Would that be acceptable? I only know cattle. But I know it very well Lilly my darling.'

'Of course,' Bradly lifted the woman into his arms to take her to bed. He had to put her straight back down again. Taking her hand, he led her to the bedroom.

'You've hurt yourself haven't you' she smiled?

'Not so much' he murmured as he turned and nuzzled her neck which brought a sigh from Lilly. God, he loved this woman and he vowed he'd not spend another night away from her ever again.

He had no doubt that Victoria was not yet finished with him, but he wouldn't be letting her out of jail until she relinquished the station. Bradley had a funny feeling he still needed to earn and earn well. He'd need another station and soon, he needed to start earning as soon as possible.

Bradley sighed as Lilly enfolded him in her arms, he made a vow also that he'd never let anyone come between them. Not anyone.

CHAPTER 13

When Tom woke up the next morning it was with a start. He sat up and looked around, it was dawn, and the men were still asleep. All except Ernie who was building a fire. He jumped out of the truck and went to the fire, he looked anxiously at the older man. He noticed Ernie was smiling at him.

'What?'

'Oh, nothing boy. Here's your coffee. Hell of a few days' boy hay?'

'Shit yeah dad and it was all my fault. If I'd…'

'Hush lad. Not anybody's fault. Nobody spoke up and said they didn't wanna go with you. We were free to follow you in there or free to not follow…'

Tom nodded, 'that says what sort of men they are dad, they followed me even though they knew better. Even though they were scared. Shit!'

'Stop belly aching we were all at fault.' Tom turned around and watched Fred step up and take a coffee from Ernie. 'Jesus I'm hungry old man.' Fred grinned and set everything right. He could do that marvelled Tom. Just with his big grin and easy manner he could do that. Take all the troubles of the day, turn them into a sentence and toss them away.

Tom looked back at the fire, 'I just want to get home and I don't care if I never go on another bloody drive.' Tom shivered visibly.

That statement told Ernie and Fred and now Bill and Nevil who'd just come to the fire how deeply he'd been affected by the recent events. Bill put his hand on Tom's shoulder 'come on son, who knew those horrors were in that canyon.' Jimmy and Jack sat down in the dirt at the fire now with a mug of Ernie's excellent coffee. 'Thing is,' went on Bill, 'now that we're all here' he looked at them all, 'do we tell any bastard about it?' Bill scratched his head and looked at them all in turn.

Nobody spoke. 'That's what I thought' said Bill dropping his hand. Then, nodding his head 'but do we owe it to people to tell what we seen here? You know maybe stop anybody else from going through that bloody nightmare. We were lucky… we had each other.'

Ernie nodded, 'you got a point there Bill. You got a point there for damn sure mate.'

They were all at the fire now and young Nevil sat shaking his head. He looked at Tom, 'just think of the reputation you'll have when everyone learns you took a herd through the Devils Canyon and only lost one cow.' He nodded at Tom, 'You got us all through Tom. You'd o got Cecil through to if he hadn't run off. And I'll be saying exactly that Tom.'

'Here, here' Fred nodded his head solemnly.

'Yeah' put in Jack as if he'd just had an idea. 'And not one of us shit ourselves hay? Right?'

The little company of drovers laughed heartily and relaxed. Tom looked around 'that's right not one of us shit ourselves. If I hear anything to the contrary, I will require an explanation.' He turned to Jack 'I'm pretty sure I'd o shit myself except I'd already gone earlier. I'm sorry about the bag of onions Jack.' There was more laughter. Tom went on apologetically, 'pretty sure that's what done it mate.'

'Me to, I nearly shit myself, but I was too scared. My clack valve was jammed shut.' put in Jimmy and laughed.

Ernie turned and looked squarely at Jack now 'you got no call to feel anything but proud of your conduct Jack. You fronted up when it counted. By Jesus you did' he clapped Jack on the shoulder and smiled at him.

Fred stood up saying as he did, 'nobody at this fire ran and God knows it would have been understandable if they had. That was horrendous back there. I have never been so scared, yet everyman here stood his ground.' He handed his empty cup to Ernie and as he turned to go, he said 'pretty fuckin amazing I think.' He walked a few steps and turned back, 'well is everybody Gunna sit on their arse all day, or do we get a bit farther away from that fuckin terror pit' he motioned towards the canyon. The men sprang to their feet, everyone there suddenly wanted to get going more than they wanted to eat.

'Thought you was hungry' Nevil said to Fred as he ran to catch up with the big man who was headed for the horses.

'Yeah well, I'm not now. We eat at lunch time when we get a bit farther up the trail.' Fred felt a sudden need to hold a woman, he shook his head. And the dark eyes smiled from the treetops.

❧

Emily sat in the kitchen making a list for the shops. She was planning a little surprise for Harry; it was his birthday on Saturday. She would make him a cake and put candles on it. It would give everybody a lift to sing happy birthday. She also planned to make him his favourite lamb stew. She felt she owed Harry as it was him who got her started. Harry often ate for free.

Janet walked into the kitchen and smiled at Emily. 'I see you've been looking on the map to see where Tom is' she said. She looked over Emily's shoulder. 'They'd be about here' she said pointing to a line on the map.

'No' Emily said, 'they would have to come around these to end up here. They'd be about two weeks away now.'

'I heard they left Alice Springs and went through Devil's Canyon. Tom was told not to go...' Janet put her hand on Emily's arm, 'I'm sorry Emily, I thought you would've known. Don't worry Emily, Tom knows what he's doing.'

Emily was on her feet her hand to her mouth she hissed, 'are you sure Janet? Have you heard those stories about that canyon? Do you think they are okay? They'd be through there by now if they are alright. Is there a post office or phone out that way?'

Janet shrugged, she wished she'd kept quiet. She was getting worried herself now, yes, she'd heard the stories but had never believed them. But still… Emily was shaking her arm now. She looked into her friends face and tried to hide her own fears which were growing fast. Fred!

Janet suddenly remembered something, 'yes Emily there is a phone at the next station which is on their way. They'll report in there if nothing else. Give it until tonight and ring there and ask if they've seen them.'

'Oh, thank you Janet. I will do that.'

So, at six o'clock that night Emily rang the station and the woman answered 'hello'.

Emily introduced herself and said 'I am just trying to find out if you've seen a droving team come through there in the last day or two. It would've been a big herd and nine men.'

'I wouldn't think so dear. They don't come through this way they go the other way through…'

'Yes, I know' cut in Emily, 'but they are coming that way. I have just found that they were planning to… to use Devils Canyon.'

There was a silence and then 'well maybe my husband has seen them. He'll be in shortly. Ring back in a couple of hours dear alright? I hope they are alright, are you sure dear?'

'Yes' Emily said in a small voice. She thanked the woman and hung up. She was sick in the stomach.

The phone rang at eight o'clock that night and Emily fearfully picked it up. She answered 'hello'.

A man's voice came to her now, 'my wife tells me you were enquiring after a team of drovers?'

'Yes' was all Emily could manage. She was trembling and it showed.

'Yes, dear they came through here at around four o'clock. I went down to see them, there were eight of them. They told me that they had lost one of their number in Devils Canyon. They were in good spirits although they didn't want to talk about what happened. An accident they said one of them fell and was killed. They asked me to call the police.'

Emily could hardly breath, 'who did you talk to?'

'Said his name was Tom.'

Emily felt the relief rush over her. 'Did they say who was killed?' she asked noticing that Janet's hand went to her mouth. Janet waited for Emily to speak. 'Cecil! Oh my God. And they are sure he is dead?' Janet let her hand fall into her lap.

'Yes. They muttered something about not being able to retrieve his body. The police are going to be pleased at the prospect of going into that place. Anyway, I am sorry to give you such awful news.'

'That's alright. How did they seem?"

'To be honest they looked haunted. I don't know what they saw in there, but they stayed close together and stayed silent.'

'Thankyou' said Emily, 'I am sorry to bother you.'

'Oh, it's no bother my dear, sorry I can't tell you more. I can tell you that, after seeing those men today, I won't be going in there to Devils Canyon myself anytime soon. I did try to get them to talk but their faces just grew more grim and they clammed up completely. There was a big fellow with them I think his name was Fred, he ushered them away and they rode off.' There was a silence and the man's voice came back quietly, 'They've seen something pretty dreadful I'd say.'

When Emily hung up the phone, she looked at Janet. 'Cecil is dead. The man just told me they are all okay but behaving a bit peculiar. We'll just have to wait and see.'

But Emily couldn't sleep that night, what had they seen? It wasn't like Fred to walk away from a good chinwag, no it was not.

The next day Emily went across the road to see Ned and his wife, she had to get her mind onto something else. Carol answered the door and invited her in. 'It's lovely to see you, Emily. Would you like a cuppa?'

Ned was sitting at the table with a cup, he folded his paper. 'Yes, join us' he said with a smile. Ned had grown very fond of the new Emily and was intrigued by the young woman. He couldn't wait to hear what she had to say.

Once she was seated at the table with her cup Emily began to fidget. Ned noticed and grinned at her. 'Okay out with it.'

Emily grinned back and said, 'I have come to ask for a huge favour.'

Ned waited and, in the silence, he said, 'what is it Emily?'

Emily cleared her throat and glanced at Carol and back to Ned. 'I… I want to learn to drive.'

'Drive?' Ned's voice was gentle but surprised.

'Yes Ned, drive a car. Would you be willing to teach me.'

Ned sat and thought about it. After a few moments he took a deep breath and said gently, 'Emily, can you stretch your left arm out far enough to reach the gears?'

'Yes, I tried it out in Tom's car, and I can reach the clutch with my left foot to, and I can get it all the way down to the floor. I have to put the seat right forward, but I think I can do it. Could we try Ned? We could use Tom's car.' Emily sipped her tea and went on thoughtfully, 'and with all this driving I do expect my arm and leg will improve Ned. See?' She smiled at him.

A smile made its way across Ned's face, and he plopped the paper onto the table. At last, he said 'why the hell not Emily.' He took a mouthful of tea and looked at his wife. Smiling he said to Emily 'when do you want to start?"

'Tomorrow.'

'Oh, of course.' Ned looked at Emily quizzically.

'Well tomorrow we go to get supplies Ned. I will do the driving.'

'Of course.' Ned laughed softly. Why was he surprised he asked himself? He took another swig from his cup.

Carol said, 'Oh me to Ned, teach me.'

Ned deposited the swig of tea into his lap. He coughed for a while and looked at his wife with new eyes. He liked it.

That Saturday Emily and the girls presented Harry with his cake and sang happy birthday as Eric played his accordion. Later after they'd finished their work, they sat at a table to listen to the music and watch the dancers having fun. Nellie got up to dance with a young station hand. Harry sat and watched Emily for a time and made a decision.

He stood up and walked across to Emily and bending forward he held his hand out to her. 'Could I have this dance young lady?'

Emily looked askance at him, 'but … What. I can't Harry.'

He smiled kindly at her 'You can't? Yet here you are driving around in a motor car. I told Eric we need a few slow tunes so you can learn the steps again. Come on Emily.' He pulled her up and Emily got reluctantly, hesitantly to her feet.

'Oh Harry, I will just be a burden. I don't think…'

'Yes well, I do. Come on Emily.'

On the dance floor Emily stepped into Harry's arms and took a few uncertain steps. The memory of how to dance came back very quickly but it did her no good. She couldn't do it. Harry felt her frustration and he said kindly 'try and relax girl. We can do a modified version of this dance. Follow me okay.'

By the time Eric had played three more tunes Emily was enjoying the dance. Oh, she loved it, and Harry was easy to dance with. Harry had learned how to dance with her altered gait and Emily had learned how to keep up with him. He smiled kindly at her 'you see young lady, you have adapted to the dance, the dance did not adapt to you. And may I say that you are quite a dancer. When you dance with somebody Emily you just have to help him to know that. Help him to dance with you, to do the dance your way. You love the music Emily, don't ever let this leg of yours stop you again. Not ever!'

Emily danced away the evening and loved every minute of it. When Harry had to sit down, she danced with Ned and then with Janet.

'You are the most amazing young woman I have ever had the pleasure to know' Ned had said as he left her to go and dance with Carol.

When Emily crawled into bed that night, she was happy. Happier than she had ever been, yes, she owed a lot to that mongrel Rodney Gaskill.

CHAPTER 14

Tom and the men reached Alice Springs on a Wednesday, late afternoon and deposited the herd, which was still only one down, in the stockyards. Tom gave them hay and water. He knew these cows needed a little bit of building up and he'd do the same tomorrow. He found he was proud of how they'd come through their ordeal. He also felt that they put him to shame, he hadn't faired quite so well.

All the men fronted up to the bar that night and Tom put twenty pounds on the bar which was a little more than he usually put on the bar for his men at the end of a drive. He went first to the phone and told Fred he'd sing out when he was done if Janet was there. Fred nodded and downed his beer in one go.

When Emily answered the phone and heard Tom say hello she cried. 'Oh Tom, I've been so worried. I found out about your plan to go through Devil's Canyon and Cecil's demise. Are you alright love?'

'Yeah, I'm okay Emme, I'm sorry I didn't tell you. It was hellish is all I can say. I found out what a gutsy bunch of men I have with me though that's for sure. Emily… Cecil died because he ran away. He was terrified and he ran Emme. We had to leave him… Leave him behind Emme. I couldn't get down the cliff face and so he's still there. I found out a large contingent of coppers left here to bring him back. They intended to camp away from the canyon a bit and work in there during the day. Jesus, I hope they're okay Emme. Jesus, I do…' Tom gave a great sob.

Emily cried with him and told him she loved him and how she was anxious to see him. 'How are the others' she asked?

'Yeah, they're okay. They stood beside me Emily, not one of em ran. We lined up and they stood their ground. Anyway, we'll be home in a couple of days sweetheart we'll talk hay? I miss you woman and I miss your bed. Okay darlin Fred wants to talk to Janet is she there?'

Emily said she was, and Fred went into the phone box. He'd downed as many beers as he could and tried to stay off the subject of Devils Canyon. He told her briefly what happened to Cecil and then told her that he loved her. 'So there woman' He finished. 'I think I'll try and buy a few acres at Damper Creek hay? Down by the river somewhere we can fish all day. What do you say woman? We'll live on fish and chickens and eggs and your wages hay? Can you afford the amount I drink? Can you afford me woman?'

Janet laughed and told him she loved him to. Fred felt his heart right itself and he made kissy noises, and she made them to. Though when he put the phone down, he went to the bar and got good and drunk with the rest of the men. Fred had a woman who loved him, and it felt bloody good.

By the end of the night the little band of drovers were almost back to normal, almost. The barman knew there was something different about them and threw in a free drink. He listened intently to see what he could hear but they never discussed their trip through the pass.

By bedtime that night everyone had heard about the drovers who had come through Devils Canyon losing one of their number to the monsters in there. They also talked about these drovers who'd come through with all their cows. And Tom the drive boss who had pulled it off after losing his friend. By morning they talked about the one cow they'd lost to a monster. How they'd walked into the dark and the mist to front these monsters and rescued their cattle. No one could truly say where these stories had come from.

The state of the police who came back seemed to bear this all out. They had the body of Cecil with them which seemed to have nothing wrong with it. They were in a mess to and though they did a lot of drinking, like the drovers, they did very little talking. Accidental death they wrote. And so, the legend of Devils Canyon grew.

The drovers left town and were given somewhat of a heroes send off.

❧

Three weeks to the day they'd spent the night in Devil's Canyon, the drovers were home. It was a Friday afternoon and Tom wondered where his car was. He said this to Ernie and Fred when they all stood beside the truck looking up and down the street.

'Hay isn't that your bloody car coming Tom?' cried Charlie.

The men all looked up the street at Tom's car coming around the corner and down towards them. It was coming fast and was obviously being driven by a confident driver. 'Who's driving it' said Fred and immediately wished he hadn't? He glanced at his old friend and his gut was in a knot for him.

Tom felt a fear grip him in the gut, he couldn't stand it again and in front of all his bloody men. He stood with a stoop to his shoulder as he watched his car start to slow up. It stopped just away from them with the sun glare from the windshield making it impossible to see who was in it.

Tom readied himself for a fight, the cheek of some bastard driving around in his fuckin car. All the rest of the men also stood at the ready, they'd back Tom to Hell and back… Jesus they already had, and they'd do it again and again. Tom could hardly breathe, and Ernie's heart was breaking for him. He was too sick to even think about a fight.

The door flew open, and Tom's mouth hung open as the love of his life stepped out and did her best to run to him. He rushed at her and gathering her up in his arms he briefly eyed the car for anyone else and swung her around and kissed her long and hard. He put her down and said in a loud voice, 'what the hell woman?' Tom couldn't believe his eyes. His heart swelled with pride for this woman who was pretty much half crippled. She never ceased to amaze and astound him.

'Yes, I'm sorry Tom. Ned taught me to drive so I could go and get my own stores. I wanted to Tom, so I asked him. Carol is learning to drive to… Umm in their car Tom.' Emily stepped out from behind Tom whose mouth still hung open and waved at the men who stood with mouths agape by the truck. They slowly raised their hands and waved back, smiles appearing on their faces.

Fred rushed across to Emily and took both her hands in his. 'Jesus' girl, you are something. You are just… Bloody… something.' Fred suddenly looked a bit awkward. 'Isn't she Tom?' He turned to Tom who was looking at her with a grin and a look of wonder in his eyes. 'Emily…'

Ernie came across and patted his son on the shoulder, 'yes Fred, she's bloody something alright. Speedy Gonzales to I might add, thought we'd all have to jump for it.' Everyone laughed. Ernie looked at Fred, he couldn't believe the saver of situations had got himself flustered.

The men gathered round her and suddenly were all talking at once, every one of them vying for her attention while Tom looked on in amazement. Emily laughed nervously and held onto Tom. Tom stared, dumbstruck at this woman of his. He slipped his arm around her waist.

Maybe, he thought seriously, he did need to stop running off on the trail and stay at home with her. He missed her more than he could easily bear. Oh, he missed her so much more now than he ever did. And today, thinking she might have found someone else was way worse than Devils bloody Canyon. Way worse than those bloody horrors that ran out of the mist.

Fred went into the house to find Janet and found her in the kitchen. He stood at the door and watched her turn around wiping her hands as she did. 'Jesus, I have missed you woman. Do you think if I got a job on the mine or the railways that you could feed me for free?'

Janet's face turned serious, and she looked into his eyes. 'And do you mean that Fred or are you just toying with me?'

'I'd never toy with you woman.' Fred's face was deadly serious as he looked back at her and said softly, 'would you mind Janet? Could you stand having me around all the time?'

Janet flew into his arms, and he laughed softly. He kissed her and she kissed him back. It was a fierce kiss, a most passionate kiss. Fred lifted his head to look at her. 'Marry me woman make an honest man out of me. Or at least make a happy man out of me. Please darlin.'

He held her tight when she nodded and said, 'you know I will.' The memory of the things in the mist abated. In his heart he knew they'd never be gone but now and again they would abate. His Janet, she would hold them at bay.

❧

On Saturday night the men were all dressed in their Sunday best and ready for a good time. Most of them had a bottle or two stashed somewhere. Only Charlie had gone on home. Word had got around that the drovers were back, and girls seemed to come out of the woodwork. They wanted to see these heroes who had taken on Devils Canyon and won.

When the food had been served, eaten, and cleared away, Eric took up the piano accordion and began to play. Everyone waited as Emily walked out to sit at a table with the girls. Harry was excited to see how Emily danced with Tom, he was fidgeting, and he knew it. He knew it would be beautiful. He and Emily had practiced every Saturday night and sometimes in between.

He waited and waited and so did everyone else. Emily made no move to dance with Tom, she couldn't her stomach was in a knot. The night wore on and everyone kept silent it wasn't their business. But everyone there wanted to see the young couple who had been through so much, dance with each other. The longer the wait went on the more important it became.

Tom sat with Emily and Janet, Ernie, Albert, and Fred. Janet and Fred had just sat down, and Janet glanced at Emily. Her heart went out to her, she could see that Emily was just too frightened. Tom sensed a certain tension but had no idea what it was about.

Harry knew of her dilemma and finally got to his feet he could take no more. He went and spoke very briefly to Eric and Eric nodded and grinned expectantly. He played a slow waltz, the first tune that Harry and Emily had danced to. People got up to dance. Harry waited to see if the tune would encourage Emily to make a move. It did not, she sat frozen in her chair.

Harry had to make a move, everyone was looking at him, they were waiting for him to do something. As he crossed the short distance to where Emily sat his heart was in his mouth. Oh God help us he prayed silently, earnestly.

Tom was puzzled when Harry came to Emily and held out his hand to her. Emily looked at him, imploring him with her eyes to go away. Harry shook his head slowly once and smiled at her. He stood there, the tension he felt he knew, would be nothing to that which Emily was feeling.

He bent 'Emily' he said softly, 'you promised me that never again would you deny your love for music and dance.' Only Emily heard him because only Emily knew what he was talking about.

Ernie and Fred could see the distress Emily was feeling and Fred was about to get to his feet. Ernie was curious and knew that this had something to do with the tension in the atmosphere. He'd caught on but he couldn't believe what was about to happen, he put a hand on Fred's arm. Fred stayed seated. He looked at Janet and saw her wink and nod to Emily, a smile on her face. If it was alright with Janet, he thought…

Emily, looking only at Harry, rose to her feet her heart in her mouth. Harry held her gaze and smiled confidently at her, willing her. He bowed and took her hand in his and lead her to the dance floor. He turned to her and bowed again, and Emily put her hand on his shoulder.

Everyone was watching. Tom's breath caught in his throat as he realised what went on, realised what they were going to do. His Emily would be laughed at, he wouldn't be able to bear it but there was nothing he could do, he couldn't even get to his feet and cursed himself for being so useless. He held his breath keeping his eyes on the two who had the dance floor to themselves now. He couldn't have looked away had his life depended on it. The clapping subsided and Eric began the waltz again.

When Tom saw Emily glide somewhat awkwardly to the beat of the music he cried out. The other dancers watched a few seconds and went on with their own dance. Harry led Emily through a dance which was not only as good as the original but better. Fred sat with his mouth opened and so did Ernie.

They danced once round the dance floor and Harry leaned close to Emily and said 'I know what a chance you took on me and I thank you. Now are you ready to take a chance on another Miss Emily? A chance on him?'

Emily smiled and said to Harry, 'once more around the floor and then we'll take a chance on him Harry. Do you know how important this chance is Harry? What if he just… If he…'

Emily heard Harry laugh softly in her ear and told her not to worry. 'He won't, and anyway I'll be nearby with Nellie there. See Nellie waiting over there? We are your support team my dear. We shall be your plan C should this go belly up. I would bet my life it will not.'

Tom got slowly to his feet as if he knew something was expected of him here. He smiled at Emily across the distance as he not only realised that they had gone to plan B but why they had gone to that plan. His Emily had doubted him, doubted herself. It should have been him up there.

As they drew level with him Harry brought Emily gracefully to a stop and without missing a beat, he turned away from her. Harry would rather have walked through Devils Canyon himself than turn his back on that beautiful girl but turn his back he must. And he must leave her on the dance floor alone. Harry had a lump in his throat and a tear in his eye and he asked himself 'what if?'

Harry flicked his eyes at Tom and was relieved when the young man passed him on the way to the dance floor, a look of wonder on his face. Tom was on the way to his woman, to his future. Everything he loved was on that bloody floor and Tom would embrace it with all his heart. Tom didn't see that Ernie Albert and Fred had tears that spilled from their eyes and ran down their cheeks. Most people did.

As Tom slipped his arm around Emily's waist and pulled her close, he smiled down at her. 'You silly thing' he said softly, 'did you think I would not dance with you? I figured this was plan B.'

Ernie sat and watched as did Fred and the rest of them. It was Jack who gave voice to what they were all thinking. 'Bloody amazing. Bloody beautiful. And that woman, she is bloody…'

'Yeah' said Ernie, 'bloody amazing.'

Fred looked at Janet, 'you knew?'

Janet smiled and nodded. 'She was supposed to ask Tom but wasn't game, so Harry stepped in.'

Out on the dance floor, Emily smiled up at Tom, 'it won't be easy Tom. You will have to get used to dancing with a cripple. I'll try and help you darling, just suit your steps to mine.'

'Emily' Tom said his voice husky as he took some small steps, 'I have known a lot of people some of them better on their feet than others, but no one compares to you woman. And don't call yourself a cripple else what does that make the rest of us?' He dropped his head and kissed he gently on the lips. All the love he felt for this woman went into that kiss and Emily floated.

As he danced her round the floor, he found all he had to do was make allowances for her one step kind of shuffle. He had only to make her one step into two. Pretty soon it was easy, and he was enjoying it. He looked down into her eyes and fell head over heels in love. No reservations no differences and no doubts. Just him and Emily. He smiled and said softly 'how I love you, Emily. More than ever, I love you woman.' Tom was giddy and he knew why.

Harry sat watching the two of them for a while until Doris, a widow from Mataranka got him to his feet. People did come from miles around to Emily's for the dances. Most of them ate and waited for the dance to begin, some came only for the dancing. Emily didn't mind, word of mouth had been very good for her business.

Albert gave a great sob and Ernie put his hand on his back. He looked at the man and realised how much the old fellow loved the girl. He also realised as he looked at Albert that they would be family when Tom and Emily married. He sighed contentedly.

He turned to watch Tom and Emily and was struck by the look on his son's face. He knew that Tom had loved Emily almost all his life but tonight there was a spark there. Ernie sighed again and thanked God for that spark. Yes, everything would be alright he told himself.

A woman from one of the stations a widow who now ran the place on her own stood in front of him. Ernie looked up, smiled, and shook his head. 'Woman I have two left...'

Ernie was hoisted out of his chair by the woman aided by Fred. Ernie laughed and said to Fred, 'no more curry for you Fred.' He stood looking down at the big man he admired so much and smiled and said distantly, 'no more curry for you huh.'

As Ernie took the woman Betty, in his arms he was struck by how good it felt. His heart was filled with a wonder and peace he hadn't known for so long. It was also filled with sadness as he sensed the ending of an era. Yes, Fred and Tom would settle he realised. hell, even Jack was talking about getting out, Cecil wasn't coming back. On instinct alone Ernie pulled Betty closer and she put her arms around him. Hell, that feels good he thought and danced the rest of the night with her.

Chapter 15

It was over a week since they'd got back, and Fred walked into the Mataranka pub. He'd bought a second-hand car so he could go and see Janet every day. It was a utility, and he had his swag in the back so he could sleep in it. This allowed him to spend most of his days and nights in Damper Creek. He hadn't told Janet, but he was buying a two-hundred-acre block near the river just like he'd promised her. He spotted the bloke he was buying it from as he entered the pub.

Fred paid the money and signed the deeds, and the land agent left the pub with the seller. Fred's head spun a little, he was a landowner, and it was good land with plenty of water. He looked down at the papers in his hand and putting them in his jacket pocket he decided he'd head off for Damper Creek. He had to see the railway ganger this afternoon to find out when he started work there.

He decided on a couple of beers first and put the money on the bar. 'A pint' he said with a grin. Life was working out just how he wanted it to. He flicked his eyes to the left and felt his blood run cold. There in the mirror was the dirty mongrel he'd always hoped he'd run into. His heartbeat faster and he got that old predatory feel in him.

He walked away from the bar and came up behind the man. His big hand came down on Rodney's back and took a hand full of shirt. 'Rodney, isn't it? Rodney Gaskill. Purveyor of the finest roots and basher of other men's beautiful women. Makes only the finest cripples.'

He slammed Gaskill into the bar headfirst bringing a grunt from the man. The other drinkers moved away and kept their eyes down on the bar. They'd heard what this bastard had done, and they were going to see nothing.

'Now what's going on Fred' the barman interceded? Fred stared at the barman and shrugged and Joe the barman dropped his eyes to the bar, 'well take it outside Fred,'

Rodney made to run but Fred had him by the scruff of his neck. 'Now where are you hurrying off to little mate? Not very nice, is it? I'd like you to come and have a drink with me, haven't seen you for ages. No, I'm afraid I must insist mate.' Fred got a better hold on the man and quieted him down. He put his mouth close to the man's ear, 'you must be fuckin mad coming here where Tom lives and walk into the local for a bloody drink into the bargain. Fuck me drunk. Large as life if you don't mind.'

Fred dragged Gaskill to where his pint was. He pocketed his money, downed the pint, and smashed the glass over Gaskill's head. Rodney all but collapsed but though dazed stayed on his feet. The barman rushed down the bar, 'Oh put it on my bloody slate' said Fred, leaving the pub.

'You don't have one' Joe sang out.

When Rodney came to properly, he had a headache and was tied up and in the back of Fred's Ute hurtling down the highway. Fred took him to the block he'd just bought and tied him to a tree. 'Now don't go running off or I'll just get really mad. I'll have to come and find you again. Wait here there's a good man.' Fred grinned at him 'I know someone who'd be overjoyed to find out you're back.' The punch Fred delivered to Gaskill's forehead before he went knocked him clean out.

Fred got in his Ute and drove the short distance to Damper Creek and pulled up at the gate. He crossed the veranda and knocked on the door. The door opened and a somewhat surprised Albert stood there blinking up at him in the bright sunshine.

'G'day Fred. Good to see you man … But … I don't think this is a social call is it, Fred? You wanna come in Fred?'

'I need your help Bert, can you come?'

'Yeah, sure Fred. I'll just get my jacket and makings, okay? Just be a tick.'

Fred watched the big man walk down the passageway. He didn't doubt his decision for a moment.

Albert didn't ask questions as Fred drove to his property; he knew Fred wouldn't ask for help if it wasn't important. Fred turned off the road and headed into the bush towards the river. A single tyre track was all they followed.

'Where is this Fred' asked Albert with interest?

'I bought a couple hundred acres here Bert. For me and Janet to settle down on. Strap yourself in Albert you're in for a bit of a shock.' Fred clapped a hand on Albert's shoulder as he got out of the car.

Albert made out a body slumped at the base of a tree. 'Is he dead or alive Fred? You want help to bury the bastard son?'

'He's alive Bert and whether or not he stays that way is entirely up to you Albert.'

Albert looked puzzled and got out of the car, keeping his eyes on the body at the tree. Fred walked to the tree and undid the ropes holding Gaskill. He lifted the man roughly to his feet and as he did, so Rodney came to. He looked up and into the amazed and horror-stricken eyes of Albert. Rodney knew he would be lucky to survive what these two dished out.

'Where'd you find this fuckin snake Fred?' Albert's voice though dripping with hatred, was incredulous. His brow was knitted in a frown and Fred couldn't make out the look in his eyes.

'In the local pub at Mataranka, can you believe it? Large as fuckin life the dopey bastard.'

'Well lucky old us.' Albert turned to the man he hated and despised and spat, 'Emily is a cripple now thanks to you.' All the words Albert thought he would say to this man, all the words he had imagined over and over, failed him.

Gaskill shrugged. 'Well come on son' said Albert 'I do want revenge. I have waited for this day. I will kill you, but you shall remain free to defend yourself.' He flicked his eyes at Fred. Fred nodded.

A sneer made its way across Rodney's face and hope made it to his eyes. 'So, you're gunna take me on you stupid old fart.' He flicked his eyes at Fred who chuckled. Albert never talked about his prowess in the ring and Rodney obviously hadn't heard about it.

Albert rolled up his sleeves and looked over at Fred, 'thanks for this Fred but why me? Why not Tom?'

Fred scratched his head. 'Well, I dunno Albert I didn't have a plan but ending up at your house seemed right. Now if he beats you, I'll take him to Tom. If he beats Tom, then he's free to go and I'll kill the cunt myself.'

The two men shaped up and finally Rodney punched Albert on the chin. He grinned at Albert, 'that's how you're gunna beat me old man, by wearing my fists to the…'

Rodney didn't speak again, nor did he throw another punch. Albert went about beating him to a pulp with ease. When Rodney was unconscious Albert kicked him to within an inch of his life, but then he stopped. He stood over the prostrate form on the ground breathing heavily. He shook his head and looked at Fred who had a knowing smile on his face.

'I cannot' Albert said simply. 'I wish I was that kind of man Fred; I really do but I can't kill him. His legs are both broken Fred. I suggest we leave him where no one will find him in a hurry, and he can suffer there as Emily did. As for Tom, I'm glad you brought him to me. Tom would be troubled by giving him such a beating, but I feel only joy. And I shall sleep tonight as a baby knowing he's out there suffering.'

Fred chuckled as he lifted the unconscious Rodney Gaskill and threw him in the back of the Ute. 'My thoughts exactly Albert. And I know just the place to dump the mongrel. And it's all uphill to find help.' The two men laughed.

When Fred dropped Albert in front of his house the old man could hardly speak for raw emotion. He put his hand out and shook Fred's hand at length. 'Thanks again son and congratulations on your piece of land, never know where that could end up hay you are no stranger to hard work Fred. And congratulations to you and Janet on your engagement, we are fond of Janet. And Tom and Emily's reunion is a salve to our hearts. We are astounded at how she has coped and flourished. My Mavis cried when she and Tom danced on Saturday night. And thank you for being there for him Fred, he is lucky to have you in his corner.'

Fred heard the sob the old man tried so not to show, but the tears flowed now. 'Well, you are welcome, Albert. Now I will leave it to you to tell Tom or not. It's a hard call but I know you will consider him most carefully.'

'Thanks again Fred, I feel a hundred percent' he smiled. 'Yes, sir a hundred percent.' Albert shook Fred's hand again 'all the best to you lad.' He got out of the car and watched it drive off. He liked Fred, he was a fine man, one of the finest he'd met.

As Fred drove away, he choked back a sob of his own and swallowed a lump in his throat. Whenever he'd thought of running into Rodney Gaskill, he had killed him, or Tom had. Why he had decided on Albert was all too clear now though. The old man loved Emily as his own. It was Albert who'd been there for Emily, Albert who had put his hand in his pocket and put in his time at the girl's bedside. And it was Albert who got her to her appointments and Albert who needed this closure more than anyone.

❧

It was Saturday and Fred, Ernie, Albert, and Tom sat at a table talking quietly as they were wont to do. It was late afternoon, and the girls were preparing for this evening. Albert, raising his eyebrows, looked meaningfully at Fred and Fred knew what was coming. He nodded his acceptance, he had given the decision to the old man to make. Fred knew they wouldn't be able to sit on this for long, not once it got out that Gaskill was back and badly hurt.

'Tom' Albert started quietly, hesitantly; he drew a deep breath. Tom smiled and nodded to him to go on. 'Umm… Fred and I had a cuppa with Rodney Gaskill a few days ago. Out there on Fred's place. We found the mongrel and took him out there and I beat the shit out of him.'

Albert put his head down and looked up again as Tom cleared his throat. Tom sat stunned, looking from him to Fred and back. Albert sniffed, 'I nearly killed the bastard and then we dropped him off somewhere he wouldn't be found for a couple of days. So, as he would suffer same as Emily did.' His voice was getting louder.

Tom shifted in his chair and Fred knew his anger was building. He tensed up and so did Ernie. He knew what this news would do to his son, and he was bound to feel betrayed, by Fred mainly, though Ernie understood why they had done it and he himself was relieved. He kept his eyes on Tom as did Fred, they knew Tom's temper, it was the stuff of legend. It was like trying to stuff a tiger back in the bag after you'd let it out.

At this moment Jimmy and Nevil walked up and joined them. The appearance of them did nothing to relieve the tension at the table. They stood back a little from the table and kept silent.

Fred coughed and spoke directly to Tom, 'I heard he has his legs broken and ribs broken, and his cheekbone smashed, and nose broken. He has concussion and lost a lot of blood. They say his own mother wouldn't recognise him. His left arm is … so badly broken he will never use it again. But he's alive Tom. He lives to fight another day if needs be… Tom.' Fred shrugged his shoulders and looked down at his boots.

Tom stood up and bellowed 'fuck you, Fred. Fuck the both of you.' He sat down again as if his legs had given out. Tears ran down his cheeks. Emily and the two girls came to the door and Ernie urged them to go back inside saying it was just a disagreement. The three women stood just inside the door. They knew these men were a bunch of hot heads.

Tom looked at Fred and sprang to his feet 'down the back you. We'll fuckin settle this down the back lane you traitorous bastard. Who'd o fuckin thought it hay?'

Ernie stood up 'no son, they did what they thought was right. Albert was entitled to it and Fred gave him it. Come on son…'

Tom stood glaring at Fred with his mouth working silently, he was angry. Tom was so angry, but he knew Ernie was right. He hated it but Ernie was right. He looked at Albert, yes, he was the one who'd been there for her while he himself had run off. Albert was sobbing into his sleeve now, 'I… I'm s…sorry Tom. I love the both… the both of you.'

Tom rushed round the table and knelt by the old man. He took Albert in his arms, and they cried there for a moment.

Tom pulled away now, 'did you do him over real good Albert?'

Albert nodded, 'just on killed the bastard Tom.'

'He's eating soft food' grinned Fred.

Tom stood up; he looked washed out. He said quietly, 'for so long I've dreamed I'd get my hands on him. I wanna go to the hospital Fred, wanna see the bastard. You take me there.'

Fred looked at Ernie, Ernie stood up and looking at his son he shook his head. 'Probably not a good idea Tom. But if you insist, I'm coming with…'

'Well, if this doesn't take the bloody cake.' The men turned and looked at Emily as she came through the door with an unpleasant sneer on her face. She stared defiantly at Tom. 'I want to talk to you before you go because if you go, I go. He did this to me Tom, not to you, to me. He did this to me. I had it coming in a way Tom, you know it.' She flicked her eyes round the table. 'How dare you all act as if this is revenge for me. It is not. You sit there and discuss it amongst yourselves and tell me to get inside? I have moved on in case nobody has bloody noticed. That arsehole did me a favour and don't tell me you don't all know that. You go then Tom, get some more revenge for yourself. And when you're done you head back to Mataranka… There's nothing for you here.'

Emily turned to stomp back inside and remembered her stomping days were over, she'd have to shuffle back in the house. She put her hand to her mouth and Tom made to go to her but stopped. Emily started to laugh, she laughed and laughed and then turning to Tom the laughter died. She said 'excuse me while I stomp and shuffle back in the damn house and do my best to slam the bloody door with my good arm. My good arm Tom.'

Jimmy caught the funny side of it and chuckled then said, 'she's right.' He shrugged and stared defiantly at Tom.

Tom turned and glared at him. Jimmy went on, 'go on then Tom. Down the back lane, is it?' Jimmy laughed helplessly and a smile made its way across Tom's face.

Fred burst out laughing and said 'by God she is Tom you know? She's bloody right.'

Ernie stared, breath taken at this mere slip of a girl who had in fact turned her life around since Rodney Gaskell hit her and caused such terrible injuries. All that she was today and all that she had was due to that one fact, Rodney Gaskill had almost crippled her. Ernie nodded and said softly to Emily, 'You are right girl. Yes, you are, and I apologise to you. We are but stupid men and it shall be no surprise to find us and our behaviour often wanting. Come and sit with us all of you girls please.' Tom's mouth dropped opened as he stared at his father. Ernie stood up and gave Janet his seat and the girls all sat down. Ernie looked around the table, 'can we begin again ladies and gentlemen.' He went and got a chair and sat next to Albert who moved along for him.

Tom remained standing; he was dumbfounded. Had the love of his life just put him in his place? And more importantly, had she forgiven that bastard and embraced what he had done? This was too much for Tom.

Tom sat in a chair at the next table as there were none vacant at the table where they sat. Jimmy and Nevil had sat there, and all talked excitedly to Emily and the girls. Nevil was focused on Nellie; he so obviously carried a torch for her.

Tom got up and walked away, he had to be on his own for a while. He had to try and make sense of it all. Could Emily despise her old self so much? Tom walked down to the end of the street and got in his truck. He drove to Mataranka and went to his hut. He lay on his bed and cried for a time then got up and went to the cupboard where he kept a bottle of whiskey and a bottle of rum.

Tom poured himself a rum, He couldn't believe that she could've forgiven that mongrel so completely as that. Something else was gnawing at Toms belly, something unpleasant. He shook his head he didn't want to think about it. It was dark outside. They'd be in full swing back at Damper bloody Creek. Well fuck em. He sat at the table.

Tom swallowed rum until his head floated and the pain in his chest eased. He started to think reasonably about what had happened at Emily's but couldn't come to a decision to go back there. Couldn't bring himself to get up and go there.

He was stung at Emily's attitude towards him, and he knew it. Had she been in love with the bastard? There it was out, loose in his head. Could he get it back out?

'You reckon that'll do it Tom?'

'Oh, fuck off Ernie' he said turning his head 'you to Fred.'

Ernie sat down while Fred got another two mugs. Fred returned to the table and produced his own bottle. Tom looked at it. 'Wasn't sure if you'd give me a drink Tom.' Fred handed a mug to Ernie and took a good long swig on his own. He went on, 'I'm sorry Tom, I dunno what to say.'

'Then do me a favour and say nothing for fuck's sake Fred.' He looked at Ernie 'you to. I can't throw you both out but I just wanna drown my sorrows. Yes, Fred I am fuckin sorry for myself.'

'Why?'

Tom turned and squinted at Ernie. 'You were there weren't you?'

'Yes' Ernie sighed. 'I saw it all Tom. I think the young lady was…'

'Right! Yeah, she was fuckin right I know. Told me I could head back to Mataranka and that is all I did. So now you can go.'

'Angry! I think she was angry Tom. She went a bit far and now, I'm sure, she's sorry for it. And she'll be worried about you.'

'Bull shit Ernie' Tom sounded tired, and it cut Ernie to the quick to look at the suffering and the confusion on his face.

Fred put his hand on Tom's shoulder now, 'you've been through a lot and you're still going through it. You got as much of a fright as we got in that fuckin canyon. You lost your friend there, Tom, your lifelong friend and you lost your woman. Then me and Albert took away something you felt was your right, something you waited a long time for, and we all know why Tom. And for the first time in my life, I betrayed you. But you didn't bloody run off Tom, you found your misses with another man. I do know what that's like mate, we all head for the hills you know. Then to cap it all off that misses goes fuckin crook at you in front of all of us. Ungrateful, just bloody ungrateful if you ask me.' Fred flicked his eyes at Ernie.

'You seen that, Fred? You seen how she treated me?' Tom picked up the bottle of rum ignoring the glass and took a long swig. At last, somebody had sided with him and not the perfect woman who was all things great and good.

'I saw it to son' Ernie put in quietly.

'Oh hell, you two go back to the dance. I'll be right here. Go on I'll see you in the morning.'

'What's goin on?' Jimmy and Nevil walked into the light of the hut. 'Heard it was all happening here old mate' Jimmy laughed and clapped Tom on the back.

Ernie spoke first 'oh strike a light!'

'How did you bastards get here?' Tom was glad to see them.

'Got a ride' replied Nevil and sat next to Tom.

'Brought me own grog to' said Jimmy and produced a bottle of gin.

'Bloody women's drink ya little woman' Nevil said.

'What do you know about women Nevil,' laughed Tom. He was feeling better already.

'Bout as much as the next man' said Nevil sagely.

'Aint that the bloody truth' put in Fred.

'Yeah, bloody women,' said Ernie.

Fred spoke 'Janet told me I was about as subtle as a charging bull. Told me I ought to mind my own business … me! Now I ask you. Had a good old go at me for causing trouble and said how shocked she was at my involvement in the grievous bodily harm of my good friend Rodney.' Fred laughed good naturedly with the others. He turned to Jimmy, 'what brings you out Jimmy? Thought you'd be home working on your next kid hay?'

Jimmy shuddered. 'My misses told me she wanted another baby. Told me if I didn't like it, she'd… '

'She'd what' asked Tom, incredulous?

'I dunno I didn't stick around to find out. Anyway…'

'Ooh fuck' said Ernie, spilling his drink over his hand as he sat forward.

The little band of drovers talked and laughed into the night. They wouldn't dream of leaving one of their own to suffer alone. The bond between these men was unbreakable and they knew it. They were stuck with each other, more so since they rode into Devil's Canyon, together.

Nevil and Jimmy didn't tell Tom it was Emily who gave them the lift out there. They'd tell him tomorrow.

Sometime during the night Jack turned up. 'Bloody man came to have a drink and a dance, and you'd all pissed off out here.' Someone handed him a drink and he said, 'what's going on chaps?' He took a bottle of brandy from his jacket and placed it on the table. 'Yiz all look like you got women problems and I'd know right?'

Tom turned 'where did I put those fuckin onions, Ernie?'

Fred threw his head back and laughed loudly along with everyone else, 'yeah things could be worse we could be still back in that fuckin place.'

'What the fuck are you blokes doing here' Charlie walked into the hut with a dozen of beer? He found a box to sit on and cracked a beer.

'What are you doing here' asked Tom surprised to see him?

Charlie took a long swig from his bottle, 'Misses threw me out.'

Tom looked incredulous at him 'well you've wandered into the right place old mate.' The men roared with laughter and Charlie shrugged and took another swig.

He looked at Tom 'Bill's just having a piss in your front yard mate n he'll be in. That's if he doesn't end up in the river.'

Bill came in and found a four-gallon drum to sit on. 'How's it going you blokes.'

'We have a few woman problems.'

'Oh, the joy of it hay. My misses told me I was no good in the sack or anywhere else twenty years ago and I aint seen hide nor hair of her since. Don't know if I'm divorced or not really. Hay Ernie, I seen you disappearing into the night with Betty. You gettin some there you old dog? Hay she's not bad and bloody loaded to.'

Ernie slid off his chair hit the floor and sat up. Peering over the edge of the table he mumbled, 'I did, I did. In the front of Tom's truck. Lovely bloody...'

'Oh, Christ almighty.' Tom pushed him on the shoulder.

Jack who had been sitting quietly suddenly spoke up as Jack was wont to do. 'I have been told no more droving or else' he said quietly.

'Or else what' asked Ernie from the floor? 'Oh shit' he answered himself.

'I was gunna retire,' said Fred. 'That's why I bought the block.'

'Me to,' said Tom.

Bill nodded 'I have thought about that exact same thing. Take a minute to imagine gentlemen. Where we'd be right now… Right now, if we didn't have the next drive to look forward to.' This was followed by a silence. A long telling silence.

Jack sat up straight as he did when he was about to announce. 'Hey, you know that big fuckin thing back in the canyon? Well, I wonder if those smaller ones were his women?'

'Oh, Jesus yes' moaned Tom as if it all made sense, 'no wonder he was in such a good fuckin mood.'

They all laughed. Jack stood up and raised his glass. 'Here's to that big ugly bastard and how he appears to be getting all he can handle, while us good lookin blokes appear to be out on our arses.' He paused as the men laughed heartily and stood up and raised their glasses.

'To the big ugly bastard' they said in unison and gulped at their drink.

Bloody brilliant thought Ernie as he giggled helplessly, Jack had normalised the bloody things and made them human with human frailties. In one foul swoop he'd taken the sting out of them. The laughter went on for a while and subsided. Jack went on, 'we should apply for a government grant Tom and go back and study him.'

'We'd have to take some cows … way that thing eats. Imagine if I took my woman out and sat there and ate like that. In front of her while she waited for the scraps.' Tom put his drink down now and looked about. 'Shit yeah, we need to study him.'

'Well try it' put in Nevil.

Ernie gave another giggle, 'what? You bastards learn something? I'd like to study that.' He wiped his mouth, 'We have some crawling to do tomorrow gents.'

Charlie passed out on the floor. 'Oh great' said Tom, 'if you bastards are sleeping in here, I'm off outside.' He couldn't get up and slid to the floor alongside Ernie. Ernie patted his head.

Bill and jack took a bottle each and went to find a tree to sleep under. Jimmy and Ernie toasted again to the big ugly so and so and they passed out at the table.

Nevil said, 'I hope yiz don't retire. Who else would have me.'

'Here, here' Fred gave a hic of a laugh and went to find a level patch of ground to sleep on, a bottle under his arm.

Chapter 16

Tom came to with a start and looked into the face of Emily. He tried to focus but found it a struggle though he was sure she looked friendly. He got up on one elbow and looked around him. There were bodies and empty bottles all over the place and the snoring was horrible. Tom could only guess at what it smelled like. He scratched his chin. 'Did you kick me, Emily?'

He was struggling to a sitting position when he felt Emily's hands go round his shoulders to help him. 'Leave me be woman I am fine. Now say what you have to say and get it over with.'

'Say' said Emily?

'Say' said Tom.

'Is that the first thing that comes into your head Tommy Cooper? What have I to say to you?'

'Yes'.

Emily looked about her now, 'what have you to say to me Tom?"

'Umm… Sorry?'

'For what Tom? What might you be sorry for?'

'For being a jerk to the woman I love.' There was a pause as he stared up at her. 'Also, because I sometimes fail to understand. But I bloody love you. I always bloody have. And you Emily, you never miss a fuckin opportunity to put me back in my place. You told me to go away Emily … so I did. And here we all are, having a little celebration. Did you have a good night, Emily?'

'Get up Tom.'

'Alright Emily. Alright my love.' Tom made it to his feet. She stepped towards him, and he stepped back until his backside came up against the table. She stood close to him. He could smell her, how he wanted her. But he didn't doubt she could smell him to. 'Like I said, I'm sorry.'

'Are you coming home Tom? Are you coming home to me? I know you didn't understand my attitude to Rodney Gaskill, but I'd just like to forget about him. I cheated on you Tom it serves my right what I got. It was my punishment and it changed me into somebody you could love. You know it. I have only one thing I want you to do for me love. When he comes round, take him to the edge of town and see him on his way. Tell him that if I see him or hear of him again, I will go to the police, and he can sit in jail for a while. But Tom, I don't want you hurting anyone in my name. Please! Please Tom!' Emily put her hands to Tom's face, and he dropped his head and let her kiss him.

He put his arms around her and pulled her tight against him. 'Oh Hell' he murmured.

'Won't be a minute lad,' said Ernie. Tom looked around to see him and Fred dragging the bodies outside. When the last one was gone Fred came in 'there you go' he said and grabbed a couple of bottles off the table.

They were alone and Emily said, 'there you go what Tom?"

'Well, you know. Oh, come on woman … do you want me?'

Her face softened then Fred came back, 'just getting Jack's makings love he gets the shakes if he doesn't have a smoke in the mornings.'

Emily turned to him. 'Are you going to put in an appearance anytime soon Fred. Janet is a little anxious.'

'Yeah, sometime tomorrow, Emily. I promise. Do you know…?

'Yes, I do. And if that's all that's bothering you, you are as big a sook as he is.' She thumbed towards Tom and walked towards the door and Fred.

Fred laughed and said fair enough as he left the hut. Outside the door he turned, 'we messed up yesterday, Emily, that's all.'

'I know' Emily said softly. 'We want you all in there, all cleaned up and sober for dinner tomorrow night. We are busy today anyway. Thanks for this opportunity, Fred but I am busy. See you later Tom.'

Emily got in Tom's car and left. 'Thanks mate' he said to Fred.

Ernie got up off the ground, 'I'm gunna put the kettle on, then I'm gunna do a spot of fishing.'

The men sat round and drank the coffee Ernie made. Tom spoke first, 'hay Ernie, weren't you supposed to see Betty last night?"

'Yeah mate. I'll phone her up today sometime. I'll be all apologetic, you know crawl. She'll be fine.'

'Yeah' said Charlie 'we all have some crawling to do. I might go and get Kathy and bring her to tea tomorrow.'

'Me to,' said Jack.

'You're not taking Kathy' they all chuckled at the puzzled look on Jack's face, he was probably the best looking of the bunch.

Nevil spoke quietly now, 'so are you all retiring or what?'

They looked at each other and then shrugged. 'I'm not' said Charlie, 'hell if I was home all the time my marriage wouldn't last a month.'

The men sat in silence. They were digesting the coffee as well. Fred picked up the brandy bottle and put a dash in his. He could feel a certain anxiety starting in the pit of his belly.

❧

The men all fronted up for tea that Monday night, all those who had wives or girlfriends, brought them. Even Jimmy's tribe was there.

Fred came into the kitchen to see Janet and she took him to her and cuddled him. A tear slid down Fred's face Janet wiped it away and said, 'Oh dear.'

'I love you woman, but I'll make an awful husband.'

'I know. So, I know Fred.' She smiled.

'Janet are you… Saying you'd…?'

'Yes Fred, we'll just enjoy what's between us hay.'

Fred kissed her tenderly and said softly, 'I do want it to last forever girl. I love you with all my heart you know?'

Janet smiled, 'yeah, I know love. I know you do.'

That night the men all went on home with their wives or girlfriend. Ernie was invited out to Betty's station once again.

Ernie had felt the sadness in some of the blokes who had felt so excited about retiring. Others were anxious to get going, Jimmy, Nevil, Charlie.

Fred took Janet to his block where they slept in the back of his Ute in the swag. He held her to him and started to shake, 'Oh Fred don't honey, it's alright. Don't cry my love, just love me Fred, you know. Now and again like.'

Fred kissed her long and lovingly, he felt her tremble. 'Janet have you been this far before?' Janet shook her head. Fred went about slowly loving the woman of his dreams and when he was finished hours had passed and she was breathless. Breathless but smiling, 'Oh Fred!' He smiled back, delighted. 'Oh Fred, I want more of this.'

'Janet, you do want to marry me, don't you?' When she nodded, he said 'well then, let's do that. I want to marry you woman, more than anything.' He held her to him, 'it's just that I might have to do a couple more jobs. Just till Tom replaces me like. You know?'

When finally, he slept beside her that night he felt at peace. He had never known such peace and one day he would build that little hut on this place for him and Janet. And he'd get those chickens. He'd fulfill all of his promises to her, even that one, he already had the ring. He told her this as he dozed off and was rewarded with a kiss, he smiled. Janet snuggled closer to Fred; she didn't doubt for a moment he would fulfill all of his promises. Eventually, and in the meantime, he was hers.

Tom loved Emily with all his might and found that her body never ceased to delight him. Emily held him to her as they lay catching their breath, 'I'm sorry Tom. For everything love. You didn't run off Tom, I drove you away. I can't imagine how hurt you must have been. He hit me because I told him he was nothing compared to you.'

He pulled her closer and nuzzled her neck, 'hush woman, we'll get there. I am yours Emme, I belong to you. It was a big thing in our lives Emily, what happened to you. I didn't know how to feel but I have given all thoughts of Rodney and revenge up as a bad idea. A lost cause Emily. It's just us now honey. Okay?'

Tom kissed her on the lips and smiled softly. 'I'm not quite ready to retire yet Emme. A couple more jobs just to get a bit more money. For cattle you know, I'll need cattle. And I have to get somewhere close enough for you to keep working to Emme. Here in your business. I'm proud of you woman.

'Oh Tom.' She drifted off to sleep in his arms more content than she could ever remember. Just me and Tom, she thought. And Fred and Ernie and Jack and Charlie and Jimmy and Nevil and Bill, she smiled at the thought. You loved the one you loved the lot it would seem. Yes, they'd be one big happy family.

And a tear slid from dark eyes in the darkness of the room as they melted away to be gone forever.

THE END

Tom with an Aboriginal grinding dish he found while droving out in the Simpson Desert. He had a bit of a time getting it back to the truck on his horse, it weighed a ton.

Tom near Lake Eyre, a Salt Lake in South Australia while moving cattle from South Australia to Queensland. This is the Northern tip of the dry lake.

Brumbies which were used extensively in the outback were often half broken. Brumbies, or wild horses, in Australia made good stock horses especially as they were used to the terrain and the conditions. Quite often you started your day trying to stay astride a bucking horse. Once this was out of the way, they would work all day. Tom here is getting his day started.

Taking a herd of brumbies to Queensland. These horses would have been mostly unbroken.

Fred and the boys loading for the Western Australia to Northern Territory run.

About The Author

Rosanna Mary Seaton 2022

Born Rosanna Mary Seaton in Pemberton WA in 1954 to parents Maida and Arthur Seaton. The daughter of a rabbit trapper (returned war vet) she grew up travelling all over Australia. By school age she had lived in all states of Australia except Tasmania.

Raised and trained by her ex-commando father in hunting and bushcraft Mary could track an animal for miles and shoot it on the run for her dinner by ten years of age. When other girls were learning to cook sew dance and school, she was out with her father learning to trap, track, shoot kill butcher and survival in the harshest of conditions. Mary always says it helped her to focus and deal with life's trials.

She was educated to high school standard doing correspondence (school of the air). Along with her sister Judith Seaton, she was taught by their mother Maida. At age fourteen she was sent to boarding school in Broken Hill and left school at end of year twelve. She was also a rabbit shooter and that was how she earned her pocket money, often coming in gun shooter.

Growing up in the great Australian outback her parents based themselves out of Tibooburra and this she adopted as her hometown. For many years Mary's teacher was her mother Maida and it was from her that Mary developed an interest in writing art and learned to play piano and piano accordion. She learned also violin and guitar from family members.

She left school in 1971. Mary married in South Australia and all four of her children were born in that state.

Rosanna went on to become a truck driver until she could no longer do it and then became a security guard and worked out on the Olympic Dam mine in South Australia. She started writing seriously in her late forties, often making up stories during her long twelve-hour nightshifts. She also worked for Correctional Services. Her other jobs include working for education department, barmaid and factory-work. Whatever pays the mortgage was her motto.

She now resides in Port Pirie SA and works for Red Cross. Mary also is a keen gardener and loves walking the chihuahua. Children have grown up and left home but live nearby.